THE WISDOM
OF BONES

THE WISDOM OF BONES

KITTY ALDRIDGE

corsair

CORSAIR

First published in the UK in 2019 by Corsair

1 3 5 7 9 10 8 6 4 2

ISBN: 978-1-4721-5439-2

Typeset in Bembo by M Rules
Printed and bound in Great Britain by
Clays Ltd, Elcograf S.p.A.

Papers used by Corsair are from well-managed forests
and other responsible sources.

Corsair
An imprint of
Little, Brown Book Group
Carmelite House
50 Victoria Embankment
London EC4Y 0DZ

An Hachette UK Company
www.hachette.co.uk

www.littlebrown.co.uk

To my mother and my father

Dramatis Personae

London

Percival Unusual George – Showman. Guv'nor. King of Quick Street

Long Bella Wickes – Trumpet. Cards. Snakes. Theatricals

Amen Stepman – Clowning. Fiddler. Cards. Telepathy

Tuesday Brown – Announcements & Conjuring. Cups & Balls. Boards

Ruby Doll – Dance. Doves. Cards & Cups. Theatricals

Bird Doyle – Bird Girl of London. Clairvoyant. Clairaudient. Mystic/Cards

Flora Wickes – Chloroform. Rabbits. Cabinet & Vanishing

Grateful Jim – Tumbler. Trickster. Singer. Messages

Pinkie Danvers – Wagon. Nags. Theatricals

Pie Clark – Wagon. Whistles & Songs. Theatricals

Albert Goffe – Proprietor of Curiosity Shop, Waterloo Bridge

M. Luc Ferrières – Watchmaker & Clock-Mender, Clerkenwell

France

King Stanislas I – Exiled King of Poland, Grand Duke of Lithuania, Duke of Lorraine and Bar. A count of the Holy Roman Empire

Nicolas Ferry (Bébé) – Personal dwarf of King Stanislas I

M. Le Chevalier de Solignac – Secretary to King Stanislas I

Catherine Opalińska – Queen Consort to King Stanislas I, Duchess Consort of Lorraine

Marie Leszczynski – Daughter of Queen Catherine and King Stanislas I, French Queen Consort by marriage to King Louis XV of France

Catherine, Marquise de Boufflers (Madame de Boufflers) – French noblewoman and royal mistress of King Stanislas I

Émilie, Marquise du Châtelet – Philosopher, mathematician, physicist, author

Voltaire (François-Marie Arouet) – Philosopher, poet, dramatist, polemicist

Józef Boruwłaski – Celebrated Polish-born dwarf

Jean-François de Saint-Lambert – Military officer, poet, lover of Émilie du Châtelet and father of her daughter, Stanislas-Adélaïde du Châtelet

Fréron – Literary critic, controversialist

Montesquieu – Judge, man of letters, political philosopher

I have always observed that to succeed in
the world one should appear like a fool
but be wise.

Montesquieu

The whole arrangement of our life consists in
contemplating who one is, who one has been
and who one would like to be.

King Stanislas Leszczynski
Penseés Diverses, *from* Oeuvres Choisies de
Stanislas, roi de Pologne (1825)
Translated by Dr Renata Tyszczuk

Part I

Zeus split them into two separate
beings, condemning them to
spend their lives in search of their
other halves.

Plato, The Symposium

St Mary, Islington, 1879, Plough Monday

I am a butcher's only son, bred to the knife. My father had a shop on the Liquorpond Road. A blunder as I never took to it, the blood held no promise for me. I have not the stomach for butchery, albeit I have the cheer of a meat man.

I am a jiggler-joggler when it comes to phrases and rhyme, phraseology I have aplenty. I have the flair, I'm told. I should rather raise a laugh than a knife. Ha! The wit flashes.

My name is Percival Unusual George. It is considered unusual. The Unusual is an addition, I was not baptised so. My reputation was hung upon me along with the moniker. It is no grievance! The unusual is bread and butter to me. I have dedicated my life to the queer and the rare. I have toiled like a slave to please the public and I have wronged no man of a farthing. Cut me where I stand if I don't speak God's truth.

The usual interests me not, it is far too usual. I reserve my interest for the hard to find, the challenging to define, the stranger by far. Monstrosities, curiosities, novelties, human or animal, alive or otherwise. My interest is broad.

Percival Edward George is the name my mother and father gave me. I was born in the January of the year of our Lord, eighteen hundred and thirty, between the brewery and the Union in Clerk'nwell near the Coldbath Jug, where the inmates are forbidden to roar.

Number eight Quick Street is our residence, a brick and tile corner dwelling squeezed between Methodists and cattle yards on the road to the coal depots and asylum.

As a lamp-lighter loves his bull dogs so a showman loves his dwarves and here's two in the back room who call me boss, plus pint-size nags to pull their wagon. We may be sawdust but we are not rag and stick. My shows are clean, good brass, first class. I am not so honest as a magistrate yet not so dishonest as a thief. I am the king of what is to come!

I shall tell the tale. Here it is.

Once upon a time I was the flash cove. Bang-up. Rings over gloves. Silver-top cane.

A nib. Customer likes a bit of polish when it comes to it. Bit of shine. Bit of prestige.

I have shops here-there-everywhere: Caledonian Road, Borough, Islington. That's a few. We are swift to spot an empty premises. Then be brisk: sawdust down. Paintings up. Gags writ large. Bucket for your coke-fire. Oil for the flare lamps. Feathers for the girls and, Tye-diddy-o! Noise is all. A chaunty din. Call the attention of a crowd!

Bang! Bang! Bang! goes my man, Amen Stepman, on the drum.

Walk up! Walk up! This way for The Strange! The Hideous! The Obscene!

The strange, the remarkable. The world for a penny! Unusuals, novelties, prodigies.

Mine are remarkables all, my company of nine.

May it please you to consider them, each at a time.

Amen Stepman

His teeth are long, his feet are small. His curls are gold and his temples greyed. Amen Steps was not born to clowning but landed himself in it upon his discharge from the army. Watch him spill tea, smash a jug and dance up a storm like Billy Pinafore. He has the manner of a curate (his Bible quotes grate), albeit he wears the long-boned face of a common bludger. He is unguarded and luckless, pious of aspect. His heart is as gold as his curls. That's Amen.

Bang! Bang! Bang!

Walk up! Walk up!

Here we stand, poised to take the shilling. Ready yourselves to be astonished, alarmed or what-you-will. Who can claim the same for a penny? Too few that's who.

My Unusuals. Under the canvas their talent is grown until before the crowd they stand in strange perfection. Unique. What do they want with the average, the dull, the reg'lar? Their like exists not. They come to me, and I tell their tale. To you, madam, to you, sir, to whomever will listen.

Ruby Doll

Ruby Doll kicks her skirts. Did her mother take cinnamon in her coffee? Or p'raps the infant Ruby was cradled in a copper, being as her hair is the colour of flame and her face is pecked with gingerbread dots. She is a marionette designed for dancing atop a table. She curses like a dodge, sings like a mermaid and her eyes is narrow as nails. A soft doll she is not, save for her puffs of red hair, light as fire. I have saved Ruby from a life of devilling.

Long Bella Wickes

Tall as a door stands Bella Wickes. A twist in her nose, a rose in her hair, bangles on her arm. Woman, goddess, devil, fiend; she dodges and schemes like a reg'lar cove. From her neck swing thrup'ny snakes by the drowsing handful, while upon a trumpet Bella blows. Cries she: I have blown bigger! And many times over! At this the girls shriek like rabbits in a gin. I abhor a foul tongue but a bit of chaff is a charm to a crowd in the humour.

Hereabouts in the proceedings I stand to address the crowd, though none is yet gathered. Address an invisible crowd and one shall soon form. Presently it does.

No matter how few. Three customers will multiply and divide. Two will still pay. And five is more than either of those. This way for the most singular stories ever told by living man!

This way, if you please!

Hurry to see of what you dare not dream! Ladies and Gentlemen!

Do not be Alarmed! We do not mean to Frighten but only to Enlighten.

We do not wish to Bore you, We Implore you, Walk this way!

Tuesday Brown

My man, Brown. His name is William but I found him on a Tuesday. Tuesday Brown is the Wizard of the South and the Wonder of Whitefriars: a man of height and elongation, whose arms measure longer than his legs. His modulation belongs to an Archbishop and his mournful gaze commands a crowd. I spied him at a low ebb, staggering under theatrical scenery at Stepney Fair. He was well imbibed yet it was clear from his tones he was a gentleman. This fallen pedigree was not Unusual in the usual sense but he proved unusual nonetheless. Watching him disappear a plate of bread and butter and a cup of tea suggested to me he might make a conjuror. It is my pleasure to report that having become adept with his cups and balls he is now vomiting pins and needles like a natural. Is his timing askew? Few notice. Tuesday will spy the prettiest girl to pull the ribbon from his mouth and grin his toothiest for the Pudding In The Hat. A song here, a jib-jab there, an oh-good-gracious-what-on-earth and a bird in a bonnet. He is no emperor of the mystic arts but he puts shillings in the purse. I dig out remarkability wherever it hides. Blessed are they. Every life is a puzzle awaiting completion.

Flora Wickes

Saints be thanked! An example of the exquisite. I present Flora, The Chloroform Child.

Elfin sister of Long Bella Wickes. Nimble as a cat upon the iron girdle. Watch her levitate before a crowd. Sixteen years of age, once seen she is not forgot! To the waist falls her hair, as mahogany it shines. See her milk skin, her bow lip, her pale eyes, clear as stars. In the French lace and ribbons she walks. At her side steps Bird, The Mystic Child, swinging her cage wherein rests a lark, trembled with song, upon its moss.

Bird Doyle

Bird is light and bony as her name suggests. A sparrow. Like the songbird she warbles, skips and flutters. Her face is dear as a wren's, two black beads are her eyes, and her hair is a nest of chestnut curls. Feathered, ribboned, pinned, she chimes with coloured glass. Many believe she will unhook wings from her bodice and fly. Yes, fly! Above the clouds hear her warblings. Spied she was, in her feathers, rested upon a chimney pot. I speak only truths. Veritas! Veritas!

I have a pinch of Latin.

Grateful Jim

Singer, tumbler, all-round trickster. A boy, wiry as a monkey. The twitch in his eye is from a lightning strike, they say. Grateful Jim will pop his own eyeball and swallow it as you stand there, all for effect. He walked on his hands from the day he was born, to make his sister laugh. Jim could entertain the dead if he chose and sell himself back to his own mother. The signal is a trumpet blast.

Upon it, miniature ponies burst forth, a-jangle in harness.

Pinkie Danvers & Pie Clark

I am partial to a midget. Here are two of the superior variety. Bring your measuring stick.

Look at that! No bigger than your thumb! Pinkie stands to drive astride his miniature wagon. His dwarf ponies trot sharpish on pot-sized legs, wheeling tight corners till the dust rises.

Up walks the crowd. A group of four, then nine, then twelve. Now ten.

Clink-clink go the coins. Now we have thirteen. Whose bad luck is it? Not mine.

Bella tempts a man and his hollow-cheeked pal. Fifteen. Give the signal. Close the door.

No smoking! No spitting! No fighting!

Blessed are these. My esteemed Remarkables. I present them with a flourish taught me by the stage actor, Harold Beaufort. The rest of my performers are in jars.

Here I stand before you: head, heart and untidy frame. Thus far have I avoided the Fever Hospital and the Union. I am thankful. By my own wits and application have I forged a living in this unforgiving city.

Here is Quick Street. A brisk wind and clouds chase over the canal.

Our lodgings are adequate, well-aired, a corner dwelling that offers a stable. Once a symphony in drab, the yard is now enlivened, as Ruby Doll has planted flower boxes, reds and pinks, gay as a fair.

The street bell at five and twenty past. Amen clamps on his hat and scampers out for beer.

Tuesday Brown pronounces: 'Every man shall receive his own reward according to his own labour.' Though he spits when he is spouting, Tuesday is blest with the wisdom of the ancients. Owing to his highbred modulation I have Tuesday reading aloud the gag for the chloroform trick. His privileged tones suspend all doubt:

'In accordance with the Cambridge University, and Cautioning Herewith those of a Nervous Disposition. And bearing in Mind this is a Small Audience for such a Rare exhibition. And requesting you Kindly to all Remain Calm. And not to Detain you further. Allow me to submit for your Inspection that Remarkable and Staggering girl, Flora, The Chloroform Child. Gentlemen, Please remove your Hats.'

Top brass. Spoke gloomy as a bishop.

As to my own limited charms, I have nobility about my forehead and my gaze is affable. You might think, Ah, here is a trustworthy type. I stand square and I talk plain. My jaw is whiskered, my brows are thoughtful and my eye-glance benign. I have observed that women are not troubled by my expression and I am much obliged.

Such talents as I possess are put to use to keep us in the shilling. We do a bit of mystification, though I do not have a skilled mystifier, but only Tuesday Brown again, who is stiff of gesture, intones mournfully in the Latin and glares horribly about.

Bang-up, I am no dark enchanter, no meddler in the black arts. I am Percival Unusual George. I have strived to entertain the people of this city, summers and winters. I have cheated no man of a farthing, and my reputation is reg'lar gold.

In the yard alone with my pipe stem, I survey the evening sky. In the west it attempts a shade of pink, though clouding fast as smoke rises, it shall be choked white as goose-down in no time. St Mary's bell chimes the hour. I send Bird for hot loaves. Bella shall buy milk off the Welsh girl on Cross Street. For twelvepence we have a rabbit. Here is oysters upon a plate, pearly fine they look. By six o'clock we shall have a stew.

I light my pipe and consider that time is too quick for me, scarpers like a reg'lar hare. Of catching it I have no chance! The pleasure is to let it sprint, which is why I rest here, dipping flame into my briar pipe, watching time flee. The firewood snaps and Grateful Jim sings a trembling song.

I open the book upon any page: *Proverbs Exemplified*. A boyhood gift from my mother. *A true man never frets about his place*, it says. An excellent maxim, a sampler for Flora to stitch. Here before you, I am that man . . . in repose, fretting not a jot. Presently, I shall recline by the fire, garbed as a gent in my red Turkish slippers, purchased for one and six in The Strand, and gorge myself on walnuts. Sovereign! Everything comes easy as honey off a spoon.

Our street is dark. A scrabbling as I open the door. A stag-eyed boy waits, whistling, at one end. At my back, Bella calls out.

'Who is there?'

'No soul,' I say.

'Not Mister Cox?'

'Not Mister Cox.'

'He is not welcome here,' she calls.

'Halt your fretting! Nobody is here.'

The girls fear Cox. His name alone bids them halt their chatter. What pigeons! Idle rumours. Piffle and hearsay. He is a charmer and a gent, bang-up. I shall observe at the door. Fortunate I am, insofar as my cast of mind is sound and my mettle is lion'ish. I might've joined the East Essex. The boy on the street is joined by another. He alters his whistling tune. I shall find myself robbed in an eyeblink. The door is heavy. I slams it.

Notwithstanding my gentleman's ease this evening, I have urgent need of Mister Cox.

I should be glad to have sight or whisper of him. There is talk of Cox's employer, Stanwick the gentleman professor, and his precarious experiments. The girls will not have it but Mister Cox is no demon, albeit his patrol is the narrow border between the living and the dead. He is a man of ideas and in this we are kin. Cox is a facilitator. He facilitates for those learned gentlemen who tread boldly upon the precarious cliff path of scientific discovery. He procures

11

so that educated gentlemen may investigate. Some say he will secure the dead as well as the living, if required. My girls fret upon it. Tittle-tattle, I say. There are those who, upon sight of John Cox, walk in the other direction but in my opinion he is broadening our horizons in unusual ways. Progress is all. Stagnation is death. A showman knows that. When I catch sight of Cox I hurry to shake his hand.

Our windows and walls, low-beamed passageways and crooked steps, all are askew, though our lodgings are reg'lar tidy, save for the havoc wreaked by ponies, doves and dwarves. All hold out their hand for the shilling. Mouths to feed. Am I to perform the miracle of the loaves and the fishes? Each hears it! No-one ever replies.

Then there are the beasts: midget ponies for midget men, assorted avians, including finchlings, sparrows, linnets and doves for the *Heavens Above!* trick. Not to mention white rabbits and their offspring and a few nuisance snakes in a bag, which must be kept separate, else performers shall eat performers.

Five shillings a pound for small snakes: Long Bella wears them for shows, says it gives her mystery. She waves them at the tallest gent to make his lady scream. Bella Wickes. She was a Venus to me once, long ago now. The City Road was ours, and every public house upon it, and all the hours and happy minutes in a day. Now I am the solitary gallant. Surrounded yet alone. A showman must carry the crowd's expectations, the performer's wages, and his own heavy heart. He must house all his prodigies or risk them thieved in an eyeblink.

My dearest dwarf, Lark, was thieved in the night from under our noses. Thereafter, not a word. I am partial to a dwarf. How I miss him. His real name was Antonio

Lupinicini and he hailed from the land of mandolins. He had a magnificent pair of oily eyes and stood lower than a walking cane. He sang in a trembling fashion, moving himself to tears. He oiled his hair but otherwise was sound as a coin.

No man was ever great without some
portion of divine inspiration ~ Cicero

I wait at the window for Cox's boy. There is no sign. The night is blustery, rinsed black by rain showers. It unnerves my bird. I keep a corvid. He gargles and frets. The idea was not my own, I am besieged as Noah! I chanced upon the bird blown from the nest as a rookling. His ill fortune recalled me to my own troubles, as turbulent fates had cast our blessings to the winds. Poor unfortunate article, I thought. For this and his inelegant strut, not to mention his slovenly manners, I named him after myself: Percy the Smaller. Who better? Whereafter he became Small Perce.

Into my pocket he went with a rag, where he thrived upon mutton fat and a pinch of tripe. A large untidy head, he grew, and a stout beak, shiny as new coal.

What is the o'clock? First show at ten. It is a quarter to. We shall play six today.

The populace of this city are jaded, crowds remain paltry. I must amuse them afresh daily.

I send Jim out for dabs and coffee.

The last of the coins. Not a copper can I grasp. I say nought of it to the others.

Mister Cox, I think. Shall I seek you out myself? Must I loiter at some location? He will have an article on the boil,

13

the man is choc-full of manoeuvres. A strategy is required. A shift. Not one easily downcast, I hold ambition aloft! A prosperous day is dawning. So said Ovid. I have all his wisdoms here in my Bell's Quotations: Latin & Greek. Those classical gents knew their north from south. My compass points me forward!

No bees, no honey ~ Proverb

Almost eleven. The clock runs me ragged. The others are leisurely between shows, thirteen minutes before the next. My thoughts bolt about like loose horses.

Jim is moving the gag-boards and singing *Flash Bob* in the wrong key. Rookbird balances on the Windsor chair, eyeing the needles of Bella and Ruby as they sew.

Remarkables all. Tonight I shall have to let one of them go. I cannot pay each and every. Quick boots I hear upon the stairs.

Bird shies in. 'Do I seem mad in this hat?' She swerves between the girls.

'Yes,' murmur both, without looking up.

'You an't even seen it.'

Bella glances. 'Oh yes. Dear me, proper lunatic,' she adds.

Jim drops a heavy board.

'Bugger that noise!' yells Ruby Doll.

'I think it's nice,' Jim comments, nodding at Bird's hat, reddening like a chambermaid.

'Never mind,' says Bird. 'Seen my birds? They was here a spit ago.'

'No.'

'No.'

'No.'

The door bangs. In steps Amen, with a small loaf and a handful of sage.

'See! I have delivered Jericho into your hands, along with its king and its fighting men,' he announces. No-one heeds it, being that we have heard it all before.

Outside in the yard I smoke alone beneath ash-coloured clouds and I think, A man may not enjoy his pipe for more than a fleeting moment before ruination strikes. How shall I choose one to dismiss?

'Has Bird lost her sparrows?' I call out. 'Does she fancy a clouting?'

'Flo! Seen my birds?'

'*Seen* your birds?'

'Never mind.'

'Sparrows all over London, Birdy,' says Bella. 'Don't know if they're yours, do we?'

Flora rises from a cushion, offers up a brass button. 'Look.' She is dear in her shawl and over-sized boots. Her eyes are wide as pansies. 'I got one,' Flo tells Bird, hands clasped under her chin. 'One of your sparras. Like this. I took it.'

Bird cradles the sides of her face. 'Yes and ... Where'd it go, Flora?'

'Flapping.'

'Where?'

'Skywards.' Flora points. 'Aft then fore. Then gone.'

'When?'

'At the time.'

'For the love of Jesus!' Bird shrieks.

'Leave her, then.'

Flora gasps. 'Shall it vex the saints?' she says.

'P'raps your sparras are tap-knockin at the door, then?' Jim laughs at himself.

'Ha-hoo. Aren't we the wag?'

'Oh, Jim! He's on the floor, look.'

At this I struggle up, mid-puff, to peer at the window. 'Is that toe-rag asleep?'

'No, Mister George. I'm helping Tuesday do the boards.'

'Bird!' I say. 'Have you lost the sparrows?'

'Blessings, no! Finely not. Resident they are, hereabouts.'

'There's your sparra! In yer frightful hat!'

Ruby and Bell fall into each other. 'Ha ha!'

'Arse-poke you both.'

'Language.'

'Love has turned Jim-boy strange,' teases Bella.

'No it hasn't.' Jim flattens his hair and slopes to the window to hide his blush.

Ruby laughs. 'Go suck on a penny, Jim.'

'Try it yerself, Coppertopper,' he replies.

'Give us a hand, Bird, will you?'

'Not on your nelliebellie!' Bird says. 'Too fagging busy aren't I. As a magpie, see?'

She takes off at the canter. 'Gone with the invisible!' she calls. And stamps up the stairs.

I blow a cloud, close my eyes. She has lost her sparrows, sure as eggs. She'll have to go.

How might I feed us all? I have no Rubini, nor even a King of the Slanting Wire.

Pennies they earn yet they are shillings to feed.

I check the o'clock. We are on.

Rose Burton. As dogs do follow the cat-meat man, so do I follow Rose. Doughy and dimpled at the elbow, sturdy in her skirts, she is a matron crafted in the image of Eve. Though she employs no feminine artifice and her hands are raw from laundry work, she cannot scrub away her beauty. Monthly she arrives for washday, lasting three days in duration. No stain dares persist!

Long before Rose I loved Bella Wickes. Upon my bended knee I worshipped her. Time took it from us. She closed her heart. A man must pick a rose where it blooms, and so I shall, when Rose allows.

At the touch of love everyone becomes a poet. Plato. Here in my book. These learned Greeks square it in a single line! I myself have undertaken ardent scribble, of late. Four and twenty hours have I waited upon a word from Rose since delivering to her my short verse. What have I heard? Nought. Yesterday I purchased her ha'penny whelks. This evening I slid her a bag of almond nuts. I have promised her a chaffinch in a cage. God above! I would buy her a nightingale if I thought she might soften just a little. Or a skylark from the meat-man, who has three caged in his window. So help me! I have unsteadied myself.

P'raps my jib is too gaudy for she. Could it be my outer aspect? For whom does she wait? Some ballroom coxcomb? I must not maudle. Times such as these, I wish I never had a show. I wish I had never been a showman. My heart is a rag upon a nail.

I wager'd my luck would change if I raised the rookbird to full grown, as corvids are brimful with the unnatural. I fancied a charm might bestow itself. P'raps Rose might rest her gaze upon me? A blunder. Small Perce revealed himself to be dishonourable, foul in temper and cunning of mind: a member of the devil's cavalry, a soul as black as his plumage. He squabbles, rattles, croaks and shouts. I thought to teach him *God Save The Queen*, but he only caws and hiccups. I venture to discipline him yet he takes to the air, cackling. The girls pursue him when he steals their buttons and pins. Demon bird! they cry. His thievings are many: feathers, ribbons, coins, rings, brooches. And how the girls shriek when their favourites go astray. Rose swipes him with her broom, yet a thief he remains: inspecting my knifeblade with criminal interest. I have bid him join his dark comrades in the trees, albeit he will not budge. I have shut him out and closed the windows, yet in the morning there he is perched on a rooftop, a gargle in his throat. Hereafter he became known as Smallpurse, on account of his criminal practices. His own mischief bids him stay. Here he comes now, as if we are fellows: head on the tilt, eye a-glitter. I light my pipe and he angles his head to see the starlings sway in the sky. I pay no heed. My toiling knows no end.

Afternoons we play three shows.

I look for Cox's messenger boy. No sign. By the window at four I wait. Fill my pipe. I do not carp. Tonight I shall have to tell her. Bird will need to know I cannot keep her.

Who can deceive a man in
love? ~ Virgil

The Fates have intervened. Luck loiters where it will. God bless him! I shall meet with Mister Cox. A temporary reprieve for little Bird, who knew nought of it.

Cox shall have a scheme, I knew it. Patience is all!

I am on the dash but I examine myself in the glass as I go. An untidy sight. My hair appears dusty, albeit it is parted with a dip of water, as it does not care to lie smooth. Quickflash, I consider my other assets. My mouth, though

18

generous, is often agape owing to the uncertainties of the world. My eyes seem to plead but that could be bewilderment. My nose, along with my ears, sprouts horsetails of hair. I am not old yet not young either.

Not short, not tall. Not handsome, not ugly. I see nothing that might dissuade.

I shall ask a woman.

I find Bella flung upon her bed, dark hair tumbled, cheroot between her teeth. Mine she was. A Venus. Long ago. How I worshipped her. Time vanishes us all in the end.

I narrow my eyes.

'How is my look?' I ask. 'Speak plainly,' I say.

She replies, one eye closed against the smoke.

'Like a stoat,' she says. And wheezes out a laugh.

A wasp, she is. I tell her so.

I take myself off.

The outer is merely the outer. On the inside I am a blade made to cut, a bell made to ring, a flame made to burn. I am a man with a heart fit to burst yet I am wounded to the soul.

Spent. Not a man, no. A rook's arse.

Downstairs the girls have a basin of water and a cloth. Ruby and Bird wash Grateful Jim.

That boy has a look of permanent surprise. His very whiteness causes the dirt to be blacker. He shall cost me in soap. A nuisance. Twitch-twitch goes his eye.

Ruby fusses him, kisses his head. Jim, without warning, throws up his arms and grins, reveals his donkey teeth. The girls scream at the splashings. His hair drips. He grimaces at the taste of soap. No such tender devotion have I been shown these years. What do the girls see in him?

'Gal-boy!' I shout.

The girls cackle and howl. My patience frayed, I leave him to the wasps. Their screams of laughter follow me to the very end of the passage. Cock-nymphs, all! I cannot abide their affection for him. He is a bootless pyke, a scraping upon a shovel. I rescued his arse from the Union, a blunder. I am used up. Vexed. I see myself out.

As my boot steps from Quick Street onto White Lion Road I catch the sound of a fiddle. How jovially it carries a tune! Sovereign. I am enlightened. I meet Cox at eleven.

I shall see a barber for a shave. A good scrape and I shall be inspired afresh.

I can report a glow in the sky, warm as brass. Sunlight slows the smoke rising from every rooftop, softening the edges. Cab horses doze where they stand.

At The Angel you must be sharp to dodge the omnibuses and sweeper boys. At the alehouse I ask for a little bread and cheese with the porter. A man with his pipe and stout is an excellent form of comradeship. Here, among the old timbers, catched in a net of smoke, a man can reflect.

If I were an honest cove I might care to admit that the lack of a true oddity among my Unusuals has blighted my progress. I have no mule-headed, lion-faced, snake-skinned individual. Not one of them offers a thrilling disfigurement, nor bona fide deformity. Crowd-pleasing monsters have I none.

I must avail myself of the showman's guile, pull the wool, angle the mirror, tap the invisible. To be savagely impartial (though it pains me to say) my Unusuals are p'raps a pinch unsatisfactory, you could say a margin mediocre, somewhat less remarkable than they ought to be. Hand on Bible, I confess! They are undistinguished. Decidedly usual.

I have, by necessity therefore, schooled myself in the magician's sticky art. Ask any in the game. True Unusuals are hard to come by.

Rivalry I have aplenty. I must jink and weave like mister fox. I must hang onto profitable midgets by the skin of my teeth. Jaybirds all, ready to flit for the shinier coin. My wits are about me! A good cabinet girl will have a new bonnet, else she'll wander. A crowd must be caught by the ankle. And yet! How London admires these foreigners astride her London stages. How we do love an accent, in particular the ladies. In particular the French variety. How they love the la-di-da! How shall I compete?

I recall Monsieur Le Bucke, he of the feminised hair and continental moustache. No sooner had he stepped out and spoke an incomprehensible phrase than the ladies were on the brink of a swoon. Emperor Of All The Wizards. Ha! Miraculous what can be done with a perch of velvet and the lamps on low gas. A rat's arse to you, sir.

For my part I should like to attempt a decapitation, not to mention a Bodiless Lady, but I have no-one skilled in these arts. Sword swallowing is tolerated by Steps but it makes him irritable unless he's first imbibed and got himself elasticated.

I am not a greedy man, though had a parasitic twin presented itself in all the years I should have moved Heaven and earth to procure it, for I am not a man to forgo an opportunity. We do *Cups And Balls*, *Cards To Pocket*, *Sands Of The Desert*. We may not be of the calibre of The Egyptian Hall, but we know how to amuse a crowd. We do not take a man to pieces and restore him by instalments to his original self, as Mister Charles Bertram does nightly in Piccadilly, but we set to with our ribbons and doves and midgets.

In the meantime, my ear is stuffed with advice from old Victor Smith who performs *The Fakir Of Ooolu*. Vic has performed Persian card tricks and Eastern illusions these many years. He informs me the future is in spirits and spooks. The Egyptian Hall is chock-full. I wager he is right, albeit lately I have my suspicions he has fallen behind. Everywhere you look it's psychic phenomena and the gentlemen of science demonstrating their catalyptic subjects in order to prove and disprove. Poor old Vic! I am ahead. I am the king of tomorrow! I shall beat him on the bend.

I walk briskly on Canal Road. The ugly din of two barrel-organs, each tasked with the business of its own tune, disorganises the head. How fortunate are the deaf hereabouts!

Here at The Pied Bull on Islington High Street I am to meet Mister John Cox of Mile End. As well as procuring suitable subjects for surgeons and professors, Mister Cox assists various amateur groups whose task it is to investigate beyond the realm of the living. Spiritualists they call themselves, reg'lar meetings they hold, by invitation only, to consider the business of psychic phenomena and the phantasmagorical. One group meets in Hampstead. Through mediumship and séance they seek to convene with the dead.

Sovereign! I am intrigued.

May fortune revisit the wretched and
forsake the proud ~ Horace

Mister Cox stands me a glass of stout, holds a flame to my pipe.

One of his eyes is pink, it weeps. He has a habit of

pulling out his watch and smiling at whatever o'clock is revealed.

Mister Cox admires my shows. He tells me so. In particular, *The Psychic Phenomenal*. Steps and Bird perform it, popular it is. Little Bird has the gift, clairvoyant from birth. She spies ghosts on the street, in alleyways, on omnibuses. I had her instruct Steps in the art and he learned quick as a whipped dog.

Belief is all! I tell them.

Mister Cox refers to my 'good reputation'. Thinks I: a reputation for which I have toiled, without rest, these years long! I do not speak that part aloud. I do not wish to come over sour.

Mister Cox is personally acquainted with Professor Stanwick and his associates. Well I know of Stanwick's reputation. The professor is versed in matters of phenomena: spiritual, magnetic, electrical. He is an educated man of science. He addresses crowds in grand halls and institutes. He does not have to raise his voice, ring a bell, nor bang a drum. And no man asks for his money back.

Offering me another flame, Mister Cox enquires, 'Know you much of Professor Henry Stanwick?'

'Don't believe so,' I say.

Who puts all his cards on the table? We dodge. It is the game.

'The professor has a proposal for you,' says Mister Cox.

'Does he now?' I say.

My sort of game. I like a proposal. The stout has treacled the blood, sweetening all.

'I shall require a down payment,' I say. 'What does the professor have in mind?' I enquire.

'Strictly confidential,' says Mister Cox.

'Strictly Confidential are my middle names,' I reply.

*

The church bell chimes the hour on Northampton Row, another joins it almost instantly on a mismatched note. Clouds part and sunlight plunges, as if released from a vault.

Mister Cox's proposal has affected in me a brain-wave of some magnitude. A thunderbolt has struck! A great success awaits. A singular marvel.

I make for Clerk'nwell Green, happy as if I wound a clock. I may take a ha'penny saucer of whelks, and another for the girls – pepper and vinegar, piping hot.

Now that luck has fluttered in, our own little Bird shall remain another day.

I am the jiggler-joggler. Top brass!

Grateful Jim brings home half an ounce of tobacco, dashing on his stick legs between dirty raindrops. Pronounces himself a good boy for the errand. Twitch-twitch goes his eye. 'What shall I deserve Mister George?'

'There's pots to clean!' I remind him.

On the turn I stumble over the sleeping hound, who has deposited himself, like a stuffed trophy, before the fire. The hound is not of a single breed but all breeds therein. He gives no pleasure nor is he remarkable. His colour is dark as tar, his paws are heavy. If he were a man you might assume he was occupied by supernatural schemes, so black is his eye-glance. In the night shadows you might mistake him for a bear. We know him as Stranger Bill, as there is none stranger than he. A fortune in tripe. Daily do we pitch over him in the gloom, and daily do I regret him, but he has a bark like an underground door powerfully closed. This unremarkable hound keeps the unwelcomes away, keeps my Unusuals safe in their cots. The stink off him puts me in mind of the river at dawn when the dead things float.

*

Bella brings calves' cheeks for supper. We dine together with a dish of bread.

All except Pinkie, who has the leaky lungs. He lies upstairs and coughs like a sheep.

'Where is Steps?' I enquire.

Amen Steps spends his shilling at the rat-pit. It's not the blood, he says. If rats weren't baited that day he'd find a cockfight. No amount of Bible-bleating will wipe this sin away. A fool he is for a smoky cellar. It's the doubling of chink that draws him on. To be the lucky man. To win, no matter the odds. This and yet he never won a ha'penny. It's all a picture in his mind. To bring luck on you must act the winner, then luck shall creep towards you.

I tuck the napkin. I offer a prayer.

Worshipful words are well suited to a voice such as mine. Perhaps I might've preached.

'Lord, our Father—'

Ruby interrupts, with a rolling eye.

'Shut your spout,' scolds Bella. 'Percy is saying his Holy words.'

'What of it?' Ruby replies. 'Ought I care? Stuff your drain'ole.'

Bella slaps her hand upon the table and looks from me to Ruby. 'Shall I wallop her? Shall I wallop you?'

I am angered by this vulgar display. It provokes in me a rage and I am moved to shout.

'Am I a vendor of oranges! Hush! Each! Now!'

They are stilled by my timely explosion. Flora begins to cry. I continue my prayer.

Dear Lord Our Father, Grateful we are. Thankful are we. Your servants. In Thee we trust.

I dab myself with my neckcloth. Holy words. Becalming.

I take Flora's fingers in my hand. 'Hush now, Flo.'

After supper we bring on the fire and fetch out the cards.

The door bangs. The rookbird flaps. It is Steps. We turn. He leans, like a scurf. A pin of light in his eye. 'May God give you the blessing of Abraham, to you and your descendants.' We make no reply. He has lost at the rats. Shortly, I shall discuss with him my Strictly Confidential scheme. Time presses. His participation is required. This evening providence has oiled his wheels. I hand him his instrument. We shall have a caper. Fate is a fiddler, life's a dance.

Amen Steps taps his toe and scrapes upon the fiddle. Tye-diddy-o!

A skip. A rollicking. Doll starts. Pie joins. We roar for the lark of Pie's grub head upon Ruby's thigh, as far as a dwarf may creep. His face in her basket. Ha!

'Chuck it out, Amen!' I yell.

Tuesday sings. Jim leaps. Bella spins. From his cage the finch chirrups.

That chickling would whistle through the Battle of Trafalgar!

The songs we all know, *Going Out A Nesting*, *Kate Maloney* and *A Bit of Old Hat*.

'Who will dance a polka with me?' cries Bird, whirling her arms.

The room grows clammy and loud with stamping. I watch them skip through the smoke. I ought to reserve my affection for the shilling alone yet it is these few who swing the heart. My own Remarkables. I watch them stamp and twirl. Their faces are shiny red apples. *That's About The Size of It* has them tumbling like ninepins. Steps whips that fiddle till the bow is warm and his arm is a rag.

After roaring comes weeping. Each finds a place to

perch. I poke the fire. Steps warbles *Paddy Don't Care*, gloomy as a knife-grinder.

The moon is hung and the gas is ablaze at The Weasel.

Rose has made a broth for my poorly midget. Its meaty perfume is sweet. I tuck my chin to deliver her a compliment on its goldness and efficacy. I tuck my hands respectfully behind my back. I offer a smile. I tip my head to a charming angle.

'You are standing in my way, Mister George,' she says. She bustles. Averts her eye. All to persuade me of her disinterest. I am more observant. A flush stains her cheek. Gives her game away.

'Rose. Rose,' I say. With tender feeling I say it.

'I shall clobber you till you move!'

Her voice is harsh. I wager it's playful. She has a ladle in her hand. I move aside, bowing deeply, offering her the flourish of my arm. And doesn't she hurriedly turn and catch me in the face with her skirts. When she is near I am a man intoxicated. To she do I surrender.

No man is hurt but by
himself ~ Proverb

Time presses on. All are gone to their beds. The fiddle lies silent upon the table.

As a matter of urgency I must speak with Steps of Mister Cox's proposal. I must persuade, cajole, I must have his answer. I fill my pipe, stand myself a flame.

Wednesday morning at The Bull, Mister Cox enquired whether Suitables might be found among my Remarkables. Quick as robbery I replied, 'Amen and Bird!'

Done. I am no dawdler. In this way it was all drawn, there and then.

The experiment, Cox said, will feature in the renowned scientific journal *Borders, Spirit and Light*. Renowned is one of the professor's words. This I know. In such fashion a man shall make his reputation. The experiment is precarious. The professor has a will to succeed. In describing the work of the professor to Steps I must be plain, but not too plain. I must remember to use the word, Renowned.

In the morning it shall all configure. I shall be electrified, nimble, fiendish. If Amen agrees we will be markedly well coined.

Returning from Caledonian Road, I stride along Canal Street. A show on in ten.

The sky is white as bone. Traffic brisk. Weather restless. My countenance the same, undecided. Barely have I time to secure Amen and Bird for Cox's beguiling scheme when a new mischief arrives.

Tuesday informs me that Dick Fisher has purchased a petrified mummy of a child. Twenty-five inches high. Thinks he's barrelled the draught! A whisper in his ear says it's a duff. Weighs less than a candle snuffer, he says. You have to laugh! Dick Fisher couldn't sell a sardine to a seabird. Punters will tire of it, I wager.

I may dream up one better than Fisher's. Here, I have it! I shall describe it: no bigger than a plum stone, a restless Remarkable dressed in dainty boots and red waistco't, with webbed hands and the eyes of a python. I house him in a snuffbox: he skips, tumbles, walks upon his hands and sings *Down Among The Dead Men*.

An elfish gem. There. I am content! What o'clock is it?

~

Have a care of a silent dog and a still
water ~ Proverb

My boot is barely stepped over the threshold and my hat scarcely removed when the disaster reports itself. Bird must replace every one of her working sparrows for *The Bird Girl Of London*. She admits it. All are flown. How could she be so careless? 'A penny a bird!'

Like a halfwit she removes the strings that secure their legs. Hey presto! Off they flit. As, loosed from our bonds, would you or I.

'Must I tell you again?' I say. 'Out of your own pocket! You shall not be paid this week!'

She gasps, as well she might. A piffling thing it is to tether a bird. My temper heats.

'Do you moan?' I cry. 'Shall you weep? Yes! Well then. Take more bloody care!'

Bird is reluctant to cage the birds, being as how she pities their feathered souls. To-and-fro they flutter, sending Rose ducking and screaming and threatening us all with a flat iron.

Rookbird lets off a croak from the tomb. 'What shall you tell?' I ask him.

He tuts. With his glossy eye he'd have likely spied the sparrows' fleeings and flitterings. Daily do I offer him the open window! Avail yourself! The sky is wide! I tell him. Yet he always returns.

The ten o'clock show lacked pep. A crowd of eleven, albeit two were babes in arms. Tuesday Brown set a child bawling, due to his lavish movements and stupendous pessimism. I send the girls out for a bag of trotters for Flora's health and turf for the lark-bird. They'll return with crumpets, I wager, half-scoffed before they get them home.

None of mine show a bone, fat as brewers' wives, the lot. They are the neediest and greediest. I cannot grasp a five pound note before it is gone! Moreover, how to pay Peter when I must pay Paul? The rents tax me. And how to prick the curiosity of these incurious crowds? What astonishment shall I present that I have not already offered?

If a crowd feel short-changed they will give you murder for it, no matter how excellent your novelty. I myself have been remonstrated with, not to mention assailed, assaulted, arrested and punched to the ground. And yet! If a crowd parts with hard-earned chink for the Unusual then how may I not deliver? This is the part which irks, for a novelty is only novel once. And this is when a crowd can turn. I must conjure, procure and invent. I must appease the appetites of those who would be entertained. This is the fact. This is my task. To find a creature part eel, part African lion, who steps the tightrope, plays the viola, frightens the ladies and sings like a nightingale. It irks and yet ... no success succeeds as surely as failure fails.

During the night I hear it. A cry. I wake and await the next. There it is.

The creak of floorboards. Bella's low voice. A sob. A quiet interval. Then it begins again.

I know the trouble. An unhappy incident. A girl, besieged by the miseries of life, hanged herself out of a high window on the Pentonville Road. What? A year ago now? Thereabouts. Time to forget. Ruby and Flora were with me, as we'd bought fabric for the *Palace Of Peking* trick from Dewars on Argyle Street. We turned the corner off Argyle Square and there it was. A saddening sight. Like a rag she hung, asleep against the brickwork, chin upon her chest, palms turned out, while the world looked up at her. I should like to forget her dark toes.

Flora it is who suffers over it. Idle gossip says the hanged girl had been mesmerised. Utter piffle. Poverty it is that takes a girl that way. Yet you may not alter the minds of young women once they come upon a version of events. They have decided upon it and fostered it shall be: an iron to poke it with and a gathering of the guileless to listen.

Only poor Flora still weeps for it a whole twelvemonth on. She is a girl made of curds and feathers; her habit is to count her walking steps up to twelve and thereafter begin again. This done she will name all the colours she sees before her. She sees faces in brickwork and messages in clouds. When obliged to sit still she will count her in-out breaths and eyeblinks. She will count the feathers on a sparrow and the scales on a fish. A softer soul God has not yet created.

'Ladies and Gentlemen! The Young Lady shall Now Appear!'

Steps scrapes the fiddle, Pie heaves an accordion, Ruby bangs the drum.

Tuesday taps the canvas image of *The Psychic Phenomenal* with his stick.

There are those who push forward, others stand on their toes, a woman laughs. A crowd of twelve, a shilling's worth.

Tuesday pronounces: *'I Caution You to Remain Calm! What You are About to Witness is Inexplicable! Ladies, do Not Become Distressed. I Hereby Beg Your Indulgence When I Plead for Hush! The Young Lady, I must Warn You, is Deeply Entranced. In Accordance with Oxford University, I Respectfully present the Unthinkable and Audacious Entertainment known as, The Psychic Phenomenal! Gentlemen, Please remove your Hats.'*

In feathers and lace Bird walks, in the manner of one mesmerised, towards the open coffin. In his windy baritone Tuesday explains to the crowd that she is guided by the phantom of an old soldier by the name of Walter Cole: the cheapest (being in spirit) I yet hired. Walter it is, from the other side, who supervises *The Psychic Phenomenal*.

Bird fans her pack of cards for the crowd to inspect. Amen holds open the coffin lid, as a gentleman would a door for a lady. Bird settles within, while Steps closes the lid with a flourish. Hereabouts comes a crash of drum, accordion and trumpet to underline dramatic sensation ... while Steps skips and wheels about in the fashion of a magus. Another crash of trumpet and drum, and Bell arrives, draped in dozing snakes, with the second pack of cards.

The crowd are restless, albeit the three at the front are intrigued. Amen shuffles the pack once, twice, thrice! He cuts and reveals his card. Amen opens the lid of the coffin and out steps Bird. Ah! What now? A crash of drums. A trumpet blast. She opens her mouth ... and there upon her tongue is the very same card, while the rest of the pack tumble from her hand. A miracle! Top brass.

Chatter erupts in the crowd. I remove my hat to shush them.

'Here comes the best part!' I call.

Steps climbs into a trunk while Bird asks the crowd for a common item to chalk upon her slate. Amen shall name it, bang-up, while detained within the trunk.

Neither Bird nor Steps makes a mistake, not ever.

The finale is a poem, spoke eerily through Bird by Walter's spirit, concerning the bravery of the British army against the Zulus while, in the very same instant, Flora rises Heavenwards, draped in silken garmentry, upon her iron girdle – the contraption must not be observed or else the efficacy of the magic is lost.

I turn to the ladies in the crowd. I gasp. 'It is a miracle!' I exclaim. I stagger, as if I might swoon. I present the rag for inspection. I gasp again. Incredulity in the crowd. Stunned incomprehension.

I fan myself vigorously. 'Chloroform!' I cry. 'Chloroform!' I swing my cane. 'Chloroform!'

A crowd will have it in threes. And they shrink from the smell and marvel at the girl, Flora, afloat upon her back, counting her numbers, talking to clouds.

Dear Flo, she has breathed nothing more than water, swiftly are the rags switched, else Flo would stupefy . . . and how then might we perform the three o'clocker?

Hip-ho! On our way. Tidy fine job, all.

The crowd chatter, jeer and begin to disperse. 'You are Astounded!' I call after them.

Curses and laughter I hear in return. The odd threat if the o'clock is after noon.

A crowd may require the fantastical explained, due to their being sluggish on the uptake.

The magic, withal, resides within the gaps (albeit this crowd are not the sort to understand higher mediums nor finer aspects). I should prefer a more refined location, tall hats, gloves and parasols – yet we make of it the best we can. And the pennies turn to shillings turn to pounds, albeit they have barely the opportunity to warm in my hand before they are turned into a mutton supper, devoured in an instant by all.

Albeit I am not one to dwell upon the difficulty, I swerve as the wind. A reg'lar night fox. I follow my cane. Off I sway.

∼

In waters where you least think it,
there will be a fish ~ Ovid

Early evening. Receipts are down and yet. Must I maudle? The ale and porter calls.

The sky on White Lion Road is grey in its countenance, albeit a sudden fall of late sun turns airborne dust to stars, illuminating each stain upon Amen Steps' hat.

'The spirit moves!' cries Amen.

'Our Lord commands it,' I reply. I am not a religious man, yet I practise caution.

Behind us stroll my midgets in fresh collars; together they will drink you under the table (their size being no indicator of their appetites) and rifle your purse for excess.

In piping voices they blether, 'Not in a month. What! Do you call me a liar?'

'A liar, yes! Wednesdays, Thursdays, Fridays. I shall cut out your tongue for it. There!'

Their prating is all disagreement. Their fights can grow violent.

Through no particular design we find ourselves at The Hat & Feathers by n' by.

'The pipe and porter calls!' I announce.

'Its cry is sweet!' returns Amen.

Whereupon he swings left and disappears into The Hat, followed closely by Pinks and Pie.

Inside it is crowded and noisy as a dog fight. As Amen disappears with my dwarves into the fog I catch sight of Albert Goffe, astounded of expression, wrapped in shawls of smoke.

He leans on some unfortunate's shoulder. He spots me.

'My word! That's Unusual!' cries Goffe. He staggers in his boots, cackling at himself.

His gaze is soggy. He re-lights his pipe, coughs, squints.

'We are not made for miracles, you and I,' he says, poetic in his cups. 'How much we toil for little,' he adds, 'while others toil little for much. Isn't that right, Mister Percival Usual?'

He leans through our pipesmoke, sweat upon his eyelid. He affects to check we are not overheard, flicks glances over his shoulder, as if he played his role in a melodrama.

I laugh.

'Do not be amused,' he says. His finger trembles. 'I have something unusual as your own name,' he says. 'Shipshape! So long as you keep mute.'

Albert Goffe speaks in riddles. He is a lurk, in truth, but I am no flat. Very well do I know the tricks of this trade. It is my trade. I know all the feints and some not yet invented.

It is a game of dice. All flimflam. I pay no heed.

Goffe leans in.

'You must not torture yourself,' he confides. 'It is not for you. Not now. Not ever.'

He licks his fingertip, runs it under his damp eye. He lifts his pipe. Taps it.

'Beyond your means and mine,' he says. Foam gathers at the corner of his mouth. He blethers. He is a demon.

I remain quiet. I wait. If I do not respond he will topple. Here he goes.

'It is not a woman,' he says. 'Nor a robbery,' he says. 'It is a curiosity.'

I say nothing. I have heard it before. I re-light my pipe.

'Of rare provenance. The rarest,' he says. 'No finer piece have I yet acquired. Nor will ever.'

He waves his pipe. Coughs.

Still, I do not respond.

'A rare and peculiar antiquity!' he cries, his hands fly up. He shakes his head at the thought. His finger drops upon my shoulder. He would like to donate it to a fine museum he says. But who can afford such philanthropy? Who? Anyone? Someone? Not us.

This is part of his scheme to entrap. He will tie you in knots with his talk of museums, antiquities, history, and you will discover yourself back at home with an eyeball or a musket ball, several shillings lighter and three leagues wiser.

I make no reply. He has tossed me a frayed rope. I shall not be led.

Loosened by porter, stout and good cheer, Tuesday and I stroll along Chapel Street, while behind us stumble the dwarves. The hours have crept. The sun is taking her imperial leave behind the Gas Works. A strange and invisible element is gas. I take it as a sign.

On a day yet to be named, Percy George shall graciously oblige Professor Stanwick in the task of his momentous and precarious experiment. Steps and Bird are the bold volunteers! I volunteered them myself. They should not dream to decline such an opportunity.

Fear not, Mister Precarious Professor, sir. You shall have your astounding spectacle by'n'by. Most efficaciously shall we deliver the scientific phenomena. We have ample expertise. In this way shall we receive the agreeable reward of the multiple shilling.

Top brass. Ride on! Ride on in majesty!

There is no great genius without a
tincture of madness ~ Seneca

'Am I charmed?' she asks. 'You are indeed,' I reply, and she is.

I have chose Flora Wickes for The Talking Head In A Box, being as how she found The Bodiless Lady too confining. Flora has the physiognomy required for the illusion. As a matter of fact, her severed head is pronounced world-class due to her unusually pale skin: in spite of the candlelight it remains pearly as frost in appearance. The requirement is that she kneel in position while concealing her legs and feet invisibly behind and, thus contorted, remain still as a corpse in order that the carefully installed mirror-within-the-cabinet may perform its duty. But I am giving away the secrets.

Illusion is the self-same article as luck: affect to be its master and it shall obey. I am of a mind to reproduce Alfred Stodare's talking *Sphinx-Head-In-A-Box*. The trick demands the strategic placement of mirrors for its success but I fear this may be too elaborate a task for our outfit. How shall I compete?

What I wouldn't give for a speckled boy from Africa, such as John Crouch has. Word is he cribbed the child from a railway carriage as it was transported from Southampton to Waterloo. Crouch, the miserable lurk, awards himself the gift of a piebald child with no jot of misgiving. Vexes me that such a noble creature could be stole like a purse.

A curious fruit is the human heart. God designed us in His own perfection but Percival George keeps an eye out for those who went awry. A showman must grasp potential and see beyond the ordinary. It matters not if it be the Armless Man performing carpentry with his feet or a weasel riding a bicycle, if it's uncommon it's on. Astound the crowd! If you can't be unnatural be unusual.

Though my own menagerie holds not one of these bona fide Remarkables, I believe yet that one will come. Nightly

I pray upon my knees. What shall it be? Where shall I chance upon it? I picture a hot-eyed Remarkable, albino furred, scaled of tongue, melodiously voiced. Yes! One to charm, horrify and delight!

Some would rather have a good pony than a legless acrobat. Not I. Albeit, the spectacle alone is insufficient. What about the ill-luck that befell the poor soul? This is what a crowd wants to see: the good fortune that abandoned it. This is why they come. This is why they pay. The appetite is never satisfied. Only the misfortune of others gratifies. That is where the chink resides.

North-westerly in aspect is our courtyard, where the odours of the canal hang about and soot gathers upon the red geraniums, blackening them in their boxes. A marshy smell reminds you of the unlucky. Here is a plum tree, twisted where the wall has crippled it, and sentry upon the wall is a blank-eyed cat, staring through you, white as a spook.

Here am I upon a bench for the weary. Ask the moss upon this wall about the tick-tocking of time. Moss is familiar with time, being that time itself is a gardener, and moss is one of its more ponderous schemes. Pondering is no good to me now. I await good fortune in abundance.

Time presses. I drag myself indoors.

'Rose!' I say. 'Will you not assist me in a lie down?'

I am waggish. Ladies like a bit of horseplay. In the mirror I observe that my eye glitters as a polished gem. She cuffs me with the boot she is cleaning. This is my reward for liveliness.

'We shall have the doctor, woman! You have bludgeoned me!'

'No-one hears you, George,' is all she says.

She calls me George though my name is Percy. She calls

38

me George though my name is Unusual. I am battered, bruised, rebuffed. I should call a constable. I am maligned by women. As my regard turns to affection, so do they turn on me. For what reason? I cannot fathom.

Here she comes! A copper-gilt maiden hurrying to my aid. Here is Ruby Doll.

'Well, well, Mister Percy George. Got a clobbering? Let's see? Deserved it, did you? Course you did.' It amuses her. She laughs, dabs at my injury with a cloth. She sits beside me to sing *Waggle Duff Peg*. In the corner Steps puts down his boot to scrape it on the fiddle.

'Has the blow settled it?' cries Flora. 'Do his head hurt? Is it bloody? Can I see?'

We have mutton chops at dinnertime, a bunch of watercress and half a loaf. We add a coal to the fire and another. Flora counts them in a whisper. Bella slides into a chair. On the arm settles Bird. In the firelight we are softened, voices are stirred with syrup. Rookbird gargles. I am soothed. Sovereign.

The camel dances ~ Proverb

I am in fierce need of a jar of Eagle to jolly my step. Amen and I do partake.

My luck is gone to blazes. I currently have two midgets on their backs and Flora is become sudden weakened by an affliction of unknown origin. I have given them all two brands of tonic. That scurf runs a tidy medicinal racket: a crocus from Kent, full of patter. Fakery the lot, no doubt. Good blunt for nought.

I intend to speak with Steps of Mister Cox's proposal,

but my midgets are dropping like flies and I must solve the predicament.

Cold pigeon pie at The Rising Sun. A second half of porter and I have a scheme almost devised. The third lighting of my pipe delivers it. The act shall go as follows: the midgets, it shall be explained to the crowd, are fallen into a trance upon their backs and cannot be raised, albeit attempts are made by our two delightful damsels. The midgets (assumed deceased) must be decently buried ... here Steps scrapes a melancholy fugue on the fiddle. The weeping damsels perform their dance! Crowd loves a death et cetera. So far so sovereign. But hang-on-just-a-minute-sir! Where have those midgets fled? What? Disappeared from their own coffin by unseen magic, you say? (And here the girls display the empty coffin.) Whereupon, Bird and her London sparrow (she has replaced only one) find the midgets asleep in a cradle. Bella sounds the trumpet. At which signal Bird awakes them from their catalepsy with a kiss. Dear God! What a pretty picture! Saints be praised! And tender!

Another half pint of porter and two penn'orth of bread and cheese. Here am I, a guv'nor and his clown, repairing the vexations of this world with invention. No man shall stand in my path!

He is wise to no purpose who is not
wise for himself ~ Proverb

None do scorn Amen Steps; he is the shilling. Pure gold is his heart, yet his head is full of dust. Girls are soft-hearted for his curls and uneven smile that creeps higher

40

on the left, revealing the gaps in his teeth, fanning the skin around his rinsed blue eyes. He is older than he looks. He removes his cap to speak, not for deference, but to scratch his head while he forms his words. Steps is keen on his Bible quotes, in particular Revelations. Psalms. Memory of an elephant.

We recline together, Amen and I. He begins with a spell of coughing.

We are amiable. Fireside. Pipes lit.

'Well?' I ask him. 'What say you on Mister Cox's proposal?'

'Our Saviour weeps!' he cries.

Steps is prone to melodrama. I must soothe him. He has his reservations when it comes to interviews with the dead.

'I am no necromancer!' he says.

He quotes Isaiah and Leviticus aloud. Spooks me with his quavering tones.

'If it's speaking the Holy Book you want you ought to have taken the cloth!' I tell him straight. I point my finger so he knows I mean it. I won't be bludgered, Holy or unholy. I will not be threatened by tall words.

He quiets down sharpish. He scratches his head, thinks.

I describe the professor's experiments with the inexplicable: the bodies that float, the rooms that quake, the furniture that creeps without human agency.

'This new phenomena,' I continue, 'it is a marvel, a wonder,' I inform him. 'Godly men and gentlemen of scientific persuasion alike are gathering in earnest to prescribe their discoveries,' I tell him. 'Why, Professor Stanwick himself gave a lecture only the other day at High Holborn. Such a crowd he drew!' I add.

I tap my pipe. I have spoken. I watch Steps. I await his answer. The fire coals pop, hiss.

Steps replaces his hat. Removes it again. Points at me. Grins. He is befuddled.

'Eh?' I laugh at him. 'You see, Steps, there is prestige in it. Distinction,' I add. 'Renown,' I whisper.

Steps closes one eye and regards me with the other. I spot a tremor on his lip. I listen to his breathing.

'It's merely business, Ames. A day's work, my friend. Another show. Yes or no?'

He closes both eyes to think.

I press him. 'You will know nought of it,' I say. 'Being that you will drowse throughout!'

Children, women and animals trust Steps. He has the plain-ness, the saintly fool about him. His heart is open, his mind deceived.

'It is yours,' I say. 'No other could deliver, given as you, alone, have an unstained heart.'

Even as I speak it I realise it is the truth. I am electrified by my calculations.

We listen to St Mary's bell chiming the hour. The chimes dignify the moment, by their end there is glory in the air.

I have produced a scheme mighty in proportions. I stand to spread my arms, as might Professor Stanwick himself, arriving at his grand conclusion. But my words are all spent.

'Will you do it, Steps?' I say.

Simplicity is all. The line is cast.

Steps opens his eyes. Grins. His teeth number few. He raises his hand to speak.

'I shall do as you say,' he replies. 'I shall do it and be damned!'

This is his answer. After which he laughs, a shrill burst, at himself.

42

'Good man!' I say.

Now we both laugh. And I shake his hand, and he slaps my arm.

'What a pal you are to me!' he says. He is amazed.

'To one another, both!' I cry. 'To one another, both!'

Nor is Apollo always bending his
bow ~ Horace

I tackle the day at the gallop. I am the Quick Street nib, my legs are a gambolling blur.

I have the fizz about me. Sunlight has squeezed through street smoke and window glass to lie in columns upon the floor, where the hound has flung himself to doze, draped in stripes of black and gold; a poor man's malodorous tiger.

I find her likewise dozing: shoeless, sprawled in a chair. I shall amuse her. I have the zest. She is bound to detect it. 'Bella!' I say. 'Do we not reside on Quick Street? Answer me! Ought we not be more aptly address'd Slow Progress Lane? Or Dead Halt Alley? Ha!'

'There. Hear my wit, Bell? How it flashes!'

Bell loves a prank. And yet she does not reply. A face like an empty sack.

To cheer her spirits I may have tapped the back of her head with Friday's newspaper, playfully. Gaily. To amuse her. To enliven the day. 'Look out, Belsie!' Flack, with the newspaper. That sort of thing.

She seems enraged. Grabs at me! Frantic hands from the asylum. I grip the bannister to steady myself. 'What has got into you, woman?'

I flack her again, not for her amusement this time. She looks at me then with a vermin eye. 'Don't touch me again, Percy George,' she warns, her skin darkening.

'An innocent frolic!' I protest, flattening my hair. But she is gone.

Saints in Heaven! Women are a conundrum buried too deep for me. Once, she would lark till sundown. Lively for a game. Loved a rag! How does a female turn innocent playfulness to war? I daresay I shall be obliged to purchase a penn'orth of vinegar'd peas to sweeten her. I shall beg her forgiveness, naturally. Beautifully sentimental it shall be and she'll offer up her best smile. Tender. There. Mended.

She stood revealed a goddess truly in
her gait ~ Virgil

He found me at Bethnal Green.

I had no acquaintance with my parents. There. That's my story. Bitter. Sweet. Short.

I am Bella. Here is my voice, then. Writ upon his own sheets.

Paper costs. From his journal I razored them, two slices: they lifted out, soft as whey.

The words shall tell my side, so he shall know I have a side. What will you do about it, Percy George? There. As I thought.

I have my letters from Bible-learning. I have a dollup of numbers too. My scribble is slow, small as cross-stitch in the corners, and scraping letters is dull as winter. It could stop a clock. I do not spell but . . . i writ tidi leters see?

44

Ruby sits, darning. I too must pretend to darn with a needle, not scratch with a pencil.

'Stop blowing, will you?' she says, and tosses her hair so it lands on her back, light as froth. I pick at its copper frizz. A shrew. I tell her so.

I recall it well. That day he yelled it, loud as ironmongery, so everyone would hear.

Bella Wickes! he said. Be my queen! He got upon his knee. And I shall be your bang-up king!

That eye fixed me directly and persuaded me with its sauce. That eye of his had shine: one glance. Later, under an old willow near the boating lake in Victoria Park, he chucked off his hat and said, What have I done to deserve such fortune as you?

A drizzle began and he kissed me. He made me laugh with his pop-eyed faces. Arm in arm we'd go, respectable as newly-weds. We saw Judy hitting Punch while, in the booth, a little dog dressed in a ruff sat guard on a plinth. We rested on a bench. He fed me whelks and onions. We laughed at the swans. There was no show on in ten, no paltry crowd, no coins in a bag. We were free as hummingbirds. I imagined no other time for us, only this. He fed me a trotter and a pastry filled with warm cherries. He sang me *Sweet, The Journey Home*. We drank stout at The Cross Keys. I told him I loved him. And I did.

Leave the rest to the gods ~ Horace

The day remains tolerably bright, hazy sunlight, a breeze that hisses in the trees and presses the women's skirts. Enlivening. I fetch my hat and take myself out.

I have an appointment. I cannot be late. My future awaits.

May the Lord have pity on Bella. She dreams of a stage career, yet she possesses not the silhouette nor the elocution of an actress. Truth is an axe – some have not the courage to wield it. I bring it down . . . not for unkindness, but merely to crack open the truth. Love has not blinded me. We have no stalls here, no royal boxes, yet I have given her a rowdy crowd, heavy with coins: thrice in a morning, thrice again in the afternoon! I have found her sister, Flora, employment at her request. The sister, Flora Wickes (as if there could be another), boasts the same mahogany hair and bow lip, yet she is of a gentler persuasion. You may reg'lar find her agape at the rudimentary. Poor Flora possesses both caprice and bewilderment in abundance, albeit she offers a faltering charm that is not to be found in Bella. Abandoned as girls, I found Bella bartering baskets for pennies at sixteen years of age, with her sister at her skirts. At the Union they would be had not I intervened. Twenty-four was my own age then, already the slang cove!

At The Goldbeater's in Bethnal Green I fell at her feet. Bella had the fire. Our story was ill-fated, though we knew good years and reg'lar laughed and contented lived together before the devil's own luck arrived. I gave my heart to her. Time has wiped it away.

I keep a low flame, for only God knows what shall come. If it pleases Him, she and I may yet find our path.

Well, I know why she torments me. Four infants lost. Over the years grief turned bitter.

I am the daily prompt, I need only appear to nudge the memories of her lost babes. And yet, my arms are ready to embrace. Not even Rose Burton shall extinguish this.

She will torment me for it, yet I love Bella still. If you

forgive anyone their sins, says the Holy Bible, it follows they shall by God be forgiven. Shall she yet forgive? Will this bring the reward of love? This narrow life does not confirm it, but I am a patient man. I will wait.

He is a king who desires
nothing ~ Seneca

On the north side of Waterloo Bridge is the shop.

The walls within are stacked floor-to-ceiling: flasks, jars, cabinets, heads, horns, hides. Hundreds of pairs of eyes observe my entrance. A stink of the river lingers; shadows lean, draughts stir. The room tilts, owing to its mud and silt foundations. The customer lists as he enters and by the time he reaches the counter, all askew, he has forgot why he came and buys the first flotsam he sees. I possess jars to prove it.

I am obliged to rap thrice upon the counter to draw out Albert Goffe, Esquire.

At last he approaches from behind a curtain, without urgency, blinking in his spectacles, a-shuffle in his footwear. A snail summoned from his shell.

'Mister George, the Unusual. So soon. A pleasure.'

His tone never moderates, as if he were reading it off the board, as our Tuesday Brown does. He reaches for a long jar containing a cloudy liquid and a pointing finger.

I rap my stick. I know the game.

'I am not here for jars.'

'Ah. Well.' His eye is restless till he speaks, whereupon it closes, as in prayer. The other eye, of indifferent humour, fixes steadily ahead. Mister Goffe, though tidy of manners,

47

is no feast for the eye. He is in possession of a large and bulbous head and his eyeballs perform independently. If nature had seen fit to complete her task with a pinch more flair, Albert Goffe might himself have become a curiosity. A pinch of juggling, singing and mystification, p'raps I might've hired him.

Goffe breathes heavily. He presses his lips together, grimaces. He raises his arms in a gesture of surrender.

'I have taken a change of heart. You cannot afford it!' he cries.

I have brought custom to Goffe many times. He sold me the eyeballs of a bona fide Amazonian. He sold me the criminal hand of a convicted murderer. Both remain afloat in their preserving liquids. Today I am not drawn by trinkets.

'Monday last, you spoke differently,' I say.

He observes me. His damp eye narrows.

'I was dazzled. I was celebrating. I was topsy-turvy. I apologise.'

'You are forgiven,' I say. 'A quick glimpse then?'

'No. God bless you. I should not forgive myself,' he says.

Goffe opens a drawer of teeth. Aromas of spent coal and saltpetre.

'It is an authenticity,' he says. 'What I have is an antiquity. Bona fide. I'm looking for a good price for the piece. No slangs!' he says.

The Piece, he calls it. Ha. A game. Well then. His concealment of it irks nonetheless. I ought to glimpse the wretched thing. I try another tack.

'It's not a purchase for myself,' I say. 'I may be acquainted with someone who is interested in your antiquity. Or p'raps he doesn't count either.'

'Who?'

'One Professor Stanwick, expert in all things scientific and phantasmagorical.'

Goffe pretends to be mystified. His hands clasp, unclasp.

'P'raps I am here on his behalf,' I say.

'And p'raps you are not,' he says.

'The professor has no interest in tawdry items,' I say.

Goffe tempts, entices, rouses, forbids. He imagines himself a master of entrapment. Happily I am wise to his ruses. I have my own dodges.

I fetch out my han'kerchief, blow my nose. 'By which I mean, is the antiquity bona fide?' I ask. 'The professor has a violent temper.'

Like a theatrical he affects offence, surprise, disgust. His pique is evident, if over-played. He raises his chin, closes his eyes. 'I have authentification,' he sighs. 'From Paris. Dated. Signed by the royal surgeon. The piece is in excellent condition, professionally strung, articulated, presented for display.'

'Ah,' I say. 'And I have the pharaoh of Egypt at home for half the price! If I want bones I shall fetch some, quick and tidy.'

Goffe looks up in dismay. He flushes, flattens his hair. I have stung him.

'Excellent idea! Go fetch your butcher's bones!' he snaps. 'Leave well alone the antiquity.'

'Hold your horses, Albert! I merely ask for satisfaction on behalf of the professor.'

Goffe is become the colour of a raspberry; a creamy froth is gathered at the corner of his mouth. He leans forward and hisses through his teeth.

Now I have him.

'A most royal and celebrated midget of exquisite antiquity is what I have,' he spits. 'A rarity. A gem! Wait a moment!'

Struggling to breathe, Goffe turns to a drawer that he fumbles open with a key upon a ribbon around his neck. Victory is mine. I only have to complete a concluding manoeuvre. Goffe removes a package.

'I shall not pay dear for the dirty bones of some wretched midget,' I tell him. A final flourish!

'You are a fool,' he gasps, reaching for his spectacles. 'I do not expect you to understand. Ah. Here it is.'

Goffe unwraps a document. I observe a seal, a signature.

'Here is the autopsy report. Here is his name. And here is a box containing the documents.' Goffe clears his throat.

'These are the bones of Nicolas Ferry,' he says. 'Royal dwarf of France. Here is his likeness. And here again. France knew him as Bébé. Baby, to you and me. Never in France was a dwarf as notorious as this one. He sat upon the knee of Louis XV. The very King of France!'

Goffe has bewitched himself.

'An antiquity,' he murmurs. 'Rare. Historical. Foreign.'

'Costly,' I say.

'You'd have it performing,' he says. 'A man like you. An antiquity's not for the stage.'

'Piffle!' I say. 'P'raps you wager I cannot afford your dancing bones?'

'I know you cannot afford it. What you got these days? A sickly girl, an ex-whore, a former soldier and two frail midgets? Deary me. Shocking. In sore need of something, are you not, Percy? Something *unusual* p'raps?'

We listen to the agitated tapping of my cane. Games is games and cheek is cheek. Yet I will not be jostled by a pickled curiosity vendor.

'It is not a street piece,' he mewls.

'I do not seek a street piece, Mister Goffe.' There. My voice is sharp.

'It would stand well behind glass,' he says.

'Am I curator of the British Museum?' I ask.

'It is not an item for a fair!'

'Should I pay the price if it were?' I say. 'I am here with a full purse!' I add. 'I seek an item of unique remarkability. If it is rare I will pay. Will you show it to me? Yes or no!'

Goffe smiles horribly.

'I am satisfied,' he says. 'I will fetch the piece.'

My mind heaves. What! Will I be toyed with? Am I a dog and cart man? My reputation is known. Is Mister Cox a fool? Is Professor Stanwick another? I draw a crowd larger than Dick Fisher's and Sam Crouch's together. Saints in Heaven. A glance at the receipts tells as much! Thinks he I am unworthy of his box of bones? When I am finished he will beg me to take his piece for tuppence. He will make his reputation upon the back of mine and be grateful!

There. I have set my heart bumping. I must take a pastille. It is all a game. He shall not have the next bout. I compose myself, quickflash.

'Here it is, Mister George.' Goffe reappears in his shuffling shoes.

'Ah. Good. Sovereign. Let me help,' I say.

And now I feel cheered by my own cunning. I shall place down a payment, a subscription, something to stuff up his spoutings and bletherings. Instalments shall deal with the rest.

I relieve Goffe of the long wooden box in his arms.

'Allow me,' I say. 'Before your own box beckons!' I add, and I laugh at my quick wit.

'Most amusing,' murmurs Goffe. 'You are caught in the giddiness, Mister George.'

He observes me with one of his drifting eyes. 'Am I to

take it you have about you adequate funds?' I note a shiver in his hand.

'Should I stand here all day if I did not?'

'And do you vouchsafe to hold in safekeeping the documents connected to this historical item?'

'Yes, yes, yes.'

'Upon that contract I think we may conduct business, Mister George.'

'I shall be the judge of that,' I reply. I tap my cane once for emphasis.

Goffe places a long wooden box upon the counter and proceeds to unlock it, with theatrical delay, by use of a second key around his neck. His hands disappear inside the box and then with exaggerated trepidation Goffe raises the skeleton into the air.

'He is beautifully articulated. You see?'

Before me hangs the boy skeleton. Ivory is his colour.

A gentle swing of the legs. Dainty as an elf. An acrobat.

'Bring him closer,' I say. I touch his hands. Two starfish. Ah! Ticklish. One rests upon mine. I close my fingers around his. How gentle is the bony touch.

'A child,' I say.

'A midget,' Goffe corrects. 'Royal. Distinguished. Unique. None other exists.'

How tidy he is! I laugh aloud. A pair of wings are his shoulder blades. A pretty cage is the ribs, where within once ticked a heart. Here were eyes and hereabouts a tongue, a voice. Did he laugh? I wager he did! And where did these feet trot? These legs kneel? Before a gilded throne?

'I should like to examine him,' I say.

Goffe lifts the midget in his arms and lays him gently down upon the counter.

'Well?' he says.

I do not reply. The dwarf bones are twigs, shells and smooth pebbles. How paltry are the fingerbones and toes, miniaturised as teeth, perfect as pearls!

Once glimpsed, I do not fail to recognise rarity. Countless times have I visited the British Museum and other institutes. Instinct persuades me that he is indeed royal. He is no duff or I should sense it instantly.

I lean until my gaze is level with the sockets. Eye to eye. Hand to hand. Heart to heart.

'Well, well,' I murmur to him.

Does he watch me? I fancy so. Arrived at last. Good fortune has delivered him. It is *he*. The truest kind of Remarkable. The unusualest Unusual. Arrived to bless our days.

Ah, Mister George! he seems to say.

'And now,' Goffe says. 'You shall sign here.'

For a moment I pay no heed, for it is now that the future reveals itself.

My good fortune. At last. He is come. My true Remarkable.

'I shall pay you in instalments,' I say. I step back to conduct the business. 'If I am late by a day you shall have him returned forthwith; a fair deal. That is my offer. Take it or leave it.'

'I am satisfied so long as you satisfy, Mister Unusual George.'

Never mind the old-cove-shuffle, Goffe has people who know people, who know people. His uncle earned his stripes in the constabulary, he has no worries there. Paid his narking dues. I shall pay up, else find us all alight and burning in the middle of the night.

Flush of fives, he is mine! The French midget belongs to me. I have the signed receipt! Cheaper it would've been

53

to marry Rose. Or buy a chaise, or two horses. But what of them? Any fool can buy the same. In their place I have purchased The Piece, along with its documents. Astounded they will be, Dick Fisher, Samuel Crouch. True as church! That I am become the privileged owner of a rare antiquity. Henceforth, my reputation shall be as curator of all that is remarkable, unusual and unique. Not merely a showman with a pocketful of midgets, doves, cups and balls. No. A master collector, furnished with rarities the like of which is most uncommon. Shall I place a price on it? It is priceless. Even a fool knows that. And I am no fool. Watch me now. Here I stroll, topper and cane. A nib. The finest! The bang-up king of Quick Street.

We are but dust and shadows ~ Horace

I journey home with the two boxes in my arms. Their burden is a joy!

The larger is the size of an infant's coffin, albeit half the depth. The smaller one, containing the documents, rests upon the larger, albeit both are cumbersome as I make progress.

At The Strand I catch a two-horse omnibus and am obliged to upend the larger box, which emits an ominous knock-and-tumble sound from within. Only I know it is the rattle of a royal skeleton. Top brass.

Rumour has it that David Prince Miller, costumed as Wang Fong The Chinese Enchanter, performed in the presence of the Cham of Tartary, the Emperor of Russia, the King of Prussia *and* the Pope of Rome. Bring me my cloak! I too may soon boast of interviews with exotic royalty in brocaded rooms. Hip-ho! The answer to my prayer has arrived. A masterpiece of the unexpected. Death has delivered it, as Life has no more tricks up her sleeve. Yes, indeed. When the flesh offers nought but tribulation, look to the wisdom of bones.

To celebrate I visit Polly of White Lion Street, whose real name is Maud, in her room above The Firkin. No sooner had she slipped her fingers under my collar and gasped in my ear than we were tipping about as if it were our wedding night. No man can resist Maud when she decides it's on. She unbuttons with a left hand, snuffs the candle with her right, and clamps you warmly in her ample thighs. It is what a bird must feel as it swoops. There is nothing but the movement of air and sudden dip of the heart, the bindings unloosed. Maud Roberts is an angel! Albeit the Church would never agree.

Her words charm him ~ Ovid

Percival George. This is me, Bella, with pencil stub. Shall I be plain?

Well then. Your eye: the glass ornament in the socket.

Have you writ of it in your scribblings?

Thought not. It frightens the girls, you see – offends his pride.

That eye got bludgered when you were a boy, Percy. He won't talk of it. Suffers with his masculine vanities though you wouldn't toss him a ha'penny for his reflection. Oh, I must not laugh! Pity, as his good eye has shine. He would win you with a line and shuffle. He had the brass then. Fresh from the barber's with the sun behind him and a clean collar, Percival George was handsome. He chaffed less. He hung on my words. He held my fingers in his hand and paid attention while I chirruped on this and that. Bella, he whispered, are you Aphrodite sent from high Olympus?

If love were pennies he spent them all on me. And I did love him back. He had the strut. Oh, he could parade: a cockerel bird! He'd learned to poke a crowd with his voice, jostle them, sway them with his intonations. He swayed me and I was happy for it. Percy could fashion an uproar with a shout and a wave of his cane. We drank at The Lion and we danced at The Crown. And I loved him.

Time makes us fools. Yes, and time grows us old till we forget.

It is Thursday today. P'raps the twenty-ninth, close to The Ascension. The girls are horsing; they'll not be bidden. You are gone again, Percy George, with Amen to The Hat.

Bird hauls on Ruby's arm, their boots drag, hairpins fall.

'I am that weary,' Bird wails. Her pale face is framed by limp curls. 'On my life!'

Ruby wriggles her off, moves closer and whispers at my cheek, 'Tell us what it is, Bell. What do you know of it?' Her mouth hangs, hoping for intrigue, her eye is fixed, unblinking.

I bend for the pin.

'Is our luck come about?' calls Flora, tripping in her boots, a rabbit in her arms.

'I don't know much,' I say to Ruby.

'Tell us what you do know.' She studies me, a grimace of excitement on her face; her cloud of copper frizz hair drifts as she moves.

'None of us shall worry over gentlemen scientists,' I tell her. 'That's an end to it.'

'Oh saints!' Flora says, dropping the rabbit, pulling at my skirt. 'Will the scientists have us?'

Ruby leans, takes my sleeve; her cheek blushes through her freckles. 'Is it true that girls went and were not seen after?' she says. 'Well, is it?'

'Will you all stop dragging on me!' I bark.

'Gone and died for their trouble,' pipes Bird, ducking under Ruby's arm. 'A wicked thing! I shall not die for the men of science. Hoity what-nots. Scout the devil! Sling yer hook, I'll say!'

'No-one asked you, Bird-brain,' says Ruby.

'Nor you, speckle-neck!'

'Stow it,' I tell them. I move away and they follow.

'I shall have a word, then,' calls Bird. 'The girl-spirit shall natter to me. She'll tell all.'

'You have no spirit gifts,' I say. 'It's just a rig for the show.'

Bird canters ahead of me, whipping her thigh. 'I have gifts. I have marvels to show the gents of science!' she cries. 'I shall blow their hats off! Twirl me whiskers, they'll say. Who is this Bird-wonder? Stuff it! 'Tis me! Nobby and charmed, I'll reply. I'll have 'em curtseying in their frock coats!'

'Is she a child?' Ruby shrieks. 'Or a halfwit? they will ask!'

'I shall be seventeen before you close your pipehole!' Bird replies, and begins to spin with her eyes closed. Ruby cackles. Flora hugs herself, screams and spins with Bird.

'God's mercy! Settle down!' I cry.

'S'only larking,' calls Bird.

'S'only!' echoes Flo. 'S'only larking s'only larking s'only larking!'

'Enough!' I move to the stairs. I sit on the blanket box. I've no craving for pranks.

Flora clumps towards me in her big boots, a frown of concern on her face. How shall I comfort her? I cannot tell her what her future holds.

'Come here,' I say.

She puts her arms out to me. 'Bella,' she says. 'Are you despaired? Shall I set the kettle?'

'No,' I say. 'I'm not despaired.' I kiss her head.

Darling big-eyed Flo, always the baby. Though she is sixteen years of age, my sister acts like someone much younger.

'I shall set the kettle!' she pipes. She closes her eyes when she grins. And off she goes, heavy hair swinging at her back, counting her steps up to twelve ... 'three four five.' Dear as daisies. Lifting her skirts so as not to stumble.

I hear Ruby and Bird chaffing next door. For a moment I am alone. Percival George the-not-so-unusual: what have you done with the girl that once was me? He has forgot. A clock shall not run backwards. Days that are spent don't return, nor does love that is cooled. Albeit, if I possessed the key, I should wind back that clock. You would take my hand, Percy George, and return us to before.

A body without a heart ~ Plautus

Three shows. Small crowds. Happily I am buoyed on account of my French purchase, royal as pearls – as yet unannounced. I shall pick the moment. Such a precious item would be pilfered in a blink. I know these streets. Word gets out.

Sally Brown Is In Her Grave. I hear it as soon as I step within. Sung and scraped, with true regret, by Steps on his fiddle. A minute longer I'd have showered him in coppers.

I tell him. He bows, the crooked pigeon.

A skittering of hooves in the passage. The shrieks of girls. 'Get that horse out!' I yell, though my countenance is cordial. A pregnant doe I discovered in my bed blanket last night. Dwarf ponies chomp enough for animals thrice their size, an African elephant would eat less.

Doll sets a kettle on the stove. 'Stand us a pot,' I say. 'I'm precious dry.'

Bird fetches out the cards. A dove crouches on her shoulder. 'I'll deal you!' she cries.

'I am daggered. Spent. Bang-up,' I say. 'Deal the others.'

I sit, and from that low angle I spy the buck rabbit scratching itself behind the door.

The girls play Cribbage, Three-up. Last night they played All-Fives. I am partial to the game of skittles, over-joyed I'd be for a game!

I tap my pipe on the wall. I am in excellent tenor. Bell calls out. They are off, she says.

Tuppence each, for a polka and a jig.

'Why not jump about here?' I say. 'Amen'll scrape a tune, for nought.'

It's company they want. The music is sweeter, says Bella, being that they have a cornopean player and some hag on a harp, as well as a boot-stomping fiddler.

All blether! It's the drink they want. Sure as Sam Crouch is a nickey and a thief. No matter. Let them spend their blunt for a stamp.

Alone in the yard with the rookbird, I note the light is on the turn: pale gold, brindled with grey cloud and ropes of smoke from every rooftop. Starlings swim the sky. A bird who never seems to tire, though he never had to entertain the crowds this many times a day for coins. A starling pleases himself. What earthbound man has time for acrobatics?

I rest upon the bench. Along the wall rookbird edges closer. He affects not to notice me till he arrives at my shoulder, at which point I bring a flame to my pipe. Close my eyes, draw, inhale. Has my luck turned? Rookbird examines me. He croaks, ticks, gargles.

'Hush,' I bid him. 'Almighty God has designed it.' He listens.

'We shall have our day, rookbird. It is coming, do you feel it?' He angles his head.

'Our luck abides! The doors shall swing ajar and you and I shall step, silk and cane, together inside.'

And mortals knew no shores beyond
their own ~ Ovid

I leave Tuesday Brown in charge of the nine o'clock. I cannot shake from my mind the picture of a nourishing jar of stout, dark and sweet as molasses.

I hurry along Duke's Road and patches of sunlight fall upon my dusty boots. You would sing to feel its warmth. As the sun climbs it warms the carcasses of sow and cow hooked at Smith's. Tom, Norman Jackson's son, runs the old yard now. I close my eyes and smell the unmistakable aroma of fresh blood.

When I reached twelve years of age my father gave me to Norman Jackson, slaughterman.

Before that I received a schoolroom education: alphabet, abacus, arithmetic, algebra.

We learned the kings and queens and the National

Anthem, the Holy Bible and the Book of Common Prayer. Now my figures are writ tall in the black book, columns of inked numbers, handsome in their uniformity.

A bout of rinderpest put paid to my father's business in the September, and it was the end of my schooling: I was with the slaughtermen now. I was proud of my blue apron. I vomited daily and this made the men laugh. Norman enjoyed a song. He sang *My Frisky Old Wife*, as he took an animal apart. Piece by piece: sheep, cattle and horses disappeared under Norman's blade: vertebrae, bone, hoof, tongue, eye. Back to nought. The cheer of the dirty song turned it worse. I closed my eyes. I stood in a tide of blood and wiped my tears on the apron. Among the spines, intestines, lungs. I thought: what is more true? The living beast or the dead? Or the quick minute that ticks between the two?

Blood smells of the iron foundry. Guts smell of the river. Fear smells of piss and dung. Only when the meat is hooked, pink and tidy, does it smell sweet as a carnation.

I delivered the cuts of meat on horseback. People knew my name. Everyone loves a delivery boy who will accept payment next time. My father said, Employed is employed. My mother folded her arms. She said, Myself and this boy are not made for meat. She washed the blood from my hands and placed there instead hymn books from St John's Church at St John's Square. My mother held ambition for me. I liked helping at church.

I liked the sermonising. I liked the astounding tales, the breathtaking miracles, the congregation, and the collecting plate at the end. At the back of the church across the square, down a side street near the brewery, was a penny gaff. One day I drifted in. And that was the sermon I chose.

$\sim$

And I will enthral your mind with the
charms of novelty ~ Ovid

Percival George. You have gone with Amen to The Hat.
Here I remain: Bella your beloved, with a pencil stub.

We are folding linens, blankets, shawls. The day is cloudy,
trees bend and a wind worries the windows in their frames.

Bird dashes in, arms out and hair a-fly.

'Bella!' she cries. 'Who will argue with me now? I saw
her!'

Ruby and me halt our business. The girls scramble over
each other in panic.

'I saw her,' Bird says. 'On the stairs. The girl. God help
us, her eyes were blank.'

'Who is she?' Ruby cries. 'Is it the hanged girl?'

Flora shakes her head, gets to her feet, begins to count.

'Hush! Calm down!' I tell them.

'She was there, sure as I stand here,' Bird says. 'Eyes like
this. See?'

We turn to look. Flora opens her mouth and releases a
piercing scream.

'Shush!' cries Bird. 'Stow it! She may be listening.'

'Bird Doyle!' I yell. 'Listen while I speak! When it comes
to the spirit world you have no more sight than me or Ruby,
do you hear? It's a rig for the show. You have no gifts in the
unnatural spheres, no talents in the realm of the ghostly, nor
abilities in the strange. You have an instinct for the cards.
That is all. There!'

'On my life!' Ruby calls. 'I swear it's the very same girl.'

'Enough!' I call.

Ruby sighs, examines her fingernails. They do not want
the phantoms banished. They want me gone, so they might
chaff more about spirits and fever themselves.

I take Flora in my arms. 'You ought to be ashamed,' I tell the others. 'Ragging with the dead.'

'I don't care a duck's arse,' says Bird.

'Mind your language, then.'

I return to the linens and my hands are brisker now.

'One two three four five six . . .'

'Flora.'

'. . . seven eight nine.'

'Flora!' She halts mid-count. 'Don't let the spook come for me,' she pleads.

'It shan't come for you,' says Bird. 'You're too goosey to tempt a spook.'

Flora grips her skirts. A tear stands in her eye. 'I am afraid of ghouls,' she whispers.

Ruby unplaits her hair and stares out of the window at the darkening sky beyond. 'A spook will go where its poor unrested soul takes it,' she says. She turns, hands on hips. 'I pity the wretched girl-ghoul. If she comes to me I shall ask her, What ails you, spirit?'

Flora gasps. 'Oh saints!'

Ruby continues. 'It shan't visit you, Bird, owing to the fact that you shall tire it with your carping. There!'

Ruby is brisk. She claps her hands, as if to say there's an end to it.

'I shan't tire it!' cries Bird. 'I shall tell it, Blessings and cheer!' Bird flaps and skips. 'Skip-dilly and nobby. The spirit shall find me droll.'

'Stop hopping like a halfwit!' Ruby scolds. 'The spook shall linger with me, being that I am perky when it comes to all things uncanny, and what's more I am congenial around the dead.' And she curtsies.

'Piff!' says Bird. 'It's only the dead who can abide you.'

'Stop squabbling,' I tell them. 'Let that be an end.'

'One more thing,' says Bird. She walks in a circle, her hands at her back. 'P'raps I know who she is. The spook. P'raps we are become acquainted.'

We straighten up. We wait.

'Well,' says Bird. 'What are you all staring at, then?'

'What d'you think?' cries Ruby.

Flora sinks to the floor, her hands over her cheeks. 'Is it the girl who did not return?' she wails. 'Is it?'

There remains a path through the
Heavens ~ Ovid

I am here upon an invitation from Mister Cox. A comfortable house in Stanley Gardens, Hampstead, draped at the sash windows in burgundy velvet and lit softly by lamps.

Out of respect for the dead and those who might convene with the aforementioned, I wear a buttonhole: gardenia. Costly! But I know the value of the first impression.

Mister Jameson is our host. He smokes a briar pipe, which he taps frequently, as if knocking for the dead. A longer neck I have not glimpsed on a gentleman, nor tighter curls upon the head. When he removes his pipe, he spreads his arms. Occasionally, he leans an elbow upon the piano, an old trick that suggests to an audience the speaker might be trusted. How often have I done so myself! Of course we have no piano, grand or otherwise.

Only the civility of his vowels and resonance of his baritone tells you Mister Jameson is an important gentleman, no stage door slang, he.

Mary Parker died four months previously and seven

of us are here to meet her and hear of her adventures. Somewhere within these rooms is Professor Henry Stanwick himself.

It is important I remember that such an invitation is a very great honour. I have need of this kind of gentleman and these gentlemen must be encouraged to have need of me. If I am to rise profitably in these capricious spheres of mystery and phenomena I must fit in snug as a ham in a dish. Not a feather shall I ruffle. No, I shall only commend and admire.

Upon the grand piano I spy an arrangement of peach and honey-coloured blooms that offer a sweet scent. In the polished gleam of the piano I see my reflection and I note one eyebrow arches higher than its contemporary. God above. I must not appear to sneer. I fashion a genial smile. I keep my hands clasped at my back. I should not like to give offence by seeming to take charge.

Mister Jameson explains aloud that Mary Parker felt no pain as her spirit left her body, but only the sensation of fleeing upwards, accompanied by a delightful giddiness. I make no comment but only attend without hint of prejudice.

The speakers are prone to excitement but I know better than to grow feverish when the shilling is involved. When it comes to the spirit realm there are those who lose their heads.

Mary Parker's spirit, Mister Jameson tells us, was met at the entrance to a beautiful garden by a High Spirit. The High Spirit was resplendent in flowing robes. The Spirit was serene of mien, says Mister Jameson. Mrs Alderton, eyes closed, nods.

Mister Jameson explains that Mary Parker was able to hear the strains of violins and other stringed instruments.

To which, a Mister Saunders in the front row, wearing an opulent beard, enquires, A harp, perhaps?

I must distract myself with incontrovertible facts, in order to keep the mind concentrated and amusement controlled.

After Mister Jameson's introduction concludes, I am presented to Professor Stanwick by Mister Cox. The professor steps from his smoke cloud and strides purposefully across a rug of Persian design. His watch chain, I note, is an expensive example. His voice, resounding as a bishop's, emerges from his wiry beard. His gaze is watchful. He takes me in and presses down his whiskers with long fingers.

'How do you *do*, professor?' I have practised this in the appropriate tone, along with the handshake. I have a congenial remark prepared. *I anticipate we have a fascinating evening ahead, sir. It is an honour to attend, professor.* But he is gone! Striding off upon his stilt legs before I can be sure our introduction went off with a bang.

I shall wait upon the evidence. As far as ghosts and related phenomena are concerned I shall know in an eyeblink if there is resort to trickery or sleight of hand. My eye is attuned to such ploys. I have seen it done, without flourish, in my own shows. No girl in a mirrored cabinet with an ear trumpet and a bag of flour will blind me to actualities. We have performed that very act to rowdy cheers in multiple locations.

The Face Séance begins. Lamps are low. Voices rise. And are shushed. And rise again. We are permitted to examine the black screen erected between the front and back rooms. We are asked to examine the back room itself, its locked doors and fastened windows. At the centre of the screen is a hole cut about a foot by a foot square. If there exists tom-foolery I shall know it in a blink!

Seated once more, I fight an urge to doze. The low lamps have loosened my eyelids. Mrs Winters speaks slowly, as if her words were bubbles and with one hand gesticulates tiny motions in the air as if conducting an orchestra of bees. Her posture is ram-rod. The sight of her persuades me to snap-to and attend. The ticking clock and windy breathing of Mister Myers threatens to drowse me once more and I resort to loudly clearing my throat to remain awake.

Now Mrs Winters is speaking of instruments, suspended in the air, which play themselves. A trumpet appears abruptly before us, apparently hoisted and blown by a bluish flame, identified by Mrs Winters as the spirit.

'Good gracious!' says Mister Myers from his chair to the left of mine. 'Can it be true?' Askance, he turns to look at the rest of us.

A sudden parp emits then, from the corner of the room. A scrabbling, and the flame is snuffed out, leaving behind a lingering smell of extinguished burning. So dim is the room that I am finding it hard to identify my own hand at the end of my arm, let alone a trumpet-blowing ghoul.

Mrs Winters continues to direct invisible bees. Her foot begins to tap to non-existent music. Her voice describes the darkened room in which we are gathered. 'Which features,' she says, 'at least two sceptics.'

At this point the cabinet releases a small white figure, flowing in its dimension. The creature steps forward, bows, and retrieves a set of beads that are tossed towards it, whereupon it retires back to the cabinet. The voice of Mister Myers again exclaims:

'Gracious!'

I must keep my opinion to myself, though I have witnessed nought but blether and bunkum. It is quite clear to me the creature in white was a female of dainty proportions quite practised at contorting herself in reg'lar fashion within the cabinet for these exhibitions. Be that as it may, an invitation to observe the professor's gentlemanly scientifics at a later date would be an astounding development. Astounding and development are two words spoke often by Professor Stanwick to explain his shenanigans. I latch on quick, albeit I may over-astound myself and thereby jinx the opportunity here presented.

Be heedful, Percival George.

At the end, while taking our leave and thanking our host, Mister Cox shakes my hand.

'Well?' he says.

'Most illuminating,' I reply.

He passes me my hat and indicates the door.

'Shall we?'

There is no fortune so good but you
may find something to complain of
~ Syrus

Bella and Ruby lark in sideways, eyes oily, hair adrift.

They have purchased gin, the room quickly ripens with the smell.

My thoughts remain lodged at Stanley Gardens, Hampstead, with the heron-necked Mister Jameson, the ruffle-bearded Mister Saunders and the trumpet-blasting girl in the cabinet.

'Attending Vespers, ladies?' I enquire of them. Solicitude costs nought.

In truth, I'd hoped Amen and I might fill our pipes together and genially consider how we might prepare ourselves for Professor Stanwick's precarious experiment, Thursday next.

Bella whirls to a standstill, hands on her hips.

'You fetched a new dwarf?'

She fixes me with one narrowed eye while the other sags, half-closed.

'Who's been blethering?' I reply.

'Never mind. Show us the dwarf.'

I glance at Ruby. Breathless she is, eyebrows high, a waggle of teeth poking beneath her lip.

God above, I think. Not *now*. A picture the girls are! Adrift, gin-soaked, full of devilry. It's midnight. My royal dwarf. I think of him. Safe. Tucked away.

'There is no dwarf,' I say. 'There is an antiquity. A Piece. No concern of yours.'

'Bones? May God forgive you. Belonging to who?'

'Some poor ratman!' shrieks Ruby. 'Bones of the dead! Beware all those who walk abroad! Ha ha!'

Bella shushes her.

Amen appears, bare-footed, chewing monkey nuts.

'There is a box!' he blurts.

Beside him is Tuesday, a blanket upon his shoulder, a small cigar between his teeth.

'Is there?' I say.

'Mister George! Will you tell us what lurks within the box?'

'I do not discuss the box.'

'What does it contain then?'

'Nothing that concerns you.'

'A body, is it?'

'Says who?'

'That's what we hear. That's what they say.'

'Do they? They are misinformed. As are you.'

Bird hurries in dressed in a man's overcoat, and a monocle

at her eye. Flora is barefoot beside her, mouthing words.

'Those who know say it is something human. Or once was human,' says Bella.

'I will explain when the time is right.'

'Tell us now!' Ruby stamps her foot.

'Look out,' warns Bird. 'Bones do mischief, that's their will. Cause a hullaballoo when your back is turned. Shall I have a word? Bid them bones behave?'

'No,' I say. 'Daft wench. Bones are locked away. Leave them resting.'

Bella folds her arms. 'I'm not spending the night with the dead bones of who-knows-who that might bring who-knows-what mischief. So.'

Bird leans in. Her eye fattening in the monocle. 'What if we all died tonight and never knew whose bones we are laying with? There's an unblessing. What a palaver.'

I close my eyes. 'Hush!' I say. 'God spare . . . What fancies! Let me think.'

'Mister Percy? How shall we safeguard it? Knowing nil of what we are safeguarding?' It is Amen. Pronouncing the only sense he ever spoke.

'Halt your chaff!' I say. 'Wait!' I rise from my chair. 'A little patience would suit you all very well.'

I unlock the cupboard. I remove the box. The room has fallen quiet.

'Do bones lie in there?' asks Flora. No-one answers.

I place the box upon the table. A pause for dramatic effect before I go on to explain, in soft tones, what lies within. I take a breath.

'Contained within this box is The Piece,' I say. 'Purchased this week at considerable trouble and expense. This is due to the antiquity of the item. Being rare. Historical. Foreign. It is no slang's trifle. No street piece this. Correctly, it ought

70

to stand behind glass. Hear me? Percy Unusual George has, at last, purchased a true Unusual! Hip-hip!'

None respond. But only stare, like a herd of mules, at the wooden box.

'Hurray,' Jim breathes.

They step closer, elbowing for space.

'Get back, everyone,' I tell them. 'I need room, I need air.'

A pause. I remove the lid. All press forward again.

'There. A dead skeleton,' says Ruby.

'Bones,' says Bella. 'Thought so.'

'Can I touch it?' pipes Flora.

'No,' say all three girls.

'Not bones,' I correct. 'History. This box,' I say, my tone rising to its cause, 'contains the articulated bones of The Baby. The personal dwarf belonging to none other than a royal king. The most famous kingly dwarf who ever danced upon a sovereign's knee. He is rare as untrod snow. I am not unveiling him to every arse-wedge who fancies a peek for a ha'penny. The dwarf belongs to me. I purchased him with heavy crowns. He is the walking bones of time. Wait! I have the authenticating certificate here with The Piece.' I rummage in the box. 'Here!' I display it for all to see. 'Nobody, and I mean nobody, lays a finger upon him or else find yourself selling cups and graters on Farringdon Road! Is that clear?'

They do not answer. Only Bella meets my gaze, her eye flat as a penny.

'The dead bones of an old dwarf shall bring us bad luck, Percy,' she says.

'We'll be cursed,' adds Ruby, shrugging. 'Evil goings-on. Murder in the night.'

'No!' gasps Flora.

'Stuff your wailing and leave the deciding to me. He will bring good fortune,' I say. 'He is come to light my path.

71

And if I catch anyone touching his bones with their fingers. Well ... Saints forgive me but I will knock their block off! Is that understood?'

Faces, blank as pies.

'Right,' I continue. 'Next. This second box is smaller. Wood. Silver-plated. Decent. A few half crowns' worth. It contains nothing of significant value.'

At this assessment, Ruby's brisk hands scoop out the contents and nimbly she flits to the chair. She sits and lays it across her lap for inspection.

'Rags?' I enquire. She does not reply.

Tuesday joins her. He and Ruby examine them, heads bowed.

'Not rags,' Ruby insists. 'Linens. And something within. Fine skin. Calf? Look at that. Leather bound. And here, pages. See? Pages and their words. Foolish Mister George! You shall not have it now for chucking it aside.'

'Look to see there is anything of value beneath,' I add. 'What words? What do they say?'

Neither responds.

'Well?'

'Foreign!' Ruby cries.

'These are French words,' says Tuesday.

'Read them aloud,' I say. 'Let's hear it.'

'I do not know them,' Tuesday replies. 'Save for the word *château*. That is French.'

'French scribblings and scrabblings,' I reply.

'In a fine block print,' says Tuesday. 'See?'

'What use have I for fine print?' I say. I lean down and tear out a page, ball it, toss it in the fire. 'There! Horse cock!' I say. I pick up my dwarf in his box.

And I go to bed.

~

Words flowed from his tongue sweeter
than honey ~ Homer

Beneath rain-soaked trees on Regent Square I wait as the St Peter's bell tolls.

Here I stand, Percival Unusual George, whose only crime is a desire to entertain a disobliging public, preparing to enter the institute itself.

Am I today crowned king of the unthinkable? I am. Need I have troubled myself over my perfunctory introduction by Mister Cox to the professor? I need not. Do I stand upon the brink of a new interlude wherein I shall surpass all the dreams I have envisioned? I do.

The rain having eased, I emerge from beneath the shelter of the trees and set off, skip-hop, around the puddles and carriages towards Bedford Square.

This important day began by unveiling itself in swank fashion with a singular vision.

At dawn, I squinted into the mirror glass to examine my disorderly beard when a picture of an act flew into my mind: in which my midget Pie (in the role of a bone collector) performs a tender family scene with my coughing Pinkie (the almost-expired) and the priceless royal dwarf skeleton (recently acquired). Pretty as a picture those three pint pots will be! The ladies will love it! I have named the entertainment *A Bone To Pick With You.*

My joy will not be contained. At the earliest daylight convenience Steps and I seized our hats. Sovereign diem! And set off for The Firkin.

Not a few hours later I find myself unaccompanied, full of bounce, sidestepping carriages in Bedford Square like a splendid toff, and the clock has not even yet struck eleven!

Here we are assembled. We are twelve, thirteen if you

count the professor's butler, who bustles with hats, canes, ulsters and umbrellas. I am in elevated company as, one by one, the gents check the timing of the professor's late arrival, whereupon I spy some fine pocket watches of the Swiss example, including a gold half hunter and an eighteen carat chronograph.

Claret is poured in the morning room, where the gasoliers are lit in spite of the daylight.

I am relieved to find Cox here, as the other gents appear to have been introduced and yet no introductions are made on my behalf.

Cox greets me and stands us off to the side. His pink eye is half-closed; his hair, waxed and combed, gleams under the gas. 'We won't make a nuisance of ourselves, will we?' he says, rubbing his eye. 'There are men of science present,' he clarifies. In response I stand stiffly, an impersonation of elegance, hands clasped at my back, and try not to ogle the bronze figurines, gilt mirrors, nor an elaborate French Boulle clock.

We are ushered into the Black Room, which is not as dark as it sounds, albeit the drapes are heavy and the room north-facing. A gong sounds and the professor enters. There is a murmuring fuss as he greets his guests, while Cox nods for us to hang back.

I turn my attention to the subject, a young woman in neat boots and a green and brown dress, sat in a high-backed chair, hands clasped in her lap. Her mouse-coloured hair is centre-parted and drawn back in a limp chignon. She appears serene, albeit wearied. I spot a small bruise on the back of her right hand.

'Mesmerism is one of the venerable sciences,' the professor proclaims behind us, in a genial tone, moving around our group towards the young woman at the centre of the room.

'It is as old as mankind itself,' he continues. 'As ancient and honourable as the pyramids. In the Orient,' he goes on, 'it is cultivated as a divine art.' How ably, I think, he elongates the words to accommodate their solemnity. His patter is polished as honest silver.

'To the feverish bishops who say such powers do not belong to man,' the professor adds in a less ingratiating tone, '*magna est veritas et praevalebit*.' A rumble of approving laughter. A marvellous retort. I cannot fathom it but it's gone down a storm. I catch myself before I applaud. I nod at the walls instead.

The professor has one of those voices gifted only to men of the clergy, courtroom or institutions of medicine, which transports its resonance through some invisible chamber before arriving in the human ear. A grand spieler the professor might have made!

'The subject before you shall become overwhelmed by my will,' he explains. 'The magnetising force will persuade her. The subject recognises mine is the loftier power and, as a consequence, she will surrender to my superiority.'

The professor walks a leisurely circle around the young woman on her chair, and continues in his languid tone. 'You will observe how rapidly this occurs. As a man communicates silently to his dog, so this subject will look to me and know.'

The professor stops to address the group directly. 'During the manipulations I must implore you to make no interruption. The electrical communication between minds is fragile and must not be broken.'

Behind him a butler hastily arranges a bowl of water and a han'kerchief on a small table beside the chair. Intriguing.

'I am able to inform you,' the professor continues, 'that the temperature of the room is sixty degrees Fahrenheit.

75

There must be no draughts, bright lights nor sudden sounds. I must ask you to resist the urge to cough or sneeze during the magnetism process, which is fifteen minutes in duration. I shall begin.'

We watch as the professor stands before the young lady seated in the chair. She raises her hands and he takes her thumbs between his forefingers. 'This young woman,' says the professor, 'is given to quarrelling with her associates, bickering with strangers and asserting herself in the presence of her superiors. Regularly dismissed by her employers and finding herself unable to hold down a situation, her only hope of rehabilitation is a cure.' At this the professor turns to look accusingly at us. The pause is dramatic.

The young woman continues to look straight ahead.

'Ann,' says the professor, while squeezing her thumbs. 'Would you tell these gentlemen about yourself?' Without adjusting her eye-glance Ann speaks. Her voice is low, rueful, you might say. 'My name is Ann Clayton. I arrived from Kent to pick fruit at Roehampton until I was dismissed from my situation. I have had situations in Dulwich and Camberwell. And from there I was employed in Limehouse. I was dismissed from each and all for my conduct. I was taken to St Luke's Hospital where I was restrained for my own good—'

The professor interrupts. 'And so. Here is a violent, disagreeable young woman, of little use to any upstanding employer. Unhappily, she has no useful place in the world. In this particular case I have, using magnetism, psychical cleansing and other persuasive methods, succeeded in modifying her disposition until she grew into the compliant, docile character who appears before you today. Passive, feminine and obliging, Miss Clayton would make any employer proud. An excellent outcome. Without treatment she would have certainly found herself, in time, arrested and imprisoned for crimes of violence and theft. Instead, she sits in a charming attitude before you. My work is done. Any beast may be tamed, gentlemen. Allow me to demonstrate my methods in this short exhibition of psychical mesmeric manipulation.'

The professor continues. 'I must first establish a magnetic connection.' After some moments he releases her thumbs and begins to swerve his hands over her face and across her body in darting downward swoops while she maintains eye contact with him. This takes some minutes and after a while, if I am honest, my attention begins to wander.

I spy a fine pair of Cloisonné vases, a pair of marble-topped satinwood commodes and an octagonal table of inlaid ivory and ormolu. The business of magnetism continues as I contemplate an oil painting of an amply whiskered man in a black silk cravat gazing witheringly into the room. My attention is recaptured when the young lady begins to appear weary and, gradually, closes her eyes.

The professor steps back and murmurs, 'The subject is mesmerised.'

The gentlemen step closer to peer at the subject. The professor, by now, is positioning her arms and legs.

'Here,' he says, raising one leg up at an angle. 'And here,' at which he raises the opposite arm to a hoisted aspect in the air. 'You will note that an unmesmerised person should be quite unable to hold such a position for more than a minute or two without finding themselves becoming extremely uncomfortable,' he explains.

An outbreak of laughter emerges among the gentlemen. I nod silently at Cox, whose left eye is now entirely closed.

'Please,' says the professor, 'examine the limbs. Take your time. You will observe the stiffness in the leg, the arm.' I

77

step forward but Cox halts me with his hand, while the others examine the subject.

'Here!' calls the professor. 'Allow me.' And he raises the other stiffened leg of the subject into the air and the corresponding arm too. The young lady appears now in the attitude of one who is falling backwards in disorderly fashion, albeit she remains in the chair. This is unexpected. Queer. Striking even! I glance again at Cox, who is examining his fingernail. I inch forward a little, crane for a better view.

'You will observe,' the professor continues, 'that the extremities are cold. This is quite normal in the mesmerised subject.'

A gentleman in spectacles turns to enquire something of the professor, to which the professor responds, 'Of course, John, please examine the subject however you wish. She will remember nothing at all, gentlemen.' At which a rumble of playful laughter sounds.

'She will neither remember,' the professor confirms, 'nor feel a thing. Observe.'

Without preamble, the professor strikes the subject across the face. She tips to the left and gradually rights herself again.

I am aghast. I flash a glance at Cox. Astounding. She is none the worse!

'Perhaps I was a little too moderate,' admits the professor. And he slaps her a second time with greater force.

A jowlish gentleman, heavily whiskered, steps forward. 'May I?' he says. 'For my own appraisal?'

'Be my guest.'

The gentleman strikes her and then, not quite satisfied, hits her again on the other cheek. Her response is the same. And yet dark red patches begin to bloom upon her face. In the room there are exclamations of: Wonderful! Extraordinary! Well, I never!

At this I confess I am queasy. I am no scientist. I do not possess the education required to comprehend this type of drill. Necessary discomforts must be suffered in the best interests of medicine. An inept doctor I'd be! We are summoned each to our own.

'Gentlemen,' calls the professor, 'our subject is truly magnetised!'

'Can we be quite certain?' enquires a tall gent with a long neck and a crown of curls. He steps forward, scratching his finger.

'Allow me to demonstrate,' says the professor. And he takes a penknife from his pocket. He lifts our subject's hand and skilfully pricks the palm of her hand, producing a bead of blood. Once again the young lady makes no reaction whatsoever.

'One moment,' says the tall gent, approaching. 'Do you mind?' he asks the professor.

'Not at all,' is the reply.

The gent leans forward and with his fingers seems to grasp her by the throat.

'Doctor Fanshawe is compressing the windpipe,' explains the professor. 'Can you see at the back? As you can plainly observe, this produces no involuntary reaction from the subject, no cough, choke or panic whatsoever.'

The young woman is now become horribly pale. Relieved I am that her eyes are closed.

Around her lips a blue-grey tinge appears and one or two of us are now glancing at the professor in anticipation of intervention. Good grief!

'If my colleague were to continue,' explains the professor calmly, 'our subject would suffer heart failure and death would follow swiftly, so deeply is she mesmerised.'

With his extended arm the professor invites the

gentleman to step back. 'Thank you, Doctor Fanshawe,' he says, 'but I must continue, if you don't mind, or risk the sound of the luncheon bell summoning us before too long.' A chatter of laughter from the group.

'If I may suggest a less risky evaluation,' says the professor. And our host takes a lit candle from the mantel and holds it beneath the subject's forearm. 'Like so.'

Whereupon, as before, we observe no reaction from the young woman, save for the rapid reddening of her skin and the faint aroma of burnt hair.

'Now! If I may have your attention!' calls the professor. 'My current work occupies the new and fascinating territory of the psychical and the telepathic. At this moment I would advise that the subject may wish to speak. Please stand back, gentlemen.'

We obey. A hush falls. The professor speaks commandingly to the young lady.

'Ann,' he says. 'Is Matraxia there?' For a moment nothing in the room moves.

'Is Antero there?' he enquires. Then, slowly, she nods. I do not dare breathe.

'Will he speak to us?' asks the professor. Once again, unhurriedly, she nods.

It occurs to me that science is the blessed wonder of our modern age. Miraculous events!

I am transfixed. By now the subject has opened her mouth and begun to speak in a strange tongue, in a voice so deep you might assume she was a gentleman not a young woman. The professor turns to us in triumph.

'I present to you Antero. An eighteenth-century professor from Eleusis, speaking most fluently through our talented subject today. Who,' and the professor raises his hand, 'being an uneducated girl, speaks no Greek whatsoever, herself.'

A burst of appreciative laughter is followed by an extraordinary exhibition by the young lady, whereupon she begins to speak a marvellous gibberish, unintelligible to me, but ripe with affects, lisps and strange intonations.

The room erupts. Astounding! Ingenious! I join in some fulsome applause. Hip-ho!

Top brass. Even Cox opens his eye. A new world is coming. Hats off to the professor.

But the show is not over. For a finale the professor produces a small spoon from his pocket. Curious. What on earth shall he do with . . . Ah, but he has begun.

The professor is using the spoon to compress her tongue. Altogether peculiar.

'You will observe,' he says, 'that the subject remains in clairaudient contact and continues to speak the words of Professor Antero of Eleusis, no matter how hard I try to prevent her from doing so.' And here the professor increases the force upon the spoon, causing the piece of cutlery to knock against her teeth, while she continues determinedly to gargle the Greek sounds of Antero.

'So strong is the magnetism,' says the professor, above the clatter of the spoon on her teeth, 'so profound is the contact that no amount of physical deterrence will prevent her continuing.'

Astonished laughter fills the room. Some gentlemen gather round for closer inspection, while others cry, 'Absurd, Henry!' and others simply continue laughing.

'Here!' says the professor to one of them. 'Hold her jaw. Yes, here. Hold her jaw open.

There. Firmly. That's it.'

I lean to see. My queasiness has returned and yet I should not like to remain ignorant of the phenomena. I crane my neck.

The poor girl kicks and flails her arm in her attempt to continue speaking. Her eyes bulge open and I think, Science is too exacting a task for me, my nervous stomach and sentimental nature would be my downfall.

By now there are great roars of astonishment from the gentlemen, and the girl is writhing, flapping, clacking and gibbering in the chair, still trying to speak in spite of the clamping of her jaw and the compression of her tongue. One wag cries, 'Is she at the winning post yet?' And the room falls into hoots, shouts and exclamations once more.

Presently, the professor calls for the restoration of calm in order that he may close the demonstration and demesmerise the subject, now contorted, reddened and breathless in her chair.

He raises his hand. 'Gentlemen,' he says. 'I shall proceed to wake her.'

The attention of the room is recaptured. The professor stands over the young woman, as before. With both hands he swoops reverse passes from her chest to her forehead and, having completed these passes, he blows upon her forehead, while drawing his thumbs along her closed eyes in an outward direction. Finally, the professor takes up the han'kerchief and shakes it over the face and body of the subject, as if he were sprinkling her with salt or cinnamon, or the like. Next he dips the han'kerchief into the bowl of water, wrings it out and holds it taut, as if it were a blindfold, across her eyes.

I'd hoped to view the young Ann awakened and none the worse for her magnetism, but we are already filing out to the rumble of conversation and dry barks of Cox's cough, guided by the butler and staff to another room wherein refreshments will be served. Over my shoulder I manage to catch her blink, once, twice, and then we are gone.

*

82

Outside I see the rain has held off. Large puddles reflect a darkening sky that is splendidly backlit by the giant lamp that is the moon. Carriage wheels shatter the image, bright shards tumble like mirror pieces. Here I stand, dapper in hat, collar and cane, at the centre of everything.

I am no expert, yet I do say this: if the dead walk abroad, if they exist in spheres unknown to us, why then we must heed them. Or accept that we choose to be deaf. Who shall forgo the marvellous? The strange? Shall we turn away from phenomena? From astounding innovation? I take a breath, adjust my hat. I have stunned myself with these revelatory musings. I swing my cane. What a miracle is this life!

I check the o'clock. Tick-tock. No man upon the earth shall command the clock, nor any other succeed in holding back the hands of time!

For he who is mortal must put up
with the fate imposed by the gods
~ Euripides

I set this down by pencil. The task is slow yet it soothes and steadies my heart.

I am rested in Percy's own armchair between shows, no darning in my hands, idle as a duchess. Next comes a commotion at the door, a squabble of voices. *'Bella! Bella!'*

Ruby and Bird reel in, blowing like cab horses.

'Well then!' Bird shrieks. 'Where is Bella? Find her, quick!'

I turn to see them scurrying and fretting in their bonnets.

'I am here,' I say.

Bird flinches. Her little face is tight, her quick eyes glassy. As they are fevered, so I am composed.

'Bella!' cries Bird.

I see how frail Bird seems without her swagger.

'May the good Lord save us in time,' I say. Droll, albeit their fear startles me.

'We heard it,' says Ruby, copper hair a-fly as she pulls off her hat. 'That last week a girl had each tooth in her head pulled by the professor—'

'That Mister Cox arranged it!' blurts Bird.

'That the girl was found on Canal Street, sat in her own blood,' Ruby says.

'Not a grumble, meek as a lamb,' adds Bird.

'What's more, a Bermondsey girl was actual branded,' says Ruby. 'By a cigar.'

'Burned. Here, here. And here.'

I watch Bird as she points at her arms, her wrist, her neck.

'And that one girl spoke aloud in the voice of the hangman of one hundred years gone.'

'One. Hundred. Years. Gone,' repeats Bird, widening her eyes as she speaks.

'And hanged herself that night on his command—' rushes Ruby.

'With boat twine,' adds Bird, eyes swivelling. 'Grrrrgh. Like so.'

'God's pity,' I say.

'Hanging off the timbers on Lock Road!' Ruby cries.

'*Hanging?* Swinging!'

'Stop that!' I say.

'They say that one of Percy George's shall be next.'

'Being that—'

'*Being that* a gaff girl will abide the discomforts, see?'

'Shush! Let me speak—' snaps Ruby.

'See a gaff girl will—' interrupts Bird.

'Let me speak! So *a gaff girl will*—'

'—*shush her mouth!*' they call together.

'Thank you!' Ruby swats Bird. 'Aye,' she adds, 'will shush her mouth.'

'Enough!' I raise my hand.

'And not jig a dance to the fadging asylum,' concludes Bird, shrugging.

'Stop!'

Bird steps forward. She whispers, 'Cox arranged it.'

A shiver floats at my back. 'What a fuss,' I say. I catch my breath.

Ruby touches my arm. 'It's only we thought you ought to know that Mister Cox—'

'Quiet!' I bark. 'I heard you! I heard what you said. Now go upstairs. Both of you!'

'But—'

'Go!'

Their boots pound as they hurry.

I knew him hare-brained but what of this? Percy George, you simple little man. Mixing with the likes of. Might we not fill the purse in Vauxhall? Truly the girls should be happy to sing for sixpence at The Gardens. Easy shillings. Where's the harm? But he will have it his way, tangled and perilous. Shall I tend him as a child in spite of his decades? Must a woman rear grown men as children, and never ask herself why?

Back and forth I walk these floorboards until I know their creaking by heart. I do not say his task is simple but the methods shall bring us misery. Once he would've asked me. Now he reckons himself the flash cove, the Islington nib, the fly-dodge king of everything. Well. We'll see about it. P'raps I shall jump him at his own game. Where there is a king there is always a queen; open any pack of cards.

~

Every man has his besetting sin
~ Cicero

Returning home I find myself in tip-top tenor. Frolic-
some. Frisky as a June bride. As if I (a mere toiling
showman with a dream in his heart) had stepped, arm-in-
arm with esteemed professors, into the realm of scientific
remarkability.

On the threshold I discover Bird, in shawl and bonnet,
peering through the bannisters.

'Do I seem this bonnet, Mister George?' She adjusts it.
'There. Well?'

It is a forlorn thing with a dowdy flower a-droop on its
west side.

'A picture!' I declare. 'A proper lady, you are!' I have the
fizz to bless a pretty girl's day.

She grins.

In a flash, her jumble of teeth recall to me a hairless horse
from Kent I once declined to buy. Hairless is not the ticket,
a crowd prefers hairier, given the option. I am obliged to
keep up with the times or be swept aside, like that lurk
Jim Crouch.

Bella waits for me in the chair. In the typical fashion of
a woman she does not display her mood until I am in the
proximity. Just then, as I set-to performing (for her entertainment) the opening moves of *A Bone To Pick With You*,
she strikes me, without warning, while I am bended in half
and defenceless. Over I tip.

'What!' I cry. 'Are you gone mad?'

Picture me akimbo on the boards, flapping, kicking and
reddening from the shock. She strikes me again.

'You will give a girl to Cox!' she scolds. 'How could you
think of doing such a thing?'

'Quiet!' I cry. I clamber to my knees to address her directly. 'God in Heaven! How dare you attack me! What is the matter, woman?'

She strikes me again. I pitch from the blow. And this has thoroughly dislodged my patience. I straighten up, clutching my face.

'There! I am injured! Are you satisfied?' I yell. 'Shall I return the blow?' I raise my hand.

At this the girls rush into the room, flapping and sliding.

'Out!' I call. 'Out, out, out! This concerns none of you!'

Bird, with hand over her mouth, freezes. Ruby steps forward with a freckled finger in the air. 'Don't dare touch her, then!' she warns.

'She belted me!' I reply. 'Clubbed me hard! Twice! Here! And here!'

Bird, in her bonnet, peers out from behind. 'We're just heedful, Mister George. God knows if anyone may've been hurt or trampled to death.'

'Out!' I yell.

The door slams. I remain on my knees. Bella remains in the chair. We are left in the silence, save for the whispers beyond the door.

'You have injured me viciously, here.' I point to the place. 'Can't you treat me with care?'

She does not reply but only closes her eyes. I struggle to my feet. Her eyes open. Square as a cobb stone is her face. Her stare unnerves me with its violent implication. I am glad the girls are nearby.

'Might we not be tender again, my Bell? A little fondness—'

'I have no fondness left,' she interrupts.

I creep to the window, for fear she may lunge again.

'A bloody fool you are,' she says. 'How could you hand over one of ours?'

'What? I've done no such thing!'

'How could you drag a stranger's bones into the house?'

'How can you accuse me?'

'How could you care so little for us after so long? Why do you pay your respects to lurks and professors?'

'No, no,' I say. My voice sounds weary. These persistent justifications. 'You have it wrongly about. The professor is respectable,' I explain. 'Well-bred, reputable, high-regarded. Scientific it is, Bell. He publishes pamphlets. Shall we not avail ourselves of reg'lar employment?'

'Not in strange practices. And you have forgot: a girl disappeared.'

'Piffle. Hearsay. Not proved.'

'Never found. Do you know why?'

'Halt your fretting! The professor is four-square. Do you not see? He lectures at the institute! Royalty itself did attend! Yet, may God pardon us all if none of this is good enough for you?'

'Girls are badly used. And you,' she says, looking at me slyly, 'ought to be ashamed.'

'Rumours! Tittle-tattle,' I say. 'I know. It is my business.'

Bella steps closer. I hold fast. She places her hand on my neck, where pain from one of her blows still throbs. She is tranquil, yet a shiver drags at her mouth and a tear begins in her eye. 'I am afraid,' she whispers. 'Do away with the dwarf stranger's bones,' she says.

'In the box lies your bad luck, Percy. Get rid of them.' She moves to the door. 'If anything happens to the girls you will suffer for it. And that,' she says, 'is my business.'

~

We are all embarked on a sea of
woes ~ Horace

Among the vapours, gloom and spiders I pass a little time. Here in the stable with the pot-sized nags stands the miniature wagon, alongside the boards and properties for the shows. Within these glass jars upon the shelves a selection of my performers abide, a few unfinished beasts that might've boarded the ark. Our Heavenly Father did not see fit to complete them. Some are suspended entire, others in parts, some part-dissected, all of them long ago. We named a few. Pop Eye Bill. He makes the young ladies scream, his scant body is dwarfed by a single eye, blown wide as the base of a flask. One poor ragged specimen is rigged by a single unfinished wing on a mast of bone. Bat or bird? None will know, the wing shall not fly. Gabriel, we called it.

When I bring out the jars Bella crosses herself. We had a song, she and I ... *Give a man a girl he can love, As I, O my love, love thee* ... Once upon a time she lay her head upon my shoulder, her hand upon my thigh. Once we lay abed together.

The birthing of our infant came too soon. A year later she lost another. Our babes took themselves to the Almighty. One day we shall reunite in the Kingdom of Heaven.

She gave me our first infant in his wrappings. I held him, light as a thrush in my hands. She told me where to go. What to do. But I could not. I said nothing. Not to Bell, nor anyone. I did not give him to the river nor to the earth to rot his untried bones. I thought, Please, let him not be dust. He is preserved. I have solace. Unholy it may be. Yet I have him with me. It is a private matter. I spoke of it to nobody.

Words I have found to comfort the poor unfinished soul. For an eternity behind glass he floats. My lips touch and the jar mists as I speak. Does the infant attend? I believe so. What do I hope for during our interludes? I cannot say. An answer, p'raps, to a question I dare not ask. Today another question forms. Again I do not speak it, though I know this is why she fears him, the French dwarf. My precious antiquity. The royal charm. In my arms arrived his tender bones, swaddled in a child's box. And thereby did return all her grief.

Nothing is wanting . . .

'The saints have blessed us, Mister George.' Chloroform Flora has recovered from her infirmity of the lung well enough to rise again for thru'pence this evening, shining bright as a new button and eager to inhale of the gas jar once more.

Here she is stepping upon her toes. 'One two three four five,' she counts.

Our dear Flora is gifted with a lisp. A charm! Upon her tongue words sizzle like hot onions.

'Shall a songbird,' she says, 'know the tune he sings a full year hence?' Her eye is a wide blue daisy. She takes my arm.

'Indeed, he shall,' I reply. 'As a bird is wont to abide by his best ditty.'

To toast the good health of the girl I invest in a jar of my own with Steps and Pinks, at The Firkin: a fine wetting. 'Sweet success shall sustain us!' lisps Pinkie Danvers, in tender mockery of our recuperated girl. Hip-hip-ho.

I order two more jars for Steps and myself. 'Next week,' I say, 'it shall be your turn to play your part for the professor, and advance the progress of scientific innovation!'

'Saints be thanked!' cries Steps, and tips back his ale.

... but a song ~ Virgil

Late afternoon. Peace and quiet. A rarity. We are between the two and the four o'clockers.

Upon the wall in the yard sit Ruby, Flora and Bird. Three wrens. The fading sun sets a glow in each soft crown of hair. At the centre, hands on hips, is Bella. What a strange smile.

Is it for me? Might this be a plot or a ploy?

I offer a wary nod in return. I am watchful.

I raise a flame to my pipe, blow a cloud. Sunlight catches the strong bone in her nose.

She sews buttons, threads her needle. Her eye swerves in my direction.

Has our disagreement softened her? P'raps she has come to her senses? Even now ... There! She lifts her chin at me as if to say, Percy, you fool! See how my heart softens!

I nod and she looks away. Guilt? Regret? A change of heart? Or p'raps plain defiance?

No mystery can match the unfathomability of women.

Bird laces boots. Her sharp eyes and quick fingers make brisk the task. She looks up. A dear face! The pointed chin is the vital aspect, avian she is, while Ruby is our own red fox.

Upon her knee Ruby stitches a costume for the French dwarf, and Flora, astride the wall, plaits Ruby's halo of copper frizz, and sings *The Old Armchair.* Her voice has a tender chime, *'Tis past, 'tis past, but I gaze upon it now.* Fizz-splash go the words upon her tongue and Ruby joins her in a harmonising key. A duet! This alone shall persuade the British army to lay down their weapons and drink East India tea with the Zulus.

Even the birds halt their trilling.

'D'you admire my stitching, then?' enquires Ruby.

'A stitch shall bind. A stitch shan't loosen!' cries Flora.

'Aye. See?' Ruby leans to show Flora her example.

'A stitch shall bind. A stitch shan't loosen!' Flora repeats. 'A stitch shall bind! A stitch shan't—'

'That's enough, Flo,' says Bella.

'Trim and tidy, pleasant and correct,' says Bird, and laughs at herself. 'Nobby-nobody shall ask to see mine, so I don't flash me oh-so-tidy-stitching to no-one.' she calls.

Flora jumps down from the wall. 'Has God blessed us this day?'

'He has, Flo. He has.'

Flora begins a chant; she names the colours in the yard. 'Grey, brown, blue, black, tan . . . '

'Hoo-ha,' says Bird. 'Where's the blue?'

'Not the fagging sky above,' quips Ruby.

Flora points at Ruby Doll, before returning to her colours from the beginning.

'Your skirt, copper-topper. Wakey-wakey!'

'It's periwinkle not blue. Where's your eye?'

Flora crosses her arms across her chest. 'I shall love you each till I suffer and die,' she says.

'Flora!'

'What she say that for, then?'

Bella jumps down. 'No rose was ever sweeter than you, Flo.'

'Daft wench,' says Ruby. 'Give me a hand, Bell. You been at the gin, Flora Wickes?'

'Feed your girls, Percy George, will you?' yells Ruby. 'Starving to death, we are!'

'I shall feed you,' I announce. 'I have bread and butter and cheese. And . . . a bit of ham hock!'

A cheer goes up. The girls are pleased. Hip-ho!

'Good old Percy George!' I shout and raise my arms.

But they are gone inside, flitted like cats.

Love is full of anxious fears ~ Ovid

When I wed Percy I borrowed a dress. He bought me a piece of foreign lace and a posy of pinks to hold.

Our first born we named Samuel. He came well before his time. I recall his waxed eyes, swelled and dark as bruises. My poor boy, unfinished as the fallen rookling. He did not live to suck but only tried to glimpse me before closing his eyes for the sleep eternal. The next, little Mary, took hearty gasps, then went the same. Afterwards Freddie, who lived till six months. Then Robert, who survived until after his first birthday, when a fever took him. Afterwards we had his photograph made. Four shillings, a fortune. Bonny he was, sat in the chair in his Baptism gown, satin ribbon tied at the chin. Would I prefer the eyes open or closed, asked the photographer.

I take the picture from the drawer. Daily I look at it. Closed, was my reply. Here he is, as if he'd fallen asleep. Upon the black card his full name in handsome letters: *Robert Percival Samuel George. In Loving Remembrance.* Buried five years now.

A bitterness came. I turned a shoulder to Percy. His heart broke. He longed for a child, prayed nightly upon his knees. A child of his own was his dearest wish and mine. I would give it all up, he said, for a son or daughter. Could not merciful Jesus have spared a single one? he said. Could not our gracious Lord, in all His redeeming glory, have seen fit to allow him his daughter? How could I answer? His heartache left no room for my own.

My hope turned bitter and love turned sour. He sickened me with his woman's weeping. I could not abide him. One night, God forgive me, I bent to slap him as he prayed. Once I'd landed a blow I could not stop. Upon his knees he remained while I belted him with my fists. That was our ending. I closed the bedroom door. Our love birthed four deaths. Four souls. And I fear we are not to be forgiven.

There is nothing advantageous which
may not also be injurious ~ Ovid

The fates have conspired. Is it possible my good fortune shall come all at once in the human forms of Cox and Stanwick and the royal French bones of a peerless dwarf?

More contrasting forms than Mister Cox and Professor Stanwick would be hard to find.

The professor standing elegant as a crane bird, while Cox is a tangled collection of fire-sticks for limbs, wire wool for hair, beetroot for a face and a bowler atop the lot.

However, the very jewel of fortune has materialised in his form and he is stood upon my path. May God bless him!

A sky full of rain. Muddy roads, rattled and clanged with traffic. The church bell on the hour. I shall paint the picture: The Pied Bull on Islington High Street. Mister Cox. Myself.

Dampened we are from a rain shower, albeit gay of spirit. We lean at our usual corner.

Tobacco for the pipes. Cox scrapes a match, I warm my hands around the flame. Smoke lies in wreaths about our hats. Congenial.

We discuss the arrangements for the experiment, which will feature Amen Steps and Bird.

Cox rests his hand upon my forearm, fixes me with his pink eye. His other hand finds a coin for the refilling of my jug. Oh, pleasant hour! How companionable, we two!

Now to the business.

'Your girl of the deathly complexion,' he says. 'She of the jar.'

'Flora.'

'Aye.'

'What of her?'

'I may have employment for that one,' he says.

I consider for a moment. 'She is a good worker,' I say. 'Of what nature?'

'Tables, spheres, levitation, magnetism.'

'Bread and butter to Flora,' I reply. 'She executes them all.'

'The girl must astound.'

'Standing on her head!' I confirm.

'The participant must be obliging, charming, able.'

I pause. I think of Bella. I still wear the bruise. *If anything happens to the girls you will suffer for it.* But I cannot forestall now.

'Thrice times, yes,' I say.

No harm shall befall the girls, I remind myself. Tip-top employment is their reward.

'The professor prefers the female subject,' Cox continues, 'for their sensitivity. No older than seventeen. The older ones keep too many opinions.'

'You are speaking to one who knows!' I laugh.

'The age of sixteen is his preference,' he says.

'Miraculous! Sixteen she is.'

'Fearless in the spirit realm,' he adds, 'accustomed to the inexplicable.'

'She would die of tedium without a spook to rag,' I tell him.

'Is her repertoire broad?'

'Cabinet, Spirit, Mysterious, Headless. Levitates all day long.'

'The professor is receiving visitors from America. A professor and his benefactress along with assorted enthusiasts.'

'She is discreet,' I say. 'Skilled and sweet as a nightingale.'

'The professor would like a new face.'

'Her face is reg'lar new each day,' I tell him.

Cox lets off a bleat that squeezes into a laugh. Merriment turns him the colour of plums; his pink eye weeps, his fingers tremble.

'How convivial we are!' I proclaim.

The ale and porter has warmed us to wax. You'd wager candles glowed behind our eyes.

'Reg'lar new each day!' Cox quotes me. He bleats, gargles. He is not averse to humour.

It is no lie. Flora has the wiles. Changeable as the sky, she is.

'We will require her for a week, maybe two.'

'Costly!'

'She will be required to work with both professors. She must oblige at all times. I have calculated in guineas.'

'Six per week. No less. Veritas! I've been offered more.'

The pink eye closes, the fingers fold. Cox's mouth forms a seam. He waits.

'Countless occasions!' I say. 'Popular performer! Flora is the exception.'

I silence myself. My girls are skilled. Remarkables all. His need is greater than mine. I wait.

If Flora holds her situation the girls shall have blouses, fashion bonnets, ribbons, pastries. Moreover, once the professor has observed our Bird about her sorcerous business, well then, by the year's end we shall have a new address around the Gray's Inn way. Top brass!

He smiles. Ah, here it is: Cox offers me his trembling hand. We shake.

What an opportunity for young Flora! Word will get out. Her talent shall be spoke of, her career will be made. Her future stands wreathed in glory. Walk this way to find her at The Egyptian Hall. Her name shall stand two feet high. Long have I suspected that discoursing with the dead is the way to win the crowd, yet, like a fool, I have ignored myself. I suspect modern science and spiritual phenomena are about to meet one another coming around the bend.

As a matter of urgency I must enlighten Bella as to the wholly scientific nature of the contract. Set her mind at rest. I shall explain it well and truly. She shall be reassured by my explanation. Yes, clarity is required. Once she grasps the gist she is bound to be heartened and relieved.

Meanwhile, a notion has been brewing in my mind, and here it is: if Professor Stanwick's Spiritual Séance is modern science then so is Percy George's Psychic Phenomenal. Who knows, p'raps I may be so bold as to proclaim it! These fadge-beaked educated crows in their morning coats and watch chains are a haughty breed, I do not deny it, yet I have found myself among them, lighting the torches of progress. In a matter of days a remarkable experiment concerning human telepathy shall occur that is entirely dependent upon two of my own Remarkables. When I am done those frock-coated corvids will wonder what type of miracle bludgered them. Timely. Darkness will be illuminated! We shall have eyes. Percival Unusual George holds his Remarkables in readiness.

The Work Proves the
Workman ~ Proverb

Come Early As A Rush Is Expected! Tuesday has the sign newly painted.

It is pie in the sky, receipts have been low.

Steps is spinning plates but it is not his forte, his ventriloquism I prefer. Pinkie is his doll, newly recovered yet racked by a hacking cough. The girls paint his face and he is almost a triumph, especially with youngsters.

For our advertisement, Tuesday has daubed Ruby in her feathers with a saucy eye and those who pass stop to admire her attributes. Tuesday Brown turns his hand to any task, happy he is to paint roses on the booth, push back a rowdy crowd, or climb up to speak the part of the Duke of Albany, albeit popeyed as an undertaker at the wrong church.

Without fuss we nightly transform Bird Doyle to *The Human Bird, A Prank Of Nature.*

She has a squawk and a dear little feathered face. Gaily she steps, birdlike she skips. Melted tallow, a few feathers, and she transforms into the perfect picture of a fowl. 'Craaa!' she craws. 'Shall I peck out your eye, sir? No? Off I flit. Hoo-ha. How about you, madam?

Shall I predict the date of your marriage? Your first-born? Your dying day?'

When the mood takes him the rookbird sits upon her finger. He likes the sound of the coins, he will hold one in his beak. Like rain falling on roofs, chimes the sound of chink.

We have a mutton dinner from the stall. The salted gravy would anchor a ship.

'Shall we have new costumes by'n'by? Or is it only dead bones who get fresh threads?'

A whinge from Ruby, her neck reddens.

I pay no heed. 'Shall Flora say the prayer?' I enquire.

Ruby flashes. 'It's my turn.'

'Well. What of it? Piffle,' I say. 'Does it count? Flora might as well speak it.'

'Why Flora? Has she amused the crowds today? Has she filled the tin?'

Bella folds her arms. 'What's got your goat, then?'

'What do you care?' replies Ruby.

Bird, in a tassled fez, examines Ruby through a lorgnette. 'Calm yourself, Coppertop.'

'Hold your tongue,' says Ruby.

'Now, now,' murmurs Tuesday.

'Well, pardon me!' Ruby continues. 'But I for one am curious as to how a dead midget is become the superior be-all in this house when his bones ought properly be underground.'

'Hoity-toity! Someone stole your mule?' Jim grins at himself. Amen laughs.

'Shut it, wet boy!'

'Oooooh!' hoots Jim.

'Simmer down.' Bella sounds weary.

'And how can you sit there?' Ruby leans towards Bella. 'Saying not a word about it?'

'Don't you start on me, madam!' Bella bangs down her cup.

I disregard them. One thing I know of females is do not interfere in their private contests.

'I shall say the prayer,' says Amen, smiling broadly, getting to his feet.

'Shut your lid!' Ruby blurts. 'It's not your turn.'

'Shall I?' says Bird. She stands, curtsies, grimaces. 'Lord—'

Ruby bangs the table. 'P'raps the dead bones shall say it!' she cries, reddening. 'Where is it? The dead thing. Shall it say the prayer? Does it speak? Might we be acquainted, then?'

For a moment nobody responds. Then we hear the scrape of her chair and we watch as she kicks a stool, grabs her neckcloth and bolts from the room. We listen to the chime of a spoon hitting the floor.

'Joseph and Mary and all the saints,' I comment. I wipe my mouth. I compose myself before I continue.

'Any of you who do not wish to perform with the historical royal dwarf are welcome to leave and seek employment elsewhere,' I say. 'I shall pay you what you're owed. There'll be no resentment on my part.'

I survey the table. Not an eye-glance rises to meet mine. Bella, arms folded, has turned to stone. We listen to the laboured tocking of the clock.

'There. To all of you I am much obliged.'

I push away my chair and leave them to it. Not a voice breaks the silence. Instead, I attend to the unfamiliar sound of nobody's opinion, and afterwards an uncommon tranquillity descends upon the house.

She appears at midnight by my chair, startling the rookbird.

I know it is Ruby, I recognise her boot. I watch her fidgeting shadow and listen to the sound of her breathing.

'Mister George,' she murmurs.

'You shall all have new costumes,' I say. 'And winter shawls.'

She steps closer, and sits on the arm of the chair. We stare at the fire embers.

'I have a scheme,' I say. 'Of the superior variety. Top brass. Not a word.' I tap my nose. '*Confidential*,' I breathe.

'Oh?' she says. 'Tell it.'

'Go to bed. Tomorrow you rehearse with royalty. Go on. The future is here.'

Once I am certain that all are safely tucked within their cots I go to fetch him.

He is a dainty companion, does not interrupt nor demand, yet only attends. My royal dwarf and I sit awhile together till the fire glow dims. Upon my knee he rests. He is a tonic. In this way I might consider matters: his costumes are complete. Now I must conjure a scene for this French midget to play for the crowd. Nightly do I dream of him upon the stage, yet the fantasies are unearthly. High above the crowd he flies and laughs, rides upon a winged horse and sings arias to our Empress Queen. By day, on the other hand, I think p'raps he might rise from a coffin and warble a ballad song about his royal life, yet it does not compare to my night visions.

This week I must present him before the crowd.

Spare the whip and firmly grasp the reins
~ Ovid

The following day I discover I have lost a living midget. This is the tribulation that follows triumph. No sooner is your pipe lit than a thunder-shower extinguishes it.

It is my dwarf, Pinkie. 'Pinks,' I tell him, 'you have broken my heart.'

He is almost returned to health, despite coughing like a river dog, yet I know what truly ails him. It began with Bella, then Ruby. It ails them all. And lo and behold, over a glass of stout he delivers.

'We are no longer the principal midgets!' he cries.

He is on his second glass of beer and is smoking my best tobacco. 'I shall not take second place behind your box of bones,' he says, and orders a third stout.

'I shall be sad to see you go,' I tell him. It is true, albeit I am wearying of these dramatic interludes.

In his Sunday clothes he departs. As their owner, he takes the ponies with him.

'How does it follow,' he fumes, 'that a dead midget has priority over a living one?'

'Royalty prevails,' I tell him. 'I am merely observing the social order, Pinks.'

'Cock!' he cries, replacing his hat, and is gone, a pony in each hand.

My other midget, Pie Clark, remains, being that he is no fool and is untormented by rank. What joy abides! We have a wagon but no dwarf nags to tow it. Daily I play both victim and villain, and this is the bootless fate of the hard-toiling showman.

The remedy is to be found locally. We have visited three public houses; The Firkin proved the most convivial being that Joseph O'Connor played the fiddle to his wife's rendition of *There's A Good Time Comin', Boys*.

Afterwards we observe that Canal Street has transformed itself during our refreshment interval. See how it bends! Beneath the chilled yellow sky we marvel at it. Like a ladle it curves! Mist stands upon the canal and greenish sludge lards the banks. Porter, mild and stout we have consumed, Tuesday, Ames and I. Not to mention the French brandy.

We are better men for it, being as how liquor improves the outlook of any who partake.

How the cabs sway, the houses nod, the sky tilts. Bang-up, this world is a marvel. And all the life upon it. Praise God for it!

I open the door, giddy as a dolly-mop. I hear voices.

I halt to listen.

'Stand him upright. Stand him up here. Ruby, look!'

'See his little legs!'

'There. See how he dances! Look!'

'Ha ha! He's a reg'lar hoof, Bell!'

'Jim! Daft boy.'

'God above, Jim. You gave us a scare!'

'Why, what are you doing with the midget?'

'Nought. It's a game.'

'Lord in Heaven.'

'Can I see, then?'

'Halt your chaff!'

'He is only bones.'

'See how he jigs? Ha!'

'Bent like a jungly ape, he is.'

'Ha ha!'

'Hold him up, then.'

'I shall kiss the bone where once was his lips.'

'You will not!'

'Who will he tell?'

'I will tell.'

'Stow it, Jim.'

'Look at him wave! God save the Queen!'

'Good evenin', young lady. Give us a kiss.'

I have heard enough. Without removing my hat, I bolt in.

'Put that dwarf down! Don't you touch him!'

How heavily he falls, my midget. We listen to the sound of his bones striking the table. Bone upon wood daggers the heart.

I look at the girls. I look at Jim.

'We thought to examine it.'

'Aye, we thought to examine the dwarf.'

'Hold your spout!' I cry.

'It was not me, Mister George. The girls took him from the box.'

'Stuff it, wet boy! Well? What do you have to say? Whom shall I punish first!'

Jim cringes, clutches his thighs. He squeezes a sob.

The girls do not blink nor answer. Three wax faces, three freckled apples.

'Tell me!' I call. 'Else I shall be obliged to wallop you all!'

Jim turns and scarpers for the door.

I am down the passage after him quicker than a cat. I hardfist the back of his head and he stumbles and falls from the blow.

'Lay a hand on him again and I will finish you where you stand!' I shout.

I turn to the girls.

'I should put you out on the street! I shall do! No jot of gratitude. Street flies, all of you!

I ought not to have spoke of it at all. How I wish I had not! What a fool was I to imagine you might treasure, as I do, a miniature wonder of this world. Rare! A marvel of history! The like of which is unknown. What a fool was I for thinking that you would understand!'

It is Bella, alone, who looks me in the eye. Puts her hands upon me.

'Hush-hush, Percy. See how Ruby Doll has polished your box. See how it shines? What a handsome box. And what a jolly clown is this foreign midget. See how Ruby has dressed him up smart in Lark's old best? Don't his bones look dashing? See! Waistco't and all. Don't he look the part now?'

My dwarf bones do indeed look sharp in Lark's best clothes, albeit they are rolled at the hems.

'Take off the hat, I say. Take off the cravat. Halfwits all!'

Bella obeys. 'There,' she says.

I wager p'raps I ought to have remained in slaughtering where a thing is or isn't. Trapped I am, instead, between this century and the last with the bones of a matchless dwarf who shall never know my name, and those who openly disdain his.

'Not one of you is to lay a finger on The Piece again, mark me. It is no thru'penny bag of sticks which you have meddled. These are the royal bones of a beloved personal midget. Verified. Certified. Respect and delicacy! Halfwit fadging pykes such as yourselves will be handled accordingly. Have I spoke it plain or is there one who remains uncertain?'

When they are gone to their beds I place the dwarf upon my knee to examine him for damage. I find none. My rookbird observes us from the window cove. He gargles, blinks. By the last of the fire's glow the dwarf and I recline companionably. I am about to return him to his box, and yet. It is pleasant to sit a while longer, his bony head rested upon my shoulder. Restful. 'Congenial,' I comment to the rookbird. 'See us here now agreeably contented, just we three.'

~

Fleeting fortune wanders with
doubting steps ~ Ovid

As a boy I loved the stage and all those who performed upon it. With a pencil I drew pictures and crafted a troupe made of paper in costumes and hats. My father commanded I decide differently.

'No son of mine will prance the boards theatrical with bangtails and Marys, d'you hear me?'

For my part I persisted with my passion and learned the words to *One Last Dance, Dolly Jones*. He would put a stop to it, my father said. He knew the quickest way to change a boy's thinking, he told me. He would punish me once only and he would do a proper job, he said, so I'd remember. I would renounce the stage theatrical, he said. I'd be grateful to him for it.

It was in the evening he began, at five o'clock. It took a fair time to break the first bone.

I held a tune in my head, same as at Jackson's yard. It went on until two bones were broken and the entire thing lasted precisely three songs. The next day my mother took me to the infirmary. I saw nothing through my left eye.

'That will have to come out,' said the doctor cheerfully, on examining it. I recall thinking, how shall I see anything at stage-right?

The process was slow, albeit I mended, good as new. In due course a beard grew over the concavity of the cheek-bone. My mother said to my father, You shall not touch him again, and if you do, I shall kill you. And he did not touch me nor speak directly to me ever again.

I began to form schemes for the future in my head. I suspected I would become a great success. I would toil, I would prevail. I persisted and yet. The golden opportunity continued to evade me. I required no more than a singular item. A twin-headed sheep? A bearded widow? An item of charm, of spectacle. I thought to myself, Do I ask for too much? Shall forbearance fail me? Lady Luck: by'n'by she stepped from her carriage, as I knew she would. She has bestowed upon me the blessing of a royal dwarf and together he and I shall become the talk of London. The purse shall grow heavy and my dancing steps light. We shall afford soft lamps and a Persian rug, like those at Stanley Gardens, Hampstead. I salute her, the Dame of All Good Fortune, for delivering to me this masterpiece! I shall honour her generosity with a show of dazzling innovation. We shall play to seated rows of burgundy velvet beneath lit gasoliers. There will be a Royal Circle, brocaded drapes, a stage door and a dressing room. All are invited. Step up!

'Tis a small merit to hold silence upon
a matter ~ Ovid

The volume is narrow, bound in polished calf and tooled in gilt.

I have examined with a lens the engraved frontispiece with its coat of arms, wherein grimaces a maddened bull and a pair of spread eagles alongside mounted knights in armour. At its edges creep decorative trees and a variety of planting I cannot name.

At the top is tooled a small crown and the curling initials *N.F.* draped in foliage. The midget's initials. Trinket to a royal king now trinket to an Unusual king.

Ah, sweet dwarf! My own dear purchased charm. Upon

these pages skip his bones. Upon these pages, in curious lettering, he is resurrected and bound anew in calfskin.

Engraved within, I discover a vignette of dwarf and king costumed in robes: *Szlachta* is the word beneath, as if the printer dropped all his blocks pell-mell! Over and over I examine it, yet their faces are weary. More clearly do I see them in my thoughts, my sprightly dwarf and his royal king striding their palatial corridors.

Tucked within my coat the volume is safe from prying eyes. My own heart beats against it.

Tick-tock.

Softly may his bones repose ~ Ovid

Here is Half Moon Alley, Clerk'nwell. You may buy a goat around here for the price of dog meat. A snap wind pulls dust left and right and cab horses fret in harness. Here you shall find breweries, brothels and burial grounds, printers, watch-makers and ghosts. A few been flicked here and bled on these stones. Hark and you will hear a sad song trilled in Italian. They say Half Moon Alley makes its own fog, even when the sun shines. Me? I am beguiled by its smoky charm. Moreover, the public houses are top brass. I hurry into The Butcher's Arms.

Why the professor chose to convene with me I cannot, in truth, tell. There are others, albeit none so discreet as I, nor blessed with four such pretty songbirds, nor as cheerful about their daily enterprise, nor as Unusual in their general machinations. Or p'raps my reckoning is flawed.

Do I hold the key to a box he would unlock? P'raps the business of science is no more than a series of dodges and capers through which the process of phenomena is revealed. P'raps a scientist is no more than a showman with a pinch of schooling. P'raps these gentlemen herons, cavorting in their silk hats and frock coats, are throwing their dice blind with no clue as to how the numbers fall. P'raps it is I who has sprinted ahead and arrived at the future before them. Modesty prevents me considering myself superior to these gallants of progress and yet reg'lar do I have a choice scheme ... and a scheme is a scientific theory all its own. There. I have solved the conundrum. I would shake my own hand but I cannot catch myself. I am out of the door!

Time, the devourer of all things
~ Horace

I require a Frenchman. Today I shall hear my dwarf speak.

My ear is cocked. How I long to hear my miniature. His foreign mutterings shall be conjured into words I understand. Top brass, English as a row of pies.

I find him at Alfred Godfrey of London on John Street, Clerk'nwell. He is a watchmaker.

His name is Luc Ferrières. Foreign. A Frenchman. A secretspringer. A finisher.

A bell clangs as I enter. An odour of beeswax and brass. And the sound: *Tick-tick-tick-tick*. A frenzy of mended clocks! He detects me across the bench of broken timepieces.

I tap my boot, remove my hat. I adopt the smile I use for the crowd.

'Mister Furrier,' I say.

His left eye is magnified, scaffolded in apparatus, blown wide as a butterfly. He has the alarmed aspect of a man interrupted. Charm is required. I open my arms that he may see a foursquare gent.

'Good morning, sir!'

He does not reply but warily observes, as if I too were a faulty clock stripped of numbers. His forehead is high and creased in puzzlement. His eyes are small, dark, steady. I wager he has a clockmaker's patience.

'Mister Furrier!' I say again, to be plain. 'I am not intruding?'

He sets down his apparatus. Rubs his face.

'You have business, sir?' he says. 'A timepiece?'

Bang-up, his English is sound. Saints be thanked! His words are delivered in a strange key, yet I know them as well as a shilling.

'No, sir,' I reply, lowering my voice. 'I have a dwarf.'

I sway my cane, for a touch of mystery. Ferrières observes, unsmiling.

'London has nought like him,' I continue more briskly. 'I have his bones put safe away and here are his words. In print! Quite alive! As if he strolled beneath your bench, sir.'

Despite my bounce, he appears wary. I place the leather edition upon the bench. I open the cloth with a flourish. I must intrigue, lure.

He opens the book with a single finger.

'Writ in the French,' I say, to reassure him. 'Quality weave. Quality print. Quality binding.'

I lean closer.

'One hundred years old.' I speak it low, so he may ponder how broad is one hundred.

His finger strokes the page. I seize the moment.

'Sir! Here upon these pages is your fellow countryman, not three feet tall. A miniature masterpiece. The priceless gem. A pearl of France.'

I bend to the page and inhale.

'The very print ink smells of French royalty. Try for yourself, Mister Furrier.'

He makes no movement. Behind him clocks tap, click, chime, whirr.

'Perhaps. Mister. Furrier.' I labour each word, dividing up the parts, as I do not wish to jumble him. 'You. Will. Tell. Me the. Content. Of. The volume? If you be so inclined?'

He regards me without expression.

'Your English is plain and digestible,' I say. 'I can pay by the hour. Yes? Or no?'

He glances up at me, considers my garb, my best cane.

'What is your name, sir?' he asks.

I stand up straight and tell him.

He laughs at the perjuries of lovers
~ Ovid

The whine of the fiddle is the sound that greets me. Steps loves a caper.

He is dancing like a dervish on the old Persian runner. Rose will whip him for wearing down her threads. Tuesday heaves a tune from the squeezebox, Ruby hits the drum and Pie rings the bells. I let them blast. Receipts are improved. And I have a Frenchman, I warrant, in the palm of my hand.

I am piss-proud! God love Rose! I should kiss her neck. I do.

She punches the side of my head. It is a lover's cuff. I withstand. It throbs, is all.

'I am your slave, Rose Burton!'

'You were in my way.'

'Please accept my sincerest apology.'

'You remain in my way, George.'

'Begging your pardon,' I say.

I stand aside.

Rose walks, her head held high, hands clasped. She does not regard me but I sense a flicker, an acknowledgement. It is enough. I lower my gaze.

'Rose,' I say. She walks on. 'You are a queen!' I call, as the door closes behind her.

Tuesday brings me cognac in a glass. Upon my head a pebble-sized lump is rising on the starboard side. Rose is not a woman to be trifled with. A hiss arrives in my left ear. The brandy flares its heat and soothes.

Tomorrow I shall return to Ferrières. I warrant he will come to know me by'n'by. He may regard me yet. I shall make my impression on him in instalments. He will discern me, by degree, as a man of insight. Aye to that!

Bella arrives, arms folded. The girls spill in behind her. She stands by my chair.

'Will you not sing to relieve me of the discomfort?' I plead. She shrugs and adjusts a pin in her hair. 'Well,' she says. 'Proper scolded, aren't you? That'll teach you.'

The girls laugh. Bella is playful. She slaps my wounded head, making me cry out in pain. She fetches me another brandy and, as she leans down, I hook my arm around her waist and she lands tidily, with a shriek, upon my knee.

'Bella,' I say. 'You have come to embrace me after all!'

And they all howl like devils. Instantly there is cheer in the room and the afternoon turns genial. I sing. *Give a man a girl he can love, As I, O my love, love thee . . .* In the yard we share a quiet pipe, Bella and I.

How long, I ask, since we did so last? She cannot recall. In her eye I detect an impish glow. I whisper her name and she lowers her chin. The stillness between us slows the breeze, halts the birdsong. Everything waits.

I lean in to kiss her and she does not stop me. How long has it been? The years have laid over us like stone. Bella. We look at one another. My own girl.

We are interrupted.

'Shall I have to drag you, then!' Ruby has her arms out, hair loose upon her shoulders. 'Amen has the tune and all but Flora know the words!'

Bird is behind her with a spoon. 'I shall tap the beats!' she says.

Bella leads me in, and I think, A new time is here for us. A little patience. Here is reward. Together the girls sing *The Swell Cove's Alphabet*. I am overjoyed! It is a disgusting song but my heart is full of roses and it eases my poor head.

S is sponging houses, Shire-lane, saloons and swiving,
T you know is thimble-rigs, and Tattersalls, enliv'ning
U is an uprighter, or hunt with hasty dressing,
And V is the venereal that follows, as a blessing!

The song and its merry filth has restored me. I am ready to receive whatever fortune brings! And yet. I cannot sit here, adrift, I must get on. I cannot hear the tumbling of coins nor the stamp of a crowd. We have no Madam Doris nor her Skating Bears, no Mrs Daffodil and her airborne furniture. We make do.

~

The beginnings of all things are
small ~ Cicero

The fates are conspiring. Just as our own doves alight upon Tuesday's outstretched finger, so an opportunity settles upon us.

The girls are grouped together on the window seat, except for Bella, who leans against the wall with Amen.

They wait for me to speak.

'I shall describe everything as it was!' I announce. 'This morning I searched out my silk han'kerchief and gloves, to which I added my wool waistco't, church trousers, polished cane, best boots. For a scrape and a shine I took myself and here I am! Shined as a nut, after attending an informal meeting at the professor's scientific institute in Bedford Square.' I tell my story with brio, cross-legged, in the armchair.

'Here I shall begin,' I say. I tell it as it occurred. Firstly I set the scene:

'Imagine the rooms,' I cry. 'They are panelled. The cognac is French. The freesias freshly cut. Bowls of them! Dizzying!'

I note their expressions: Bella, Ruby, Bird, Steps, Brown. How attentive they are!

'I am served a dish of plums by a servant,' I say. 'When the gentlemen take their leave in order to attend a lecture in the Red Room, I eat the lot. Oh, the stains upon the napkin! I have it here, see?' I display it for the girls. They lean to inspect it.

'Thieved it!' says Ruby. 'Give it here. Look at that. Irish linen, as I stand.'

'Well? What of it?' says Bella. 'Get to the point.'

I exhale and close my eyes, as the tormented do.

'Just tell us what they wanted.' Bella speaks in a woman's tone, arms crossed.

I wager'd it'd not please her at first. She is turning by degrees into a suspicious goose. She does not trust anyone: neither myself nor the esteemed professor, who attended Oxford University and was presented to the Queen. Yet still this does not satisfy Bella.

'I saved the plum stones,' I say. 'Seven. There. Count them!'

'Percy George. What did they want?'

Indeed, I had a suspicion she would bang on like a church bell about it. Dingalingaling.

'Well. They did not request you, Bella. And they did not request you neither, Ruby Doll. And, peculiar to say, they did not require me! Albeit not directly.'

'Who exactly did you meet?'

'Men of science,' I retort. 'Gentlemen. Experts. Professors.'

'Codswallop,' says Bella.

'What did the professor want you to do?' Ruby asks.

'He is conducting scientific experiments of unusual complexity,' I say.

Bella steps forward. 'Yes. And what did he want with you?' she demands. 'You'd better not say it, Percy George. Upon my grave.'

'It's not you or me they want.'

'Who, then?'

'Flora.'

'Flora?' chirps Bird. 'Why Flora?'

'I knew it,' snaps Bella. 'My God, I thought better of you than this.'

'Hush, while I speak!' Blood has heated my face. She has agitated me with her fretting. 'Can't a man speak?' I plead. They wait.

' . . . I was saying. A game girl is required for demonstration purposes; one who is unimpeded by *doubt*. Open of heart and mind. *Unstained* in thought! Cheerful of outlook.

115

There. Satisfied? They seek one who does not trouble her-self with suspicion!'

The others have raised their heads upon the word suspicion. Bella leans down to me.

'And you gave her up?'

'Quiet! Gave her up? She will be paid in guineas.'

'What will she do? Dare you say it?'

'What! What? Whatever he will have her do! Investigation of a scientific nature. These fellows are scientists! What would you have them do? Science of course!'

'And who will protect her once she is among strangers, then?'

'What! Will you deny her the chance of success among the educated classes? Will you deny her a guinea in the hand? Oh! Hold your horses! It's all over town. Flora is a triumph! What say you then?'

I feel my blood leap. I am on my feet. No reply has she, nought but the silent judgement of the chary. I approach her. We are almost nose-to-nose.

'Well?' Only a showman's shout will rattle you to the bone. She flinches. I must drive home my victory, or else she will come at me ferociously when I am unprepared.

'Well!' I repeat. I have the caller's shout. Her ears will ring.

'It's not safe,' she says.

'What? Not safe! It is perfectly sound. She is not expected to walk a wire or scale a steeple in her petticoats!'

'We have heard stories.'

'Stories?'

'Girls that are used against their will. Ill-treated. Cruelly dealt. Abandoned. Or worse.'

This is Bella. Bang-up. I catch a scheme: coins in the purse, food upon the table, and Bella will unpick every stitch until all is rags again, and when she is done she will ask what on earth is there to eat and why, in God's name, have I not devised a scheme?

'The professor,' I reply, with all the patience I can force upon myself, 'is a man of eminence and distinction. A man of position. A man of honour. While you, Bella, are a blethering dipper from Bethnal Green who will finish the gin from a dead man's bottle. Enough!'

She closes her eyes. With no more words to spend, she turns to leave.

I suspect that was my rage talking. Well, now. She brought it on, I still have the bruises, I remind myself.

I listen to her boots upstairs. I wait for the crash of an object, a shriek of tears. There is none. I hold my head in my hands. I have won the argument and yet. As swiftly as it returned, our tenderness is, as quickly, erased. My heart is ash.

The voice of the stars ~ Virgil

The next day Tuesday Brown escorts our own dear Flora to the institute.

Irresistible, is how a gent once described Flora Wickes. A charming scrap, he said.

Beneath her chin runs a blue vein, trace it with your finger, it travels down her throat. Gentlemen seem deeply moved by it. One fellow gave her a drawing he'd sketched during a show, in charcoals. Flora had been attempting the decapitation trick, which is devilish; she returned to chloroform after that. For this kind of spectacle a gentleman prefers a young girl's head to any other variety, it is their fancy. The more educated the gentleman the prettier the head preferred. You pick it up as you go along. I don't invent the form. Thus far I have met no gentleman who did not appreciate the exquisite sadness of a child, pretty of face, performing a tale of cruel misfortune: penniless, beggarly, cast out, crippled or close to death in innocent misery, the more pitiful the better. Such scenes pluck a gentleman's heartstring and prod his charitable purse. It is the stuff of shows, and therefore the business of a showman.

It pains me to lose Flora, albeit temporarily, yet the professor pays a decent bag and she will likely have meat twice a day and apricot pastries whenever she pleases. A gaff girl's theatrical reputation may be made upon such a prestigious engagement. She will not be gone long, three weeks at most. Comfortable as the Archbishop of London she'll be.

That night I spend extravagantly on a beef supper for all, with gravy. Who's complaining now, Bell? Dingaling. She does not meet my eye but she eats a plateful and wipes up her gravy. I wait for her to comment on the deliciousness of the food, to place a hand on my shoulder. Nought. A woman keeps her dignity in a box labelled, Silence.

> Nor, even if a faithful translator, should
> you make it your care to render the
> original word for word ~ Horace

His workshop faces north to obtain a steady light and avoid the glare of the sun. Mister Ferrières has a low bench and a high bench. *Tick-tick-tick* is the sound of the mended clocks. A nest of drawers is fitted to his right and a shelf holds a lathe box and his tools. He keeps his eye on time, yet time dashes off all the same.

His fingers, gold by gaslight, tremble over gear and cog. Mister Ferrières coaxes a timepiece to tell its numbers. He observes time as it runs its daily race until, at the twelve, it all begins again.

'I was born in Picardie,' he says, without looking up.

'Ah,' I reply.

I think, Must I care? I never heard of such a place. Heavy coins I have made in payment.

Ought I demand he speaks only of France as it concerns my dwarf? I have no use for the whole of France and her other districts.

He has lit an extra lamp in spite of the daylight. He fusses with pliers: snip snip. I must endure. The patience I am about to conjure is born out of necessity. God above. Vexing. Yet, I fancy patience becomes me quite well.

Mister Ferrières glances up.

Quickflash, I affect an ingratiating smile. Words alone do not persuade. I must seem befitting. I play the part. Once I did consider the stage but who would manage the shops, lodgings, performances, outgoings? Must I spin the world and blow her north winds too? I picture briefly my mother, whose phrase this was, with a han'kerchief ready at her eye.

'Monsieur George. You bring a dwarf for me?'

I smile. He has understood.

'Mister Furrier, I do.'

His gaze returns to his pliers and screws. I observe the accuracy of his long fingers, as their ticklish work bids mechanical hands to tell the hours. As he works, he speaks. His voice is a grumble that rises unexpectedly to a higher note of enquiry.

'Time is all, Monsieur. Alors, I must remedy time, but there is not time enough. She escapes. Daily, she

119

disappears,' he says. 'Where does she fly? As I speak, she is gone. *Pa!*'

I do not answer. The Frenchman speaks in riddles. He grins, without amusement, showing a few good teeth.

'I can pay by the hour,' I say.

'Time halts,' he says, 'at the grave, Monsieur.'

He stops at his own pronouncement. Fixes me a stare. I detect self-satisfaction.

'We could begin with half a crown,' I say.

At this Ferrières removes his eyeglass and rises to his feet. I am pleased to observe that I am the taller.

'Your dwarf,' he says, 'le petit pauvre. Does he wish for you to listen? Do you consider this?

In one hundred years shall a stranger know you, Monsieur? Time will tell, yes? Time tells.

The fates alone know where our destination lies.'

Piffle, I think. Riddles, I think. Frenchman, I think.

'Patience, Monsieur, she alone will steady the hands of time.'

A speech! I think. As I stand here! To be deduced by a stranger! He toys with me. For pleasure! My smile wilts. He prates on. Even now, as my eye-glance deadens, he blethers.

'Do you ask yourself what it is you hope to hear from your little dwarf?' he enquires. His head tilts. 'What secrets do you hope he will share?'

I see it now. Mister Ferrières considers himself a philosopher and a connoisseur of human temperament. He considers his magnifying eye takes in people just as accurately as spindles and gears. How may this ticking clock-fiddler reveal the foreign ramblings of my dwarf when his own spew of ruminations threatens to drown us all? The fact that clocks tick at his command swells his conceit further, he considers his dissecting eye can take a man to pieces as well as one of his clocks. Imagines he has invented Time itself with one of his little tools. Wagers himself a philosopher to boot!

'Mister Furrier,' I say. 'Between the tick and tock of one of your mended minutes I produce entertainments across London. My acts are astounding. Highly esteemed. Time, sir? It chases us all.' There. Does he wager his tick-tock spoutings will impress a man such as myself? English-speaking Frenchmen are two a penny in this city. I will not be his kickshaw. I replace my hat.

'Good day to you, Mister Furrier,' I say. 'Tick-tock.'

The mocking bell announces my departure. I am gone.

I walk home. I have my mother to thank for my intuition when it comes to character types. She could narrow her eye at an individual or a circumstance and sway either to her advantage in an eyeblink. Percival, she used to say, each man upon this earth has a desire, a secret and a regret: discover what they are and he is yours for the taking.

Mister Ferrières may rue the morning he disdained good chink for a handful of French pratings! At the very least I am a man who may spot a peerless scheme, even as it dashes out of sight around the corner. I have it in sight!

There is nothing advantageous which
may not also be injurious ~ Ovid

Mister Cox has invited me to a table-turning, which is due to take place on Thursday this week. It is hush-hush. Cox explained it, his pink eye sealed. Unsavoury characters may hear of it, he murmured, and arrive uninvited. I shall not breathe a word, I assure him.

In confidence, I tell Rose, as the intrigue may excite some unacknowledged interest in me. It will be on Thursday, I inform her. It will be well attended by educated gentlemen of world renown. 'Professors!' I am forced to hiss, as hereabouts are eavesdroppers, lurking.

'Why do these gentlemen care for your attendance, then?' she asks in a bold voice.

'Hush!' I hiss again. 'I cannot be certain, save for the fact that the professor admires Flora and Bird, and their psychical abilities.'

'Well then!' Rose cries out. 'You shall be there on false pretences, shan't you?'

She could not have called it louder. Robustly I laugh.

'Ha! Rose, you are a skirted-scoundrel! A reg'lar jaybird!'

'Bella is distressed,' she says, folding her arms. 'You have upset her.'

These games. Giving me chaff. I am besieged. I ought to upbraid her. Wearily, I lower my head. 'What would you have me do?' I say.

'Kin comes before the shilling, George Percy.' She speaks my name backwards. I wager it is her way to mock and reject me. For what? For admiring her? For upsetting Bella?

'You have it about-face,' she chides. 'Poor little George Percy,' she wheedles. 'Who will you have left?' Her blow is delivered. Her back turned, departing. It is her small violence.

~

The wave that approaches overtops all
the others ~ Ovid

Must I possess the boundless patience of a venerated saint?

Rehabilitated by the restorative powers of porter and stout, my outlook is improved and I have returned home charitably disposed when, as the toe of my boot meets the threshold, I am greeted by another muddle.

Amen has mislaid one of the foreign snakes, which is a confounded nuisance, and most dearly do I wish I had the serpent at my disposal to wrap it around that fadger's windpipe. Amen has no apology but only stands before me with his hands aloft in a gesture of helplessness. Naturally, he has a Biblical quote to hand. *'Now the serpent was more subtil than any beast of the field which the Lord God had made.'*

I walk by him without comment. He may stand there quoting till the sun goes cold. I have no interest. Nor shall I seek to replace the viper. These reptiles are popular with the ladies for the hullaballoo, but reptilians are apt to travel abroad. Sniffed a rat, I warrant. So be it. Personally, I am not partial to serpents as, amply proven in this instance, they are not to be trusted.

On that same subject I trust no man, earthly or otherwise, since returning from the table-turning, as, on the night, our particular table did not so much turn as leap about under the manipulations of one or more of the invitees. I wager spiritual standards in Hampstead are on the slide. Vexing, as I expected a top class evening and experienced instead a gaff show.

Meanwhile, we must endure the muddle of a liberated serpent that may coil itself in my hat or boot should I be careless enough to take them off.

And now, on the subject of muddles – Frenchmen I have found: one drunk, one blind, the other violent, all incomprehensible. Ferrières will have to do. I am obliged to return.

And so I shall. And no jostling taunts nor chaffing nor mockery will I endure this time.

The clock-fiddler shall see before him a shrewd Englishman, a witful man of bounce and substance. Let him try his French-fingered pirouettes this time. He shall not catch me.

Part II

Earth sounds my wisdom, and high
Heaven my fame

Homer, The Odyssey, *Book IX*

I return to my Frenchman at Alfred Godfrey of London on John Street. I prepare myself for the inharmonious bell, which announces me as if I skip with an accordion.

I shall endure! No matter what occurs. No matter the length he prates. No matter how murky his riddling. I shall heed none and when he is done . . . I shall open the historical edition. And there shall lie a shilling. And so it will begin. For the trouble of an honest coin my dwarf shall speak.

I enter and am ridiculed by the bell. A tickle! No matter!

As before, the air is frenzied. Tick tick tick, as if a million insects toiled.

'Mister Furrier!' I call. I remove my hat.

I approach his bench. This time I do not hesitate. I tap my cane. He glances up.

I set down the book. I pay no heed to his bench instruments that pierce, nip and tighten.

A screwdriver falls to the floor.

I open the book. The shilling winks. He looks at it.

Now young Miss Bright, the Lion Queen, was mauled to death by a tiger somewhere near Chatham. It is said she tapped it with the whip once too often. An experienced Lion Queen knows better than to prod-prod. Young Miss Bright was a novice. According to her cousin, Lizzie, Miss Bright wanted to sharpen the big cat's movements. You could say she achieved this with spectacular results. The trick is to know when to prod-prod and when to step back. Me? I am well practised.

P'raps a casual observer might suppose Ferrières and I to be old friends. They'd be deceived. He leans back to receive more light upon the page, I tilt forward to catch his murmurings. The shilling rests in his pocket. Prod-prod.

'A page here is missing, torn,' he murmurs.

'Never mind that,' I reply.

Ferrières regards the words, his eye-glance dodges right to left. He is taking his time!

I have prodded and prodded. Now I step back.

He begins to mutter the words as they are writ, French, indecipherable and foreign as mayonnaise behind his teeth.

He reads . . .

Mémoires d'un Nain Royal au Château de Lunéville ~
Les Souvenirs de Nicolas Ferry.

    Transcrites par M. le Chevalier de Solignac, Secrétaire perpétuel de sa Majesté Polonaise, Le Roi Stanislas, Duc de Lorraine et de Bar. Prononcés le 7 septembre 1764.

    À Nancy ~ Chez la Veuve & C. Leseure, Imprimeur du Roi. Avec privilège du Roi.

I tap my cane. 'English,' I remind him. 'For the shilling.' He regards me with an uncivil eye. He takes a breath. He translates . . .

Remembrances of a Royal Dwarf at the Château
of Lunéville ~ The Recollections of Nicolas Ferry.
Transcribed by M. le Chevalier de Solignac, Permanent Secretary to His Polish Majesty, King Stanislas, Duke of Lorraine and Bar. Published 7th September 1764.

    In Nancy ~ At la Veuve & C. Leseure, King's Printer. With the privilege of the King.

Château de Lunéville, 1756

The click of buckled shoes upon parquet. Tat tat tat.

The sound of a beloved dwarf approaching. Tat tat tat ...
Unvarying, as if he were one of Monsieur Héré's clockwork
men. He grows nearer. Observe.

His figure is elegant, defined. What an excellent stride. He
carries a neat head, a romantic heart, discriminating brain and
a well-curved ankle.

Sssst! Par les saints, I confess! The dwarf is *me!*

Ha ha!

I am arrived! Vraiment! It is I! Flown here by these duckling
wings. *Coin! Coin!*

Ha ha!

My gestures are graceful. My countenance charming. My
passions unregulated.

My life is a riddle, my rank a puzzle. Voilà, I am small yet my
world is large and my reputation larger. My wits are sharp, yet my
king-the-duc prefers them halved, for amusement, so I am a halfwit.

I am Bébé.

Enfin! I am the favourite clown of toutes les Mesdames. Les
pauvres! They cannot resist!

You are a ravishing dancer, they tell me. It is true.

I was born among goats yet kings fall to their knees! Un
miracle? Un jeu? Alors, attends! I tell the tale.

God sees me. God sees the King of France.

Upon the throne sits Louis XV, a fat ape in mesdames' petticoats. Ha ha! At his side sits the Queen, Marie Leszczynski,
the daughter of the crownless, stateless King of Poland, ah! My
king-the-duc!

Alors, poor Stanislas! Once a nobleman then a king. And
afterwards?

Exile. Refugee. Beggar.

Today he is the Grand Duke of Lithuania, Duke of Lorraine and Bar, Count of the Holy Roman Empire, father-in-law to the King of France, fat Louis, the Beloved.

He dare not sign his name: King Stanislas I of Poland. It is lost.

Be heedful. It is a sad tale.

My king-the-duc was crowned twice, overturned once by Augustus II, overturned twice by Augustus III, by which I mean he regained the throne a second time, by which I mean he is not the king of tomorrow, but rather the twice-crowned king of yesterday.

A once-king twice over! Ha ha!

Alors, attends! The story.

I was born, smaller than a quail bird, in the Vosges, in the village of Champenay.

I would not survive, they said. My mother wept. My father wept. I survived.

I slept in a clog. I suckled a goat. Upon the occasion of my Baptism I was presented upon a plate at the stone chapel in Plaine.

My measurement was as long as my mother's right hand, my weight was less than a river trout. The smallpox could not take me.

Nicolas Ferry, my mother and father named me. God's little miracle, it was said.

Enfin! Today I am grown tall enough that I may look a goat directly in the eye.

And I am too quick for the scratch of a pen. My words are writ by Chevalier de Solignac.

He is slow! His face hangs as an old man's ball sack, his hair is two threads, his eyes are yesterday's oysters. De Solignac!

Have you slept in your grave? Do you write my words as I recite them? Ha ha!

Let us leave the chevalier.

Attends! I shall enchant you.

Closer.

See here the bend in my chin, the twist in my nose. My silks? Blue as Heaven's walls.

My face? In the blanc. My complexion? Rouged as a duchesse at the Comédie.

My eyebrows? Mouse fur. My periwig is à la mode du court, Pompadour weeps for envy!

My lips? A single cherry.

I consider it is the melancholia that lingers in my eyes.

Ha ha!

Observe here my movement! I am told I have the talents of a courtesan. My feet trip lightly as a stepping bird . . .

. . . I leap as a deer.

I land . . .

. . . soundless as a leaf.

Here I halt. It is too great a distance, though I am swift as Hermes.

Tat tat tat.

I have crossed a furlong of parquet. Windows. Nombreuses! Shining as water, tall as Heaven.

My steps are many. These wide rooms test my delicate health. Halls without end!

My breaths are short. Attends! Like a lady's spaniel, I gasp. Ssst!

Hear it? A female scream. My name is called. Fa! That monstrous witch from the Ardennes.

I shall be found. I shall not be found!

I run. I run. I run. How like the wind. I flee.

Ha ha ha! Ventrebleu! I run. Come! Follow! I am a sprite. A

puppet. See my dashings! Oh, fine legs! See? I have the figure of Apollo.

Bonne soirée, Mesdames!

I enter. I depart.

I possess the dancer's joie!

Room, room, room.

Au revoir, Mesdames! Toutes les bêtes!

Ha ha ha!

I am gone before I arrive!

My cry (a peacock). My laughter (a monkey). My body (a dancer). My self (a riddle).

Never to be solved!

Dainty are the shoes who dash me. Across parquet, terrazzo, quartz, I go.

Listen! It is my name. Hear you that? They call me.

Bébé! Bébé! Bébé!

Yet, I am gone. Gone. Gone!

Ha ha ha!

I burst from the house.

Alors, attends! I give you a forest, lakes, palisades, canals, fountains, allées.

Et voilà, my fleeing self.

Look at me! I am Zeus. I am Ares. I am Hercules. I leap the domed sky and . . .

. . . I arrive!

Too late . . . I am departed! Ha ha!

Weary are my bones. Open your eyes.

Cordieu! I have gone. Où est le petit?

Ah, miracle! From God! A miracle!

Bébé! Bébé! Bébé!

Here I am!

St Mary, Islington, 1879

Upon the page the words lie, foreign as camels, yet from the mouth of my clock-mender they emerge in plain English, if a little tossed about. My breaths come in gasps. I cough, sigh, clear my throat. I search for my hat. I am ablaze. Fevered! I do not trust myself to discuss the detail with my clock-mender. He watches me with a chary eye.

I wrap the edition in its cloth. I grasp my cane. I bid Mister Ferrières a good day, until our next appointment.

The big clock chimes as I walk through Clerk'nwell. Upon this day, this hour, this almost-very-minute, I heard the voice that belonged to the bones of my midget. Voice and bones is all that survives. Voice and bones is all we are, mark me. We are birthed into air, and death delivers us unto earth. Where all the hullabaloo and heartache goes, I cannot say. We are left with the wisdom of bones.

The stage was devoid of art ~ Ovid

Ruby and Bird are carping to see the melodrama at the Apollo Rooms at thru'pence each! Cheaper to see the wire dancing and dissolving views at the Victoria Saloon on Ironmonger Row, yet they will not be swayed.

Not for me, the sock and buskin! Give me a show or exhibition in place of a rendition on the boards-classical. A tiresome event is a theatrical, it elongates as it proceeds, is expensive to stage, and needs must be written out for actors to speak. I myself fall a-doze even now, as I remark upon it. I know what I speak of. We stage a play once a year, as they are popular with the ladies, commencing the week before Pentecost Sunday, ending the week after Corpus Christi, more or less.

Last year I staged The Comedy. Next year, The Tragedy. This year it is The Mystery, a well-known theatrical and performed reg'lar.

Here I offer the pamphlet of our most recent caper to paint the picture.

Five acts rendered in less than a minute apiece, tolerable for all.

A Tragedy In Five Short Acts!
The Players:
Virtuous And Handsome Lover
Vicious And Ugly Ditto
Weak-Minded Father
Innocent And (consequently) Injured Maiden
Somebody's Ghost

I shall speak out the lines, as they are committed to memory these years long.

'*Avaunt, caitiff! Thy black mustache cannot conceal thy still blacker heart!*'

This is Ruby in the role of the maiden. She cavorts as if marvellously pleased. Ruby is experienced in theatricals. I wager I undervalued her talent!

The audience whistles and calls.

'What, ho! Do I behold the base persecutor of innocence?' Tuesday plays the Virtuous Lover with verve, a masculising performance.

'*Perish, vile slave!*' Steps plays the Vicious Lover with stern apology and precise gesture. '*Oh, misery! Why do I survive this scene of horrors?*' Ruby again. Stabs herself post haste. All are expired.

Act Five is utilised for their speedy resurrection, this being the grand final effect. Somebody's Ghost (Grateful Jim) hurries on and frightens everyone into a Tableau.

The Ghost pulls a string. The curtain falls.

Any more than that and I too am liable to stab myself, post haste. True as a church stone.

As I make my way home along Canal Street, following a short restorative detour via The Hat, heavy raindrops begin to fall, splashing the wool of my best coat and two'n'nine hat. A day of blackness, mist and thunder.

The warmth of a lit fire! What cheer? I hurry in. And there sits Flora, stiff as a doll, tucked into a chair before the hearth, a rug over her knees.

'Flora,' I say. 'Were you dismissed?'

She makes no reply but only holds a stare at the flames.

'Flora? Have you no more duties at the institute? Shall you be returning to the professor?'

'She shall not be returning to the professor.'

Bella steps into the room, a rag in her hand: brassy, chin up.

'She was dropped off by cab,' she says. 'No reason given. She does not speak a word, only stares, like a person after a nasty shock.'

Bella is reproachful, as if it is I who am responsible for the girl's faint-heartedness!

'Leave her be,' I say. 'It is only fatigue,' I add, whereupon Bella steps forward, her finger wagging.

'Is that it?' she says, as if performing the line in a

theatrical. Galling, as her talent is woefully limited, yet her busy-bodying knows no bounds.

'Leave the girl alone, stop fussing,' I say. 'You could send a saint to hell. Leave her be.'

'I shall leave her be when you fetch the doctor!' she cries.

In disbelief I clasp my head in my hands. 'Must I always be the villain?' I implore her. 'I am a simple, toiling, steadfast man, who loves you, albeit you no longer care for me.'

She turns. I let my hands fall, adjust my aspect.

'I see,' she says, blinking. The tilt of her head suggests enlightenment as she walks away.

No man shall ever out-step a sharp-witted woman. Fact of life. I wish only that she would be tender. Where did she find this ferocious heart? Might we not fall in step, as once we did? Might we not, now and then, agree? How I should love to swing a polka, the way we did, easy as air.

Who shall rescue me from her? A foaming jar appears in my mind's eye. Only the stout and ale. I fetch my coat and hat.

Can you laugh at dreams, magic
terrors, wonders? ~ Horace

The foreign dwarf is the bona fide article, and strange as if he'd stepped out of an acorn.

A capricious worm, not unlike my midget, Lark, and just as unpredictable in his behaviours, though Lark had not the panache of the French miniature.

The French Baby is a dodge, a jaybird, a clown. His written musings are ticklish. How the ladies of Whitechapel and Caledonian Road would admire his hundred-year-old babblings, his tantrums, not to mention his foreign flam-flirtatiousness! Every man, woman and child would toss their hats in the air at the sight of him. A star in the firmament and quite the little ladies' man, a miniature spooner! The Queen herself would remove her glove to rest her hand upon the dwarf boy's head. How he has touched my heart. Pity the one hundred years between he and I, those years have denied and betrayed us. Time has his numbers cockeyed.

Nine days and she has not spoke a word, no hint of expression plays upon her face. As if she were a porcelain doll Flora remains fixed, unalerted. By turns each of us claps at her face, stamps, calls, waves. She appears not to see us.

'She is merely resting after assisting the professor with his experiments,' I suggest.

Bell rewards me with a dead-eyed stare. This is womanly behaviour: silent yet ear-piercing. 'These matters of scientific investigation are draining for a girl,' I explain. 'She needs rest, is all.'

'Is it rest you are missing, Flo?' Bell enquires in a mocking tone, rubbing the girl's shoulder, patting her hand.

'If you would only leave her for a minute!' I chide. 'Leave off your poking and prodding. Little wonder the child won't answer with all your fretting and fussing.'

'And you,' Bella cries, 'would rather a shilling rather than her! Deny it! What do you care?'

I do not say it yet I care enough that my appetite is gone and sleep along with it. Flo is our youngest and her blue gaze haunts me at night.

As for Bella, there are those who'd say I ought to discipline her, to which I say I have seen enough of her tears. When pushed to the brink I show her my cane. In fact, I move to fetch it now, and she mocks me with a laugh and ducks upstairs. She knows I would not use it. I would rather have her in my arms and yet I cannot tell her – she would use it to grind me to powder.

I call for my rookbird. 'A showman's life is arduous,' I tell him. 'Not crowds nor performers will be satisfied. Remember what I say.' He sidles. He is looking for buttons, pins. He is a dark thief, yet a genial companion, albeit he hides my pipe, startles the girls, steals food and teases the hound. He gargles and mutters to himself. He will not obey the simplest command. At night he mimics the sound of the clock in the parlour. Tick tick tick. I am obliged to command him, 'Enough!' as his ticks fall between the clock's tocks until I am utterly maddened. 'God in Heaven!' I cry out.

Scolded, he sulks, broods, turns himself to the wall. When dispirited, he grizzles like a baby. 'Our day is coming, Smallpurse,' I explain. He creeps and hops. 'My friend, we shall be in good cheer when it arrives!' I know it to be true. Next week we shall perform the precarious experiment for the professor. We are ready for success.

I pay three shillings to the doctor for a visit. He tells us what is already abundantly clear . . . that Flora is mute. Does he offer a potion, lotion, a powder, for the cost? He does not. He suggests beef tea, bed rest, fresh air and no working for a month. A month!

'Aye! Let us all not work for a month,' I suggest. 'And not eat neither!'

I appeal directly to the doctor as he searches for the door. 'Shall you, doctor, take the month off and forfeit your kidneys, brisket and hock?' To which he makes no reply.

I ought to have brained him where he stood. He's no

more a doctor than I am the King of Constantinople. I'll have no more of it.

In the meantime I have conjured an act for Flora where she is presented upon a chair as *Poor Mad Flo, The Experiment That Went Horribly Wrong*. Well, what would you have me do? Obliged I am to inform the crowd that an experiment too dreadful to repeat in its detail was performed upon the girl, leading to her present ... et cetera. It shall be hush-hush. I must keep it from Bella until it proves a hit with the crowd. One by one the others will attempt to rouse her with a splash of water, a loud bell, a mouse down the blouse and so on, all to no avail. Thus shall the sympathy of the crowd be fostered. An audience is partial to an injury, in particular the hysterical variety. I am astounded at the ingenuity of this one. True as church, I could shake my own hand.

He scratches his head with one little
finger ~ Proverb

This is me, Bella. He thinks I do not know. What an untidy predicament, Percival George.

Bella Wickes, he says, what an imagination you have! And yet it is you, Percy, who invents these meagre illusions. Where is your head? Foolish clown. Where is your heart?

You'll not use Flora this way, I shan't allow it. There. You shall have to dispose of me first. When a man has a merry design in his head he does not stop to reconsider because a woman doubts it. Ought that he might. A man devises his shifts only as far as he sees them, which is as far as the day ahead. A woman devises with all her history, past and future (for these are always on her mind). A woman prefers to leave all and nothing to fate and yet fate remains her friend, for what else does she have?

A woman prays on her knees, births on her back and thinks on her feet, and she requires no armchair, pipe nor witness.

I'll say not a word to Percy about it, yet when he comes, with chair, mouse and bell, Flora will be nowhere to be seen. Fate shall see to that.

Bees also conceal their swarms in the
hollow bark ~ Virgil

The toil of scribbling has bent my fingers to a claw! I resolve to have Tuesday inscribe for me, just as the fellow inscribes for the royal midget! I shall be liberated to contemplate agreeable content to be set down. Why didn't I consider it before?

Tuesday's education has not deserted him; his calligraphy is bold whereas my own scratches are, by comparison, poor. Henceforth Tuesday shall inscribe the personal journal of Percival Unusual George. Top brass! I shall furnish him with the dip pen and the jar of ink.

In this way I shall tell the tale of my considerable success, albeit yet to come. I shall tell it before the ending is confirmed, to lure good fortune. I shall entice luck with daring and dash. I make the usual unusual. I make the unremarkable remarkable. Alone did I elevate myself. Alone I remain, save for my little French bones. His kinship has brought me happiness and I shall protect him mightily in return.

*

140

The midget skeleton, in bright satins and wig, describes how many fine ladies give him the saucy eye behind their fans. The scene is charming! I prepared it myself for the first appearance of my royal miniature. Tuesday repainted the boards and we have a rollicking crowd of twenty.

Upon the stage Bébé, the royal skeleton, sits upon his sovereign's knee as a kingly midget is apt to do. Steps portrays the stately sovereign with haughty indifference in a silk cape and crown. The midget confesses how many more fine ladies he wishes to have in his arms. The sovereign is aghast! Ruby speaks the midget's voice from behind the curtain, while Steps flaps his jawbone . . . it is ticklish, truly! Merry as Christmas!

To follow, the French midget dances to amuse some bawdy noble ladies, led by Bella.

Bold as Punch, my miniature pitches under Bell's skirts while the others search for him. Sovereign. In the closing scene the midget is upon his deathbed and all the ladies are weeping, begging him not to expire. The final frozen tableau is a melancholy masterpiece that daggers the heart. I wipe a tear.

Afterwards, the dwarf chooses three ladies from the crowd and invites them to touch his royal bones, for luck. This part of the proceedings proves popular, albeit for the rest I have observed only moderate enthusiasm from the crowd. Vexing. Baffling.

What would they have? My royal dwarf is unique in Europe! Is the London crowd become so jaded that royalty itself is not enough? Do they not grasp the significance of so precious an item? What must I procure for them? The pyramids? The kings of Egypt?

London crowds do not appreciate quality when it is

presented. Griddlers, flats and dippers, the lot. They do not deserve royalty. Happier they are with Tuesday's cups and balls and Bella's serpents twisting in her cleavage.

And this too gives me cause for worriment, as I wonder if Bella's performance is the catch, being that she gives no pep to her rendering whatsoever. I inform her so. She is marring the proceedings, diminishing the value of my royal article. I tell her she will no longer perform the scenes and that Bird shall play her role.

I know the reason of course. We fought over *Poor Mad Flo, The Experiment That Went Horribly Wrong*. Twice she hid Flora. Twice she attempted to prevent proceedings. How she yelled and kicked. Obliged I was to have Steps and Brown remove her from our little stage (what a fight she gave). To our surprise the crowd cheered and caroused to see it. So to follow, without delay, we played *Poor Mad Flo, The Experiment That Went Horribly Wrong* to capture the mood. It caught the imagination of the crowd, a fresh entertainment never fails to deliver. Alas, a new contrivance therein involved inviting a wag from the throng to try his luck at awakening our sleeping maiden and when one depraved halfwit began to perform a lurid mime I was forced to end things abruptly.

That night I suffered the torments of Bella. In this way I was obliged to offer her, head bowed, my meekest apology.

Thereafter I resolved to retire young Flora to a life of permanent convalescence when, the following day, arrives a reddened Cox, fidgeting and blasting into his 'kerchief. He sputters the terms of an instant cure, free of charge, for our Flo. Well now. This treatment is to be administered by a brilliant young doctor from Belgium, a high-ranking guest of the professor's at the institute, who would return Flora to us in her original form, unmesmerised, good as new and shiny as a new penny.

'There!' I inform Bella. 'What did I tell you?' The professor is an esteemed authority and an honourable gentleman. Flora shall return as if she'd never been away, albeit my arrangement of bruises will linger. Not a word from Bella but only a deadening glance.

Am I to remain guilty forever? A spider dangling in the eaves enjoys more regard!

In their shawls the two of them go. Bella has taken her gloves out of tissue paper. I do not recall her wearing them since our wedding day. She has woven Flora's hair into wheat-shaped plaits and dressed her in her best embroidered blouse. She polished their boots and brushed down their coats. How to fathom it? Bella's disdain for the professor is ill-matched by the tidy perfection of these outfits. Does she wish to make a good impression? Wager she does. What, then, does she hope for? I shall have to ask a female. It is a mystery. Flora shall receive treatment at the institute, thereafter she shall be blithe as bluebells.

I bid Bella return by the twelve o'clock bell, as we have already lost a performer and the mouths remain open at feeding time, no matter what.

In four days' time we are due to perform the precarious experiment on behalf of the professor. I shall have no sleep. There is an element of risk involved, I do not deny it, albeit our outfit has the practice and skill. Nevertheless, I shall have little comfort until it is over.

~

No man ever lived so poor as he was
born ~ Seneca

En route to Clerk'nwell I find myself considering whether
Ferrières might be trained in necromancy. It is not beyond
him. He has the airs of a gentleman seer on account of his
insolence, foreign accent and long sinister fingers. He is
designed for the dark arts. He crouches, a magus-in-waiting,
under our very noses! And yet. He would bide his time. I
should be swiftly dispatched by'n'by. Disaster would follow.
I dismiss the thought.

The manuscript under my arm is a small weight, p'raps
the near-equal to that of the miniaturised dwarf himself. It
is irksome that the French go one better than the English
in certain categories, even dwarves. I have heard nought of
so pint-sized a dwarf in England; to be sure, if one existed
Dick Fisher would've thieved it and all and sundry would
have to hear him brag of it, the scurf!

The bell rings. The clocks chirrup and whirr.

'Good morning to you, Mister Furrier.'

He removes his magnifying eyeglass, rises without a word,
and moves to the back of the room, where we may remain
undisturbed. A red ring around his left eye, doubtless an imprint
from the eyeglass, lends him the aspect of a Peeping Tom.

He disregards my grin.

'Your dwarf,' he mutters. He holds out his hand.

I remove the cloth from the edition and offer it. We sit.
I place two half crowns.

He begins.

Château de Lunéville, 1756

In a basket was I taken, like a Menschterkas cheese, to His Majesty the King of Poland, who was no longer His Majesty the King of Poland, but the Duc de Lorraine. The king of yesterday. A king of nowhere and nobody. His wife wept.

Stanislas viewed me asleep beneath a piece of linen, as inconsiderable as the king's last hope. He reached in to lift me from the basket and wept as he held me to him. Nothing is more mysterious than a dwarf, not even the moon.

I give you a cloudless day, tall and blue as Heaven. A dream you have forgotten. A brass sun. Birds turn and loop, I observe their winged geometry.

Lunéville, le petit Versailles, a court in the image of the royal one ninety leagues away.

Stretching into the distance the gardens unravel, as far as the eye may see: palisades, allées, bosquets, parterres. The garden grows her symmetry alive: octagons, pentagons, diamonds and squares, halted only by the standing horizon, chalked in mist, shrouding the hills where I was born.

Among so many lines and serpentines must be placed some irregularity. At Lunéville the task is performed excitably by water! Columns and plumes explode Heavenwards and fall. A permanent mist hangs from the droplets. Ventrebleu! Ha ha! Canals flow, fountains burst, boats punt. Watercourses float into deep reflecting lakes that are bubbled with fish, feathered with fowl. Sheets of water reflect the blank sky. The sky throws her blue towards Verdun and the fountains roar as if they had taken the task of the sea itself.

I have hidden myself in the place of mirrors where I now observe many versions of myself, hopelessly weeping. I am a melancholy masterpiece. Follow my tear-stains beyond the marble, jasper and agate, past Doyen's love stories of the gods, where all Olympus gathers, spied upon by Ganymede.

My poor king, Stanislas, the uncrowned. I am the light to his dark, his elf, his babe, his best humour. By this accident, au nom de Dieu, am I honoured.

The Mesdames arrive! My powder is fresh and I walk comme ça, in the way of the fighting cock, the better to display my stockinged legs, blue as the skies of Bar Lorraine.

Here, by tumbling fountains where marbled Orpheus and Apollo attend, I stroll, attired in the latest Vernaillen Bleu. My face is agreeable in the blanc, non? Dieu soit béni!

This periwig, a coiffure modelled à la mode de la court, offers my features uniformity, delicacy, nobility. Artfully do I personificate, fooling all into believing that La Gaussin has entered the room.

Behold! The dwarf? La Gaussin? Which?

Often times have I been compared to La Camargo. Like she, I wear the tulle and ribbons when I perform the movements. For my face, think of La Gaussin: grace, poise, nobility of carriage. My expression? A mask. Contempt? Certainly. I display the hauteur.

Comme ça.

The Mesdames weep. The reason? Envy. Les pauvres!

I inform them that at my birth my mother cried out, *Ai! Cordieu! An aristocrat!*

A blaze of thirty-six chandeliers. Fifty-two sconces. You must search among sixteen gilded capitals and beneath the gilt balustrade of a minstrels' gallery to find me.

I rest upon a tower of cushions!

I see my own sharp reflection in the giant mirrors that rise taller than the forest near my mother's house. I pause to observe

146

my eyes moving this way and that. My beauty is not of the Venusian variety. I regard my face: crimson'd, chalk'd, furr'd of brow, and my own small eyes a-glitter. I perceive in my expression a hint of weariness. I remedy it at once, replacing it with an air of refining gaiety!

Enfin! *Per gratiam Dei*, I continue the tale ...

C'est une tragédie de mouchoir! Il est vrai. True! Yes. All.

Poor Stanislas Leszczynski, once-king of Poland. To his daughter, Queen Marie of France, he composes letters, offering daily counsel, guidance, prayers.

My dear child,

We lose you and we are proud and happy for your glory. We pray that you will receive blessings, many graces, and that God may bless you with sublime things and happiness.

He hopes to counsel, guide, reassure.

He hopes to provide unambiguous answers before her questions, as yet formless and unspoken, dare to emerge.

Beware of flatterers. Beware State secrets. Beware self-love. Avoid the dangers of throne life which harden and spoil.

He signs, *Your loving father, Papa.*

Poor Stanislas. What is left? His lands? Ravaged. His possessions? Robbed. His future? Ruined. A king who was once remains a king always, and may become a king once more. He remembers a future that is the past.

Beside me sleeps a once-upon-a-time king, upon a daybed draped in fabrics from Anatolia. I too sleep. I dream of the Vosges, the rivers of Alsace. His fingers rest upon my head, his belly rises and falls like his own fortunes.

'Ignoscat mihi, Deus,' he murmurs. May God forgive me.

'Deus ignoscit,' I reply.

Asleep, he weeps. Awake, he prays for the past. For his home in the Bas-Rhin, the little bridges over the Lauter, for Leszno and especially Castle Rydzyna, where dead-eyed sphinxes, carved in stone, guard the deserted grounds.

Here, among the moulded panelling, Turkish fabrics and crimson taffetas, I endure the scrape-scrape of the king's pen and the heavy sighs that accompany his concentrated epistolary labours until, at the clock's chimes, we gather ourselves to attend chapel. Upon cold stone we lower ourselves for High Mass. We lie together, prostrate. My bones grow whiter. The Mass is spoken. I speak only threads of Latin but my heart knows truth.

The king composes his pamphlets upon which he does not inscribe his sign-manual, yet all know it is he who, in his own script, writ them. Each pamphlet condemns the court of Vienna and her pernicious councils. In this way his crown was lost. Cruel Vienna, with her ill-intentioned principles! Her indecent expressions! Her projects against the Polish Liberty!

He writes his essay, *Conversation of a Sovereign with His Favourite Upon the Apparent Felicity of the Human Condition.* The favourite? It is not me. Fa! The favourite is him.

My once-king converses with himself. Ha ha! Who else might a sovereign favour more?

Here in the library the wood snaps and creaks as the day warms. Daily from this room I watch the sun swing over the wooded hills and plunge into the Vosges.

Having, as he does, an agile mind, the king devotes long hours to the gentleman Locke, and *An Essay Concerning Human Understanding.* Later on Stanislas takes his sketchbook and redesigns the plough, the phaeton, the calèche and wind-propelled boats. He prepares his essay, *Incredulity Combatted by Sheer Common Sense*, for publication.

Later still, he turns his attention to the philosophers. From the printing presses of Holland arrive, via pamphlet and volume, the thinkers of England: Temple, Bold, Tindal, Toland, Shaftesbury, Wollaston, Collins.

'Englishmen,' says my king, 'bespeak themselves in commendably unyoked fashion.'

'Scientiam et eloquentia,' he adds.

He admires the English and their lack of etiquette. He admires their little country, its many rivers, its seats of academia, and its slovenly populace.

The Queen wept for Poland. I was a child. I placed my fingers in my ears. I wailed to drown her out. She did not leave her rooms for a month. She was attended by her confessors and chaplains and her ladies-in-waiting from Wissembourg. They talk of the past in the Bas-Rhin, of Leszno and especially Rydzyna, in whose castle she was once happy. She weeps to remember the giant willows over the green reflecting lakes, the parkland canopied by ancient oaks, the ballrooms, moats and the clouds of butterflies in early summer.

To this she cannot help but grieve for all she left behind: the porcelain, the jewels and portraits, the tapestries, the Lithuanian hunting dogs, the northern furs and Argamak horses in ceremonial dress. Her ladies of Wissembourg join in her weeping. The noise is terrible! Ha ha!

Only her chaplain restores calm twice daily at Holy Mass.

The Marquise de Boufflers, who warms the king's bed and hosts his parties, remains happily focused on her duties as the mistress of the exiled Polish king. I travel beneath her skirts. Zeste! I kiss her feet. Before I reach seven years old the Polish Queen is dead.

The morning is blue and gold, a merlot sings. My sovereign and I are matched in apricot coats over oyster satins, stitched in broderie d'or.

At our backs a throng of architects and draughtsmen drift in our wake, arguing like sea birds. The sun bakes the ground, the fish sink deeper into the lake.

Sedately we progress, His Majesty aided by a cane, to the king's desk, where he attends to his letters from secretary Hulin at Versailles with his own permanent secretary and mine, de Solignac. He of the rotting face!

De Solignac was my professor. From he I learned to speak, though not, convincingly, to hold the pen. In my mouth once sat the Bavarian dialect, spoken by lips that suckled goats. We have washed it into the streams that run back to the Vosges!

My French is exquisite. Of the Quality is my conversation. I am re-fashioned. French. Royal. You may kiss my ring. Ha ha!

I am no fool. Though none do play one better.

A dwarf is amusing only if the book he reads is upside down, he is better-loved this way.

By halves do I live: height, wits, strength, size. Half-man. Half-wit. Is he half-animal? they ask. How amusing!

A supper. A theatrical. Musical interludes. Gaming. I am garbed in the military uniform of the Polish cavalry officer. My sword curves like a crescent moon. My monkey, Jacquot, is uniformed in identical fashion. He gallops and leaps upon fauteuils. He has no weapon, yet he has eaten the tall feather and braid from his helmet and soiled his battle dress.

I enter beneath the skirts of Her Highness the Princesse de Beauvau.

The screams when I reveal myself! Splendent!

Here are assembled the nobility of the sword, the ladies and gentlemen of the Quality, esteemed philosophers and a serving of actresses from the opéra.

The Model of the Graces is the daughter-in-law of the Marquise de Boufflers. The girl's face is blank as marble. She plays upon her harp, a stooped angel, enslaving all, comprehending none of her power, comprehending little of anything. She wears pink satin, at her elbows hang heavy flakes of lace. She has washed with rosewater yet she smells of rain.

In their sconces torches blaze, musicians quicken on their strings.

I enter, mounted upon Féroce, the goat. I ride him between the card tables. Joie!

He will not steer but only drift sideways, yet I have delighted the Mesdames. Ha ha! Hear their piglet squeals! Arriving at my king-the-duc I dismount. The mastiff, Griffon, attends me. I salute our host: Polish majesty, duc, exile, poet, architect, philosopher.

Roi bienfaisant. Ah, voilà! He is pleased. I stand upon his knee.

His guests, powdered and satined, stuffed with shellfish, three types of game, orange blossom praline, brandy fruits, cheeses of the Alsace and wines of the Bourgogne, salute me. All adore Bébé!

When the once-king beholds the half-man, he sees himself. Over and again he glimpses his long fall into the abyss. In my crownless king I too see myself, a folderol.

Here are illuminated salons, stairs of water, Turkish kiosks, fragrant groves and the flickering of five thousand wax lights. Within grottos water cascades while fish dart.

From the grand table centrepiece a fountain issues forth, glittering in the light as if it were Heavenly blessed. Upon every wall hang mirrors for giants while upon the ceiling Apollo thunders in his chariot. I observe myself, reflected in the glass.

My hair is dressed, à l'enfant, curled around the ears. Mistaken I could be for a Petit Prince de Sang, a coquette at la Comédie or l'Opéra. I wear satin in a shade of damson, gold

151

moiré, and foaming lace from Brussels. I display the melancholy expression of a suffering child. It is touching! Unless . . . I choose to laugh.

Ha ha! All is transformed! I am gay once more.

'Mesdames!' I call. 'Here is Bébé! See me!'

Laughter. Games. Love. My task is wearisome. Laughter. Games. Love.

I collapse into a brocade chair from where I ask marble-eyed Jupiter what he will do to enhance my immediate fortunes. He answers not. Mercury and Mars look on. I condemn them all to a life of cold silence and stillness!

A gentleman of inferior rank is speaking. I am alerted. With self-importance this beast calls the attention of all. In his speech he proclaims his house, his furniture, his horses, his equipages. As he begins to list the princes who attend his dinners I move away to attend a group of ladies. One, in particular, is flushed around the base of her chalky neck and, as I approach (lightly, upon my toes), I observe the gold hairs upon her forearm rise. I search out the fingers of the pretty mademoiselle and place them daintily upon my cheek, where they rest with the ticklish uncertainty of a creeping nursery spider. When we are called to supper I escort the young lady. Possessing her hand in mine, I slip the corner of her finger into my mouth, so that I may suck as an innocent babe and meet, with my own lustful smile, her widening eye.

Laughter. Games. Love.

Here arrive their giant faces, rouged, chalked; their yellow teeth, the ribbons, pearls, and parfums to mask their odours. I hear their steps upon the parquet, their animal cries, their silks rushing like fountain water. They look for me behind pillars, in the gilded salons, under tapestried chairs.

When they find me in a Chinese cabinet I must rejoice and tell a riddle or sing a song and kiss their dry mouths. How they

152

laugh. I count their teeth and tell them the number remaining. I proclaim their beauty. I remark upon their wit, style, their singular charm. I tell them how weak I am under their spell! They laugh. And I must count their ivory yellows again from the beginning.

'*Rou-rou-a. Rou-rou-a.*' I am a turtle dove. And a lover many times over. Ha ha!

I play the flute. I perform the movements and then I display the efficiency of my little trompette. Delightful! How the Mesdames scream to see it played!

They kiss my eyes and dip their tongues into my mouth. It is a game. We must fight the ennui, the despair, the emptiness. Voilà. I ask that God bless me and protect me.

St Mary, Islington, 1879

I am fastening to the French dwarf, as if one of us were a key and the other a lock. Why should it be? I have no answer. Had I opportunity to charge such a creature in a show career, I should not rest until he was top of the bill at The Egyptian Hall. A sensation the French baby might've been! Upon my knee stood! The world at his feet!

The unfortunate scrap was born too soon by one hundred years and in the wrong place.

A fine example of the caprice of life. Though it is never too late. A crowd is a crowd.

Why should such an unusual remarkability lie low in

darkness, forgotten? Why should not the baby dwarf of France, once beloved of a nation, albeit foreign, find a new horde that would love him? Must a remarkability stand only in its own time?

Arriving in my mind is an inkling, it illuminates. Strike me, but here it is: can it be, I wonder, that God in His divine wisdom awards me the French midget and inflames my curiosity so that only I may hear his words? He did not bestow the dwarf upon Dick Fisher, Sam Crouch, nor any other.

The dwarf speaks and I listen. Among his riddling words I find myself dumb as a boatless fisherman in a foreign sea. And yet, as Elijah found Elisha, I have found one to turn back the hands of time and untangle the riddle. God sent me Mister Ferrières, in all his queer irreg'larity. The clock spins, the dwarf whispers, I bow to listen. Who shall prevent him receiving the audience he deserves? Time itself shall not stop him. Time itself has brought him to me. I shall not fail him. In my hand has the French midget laid his soul.

Nor will the arrow always hit the
object aimed at ~ Horace

Tuesday Brown has a legible hand, I draw your attention to his tall f's and l's and tidy a's and e's. I devise a befitting anecdote and I speak it aloud. Scratch-scratch goes his pen and the words appear. Upon the page they form in loops and curls. Reg'lar and steady come my pronouncements and the ink dries at a kindred pace. Here lie the pratings of Percy George.

Twice-weekly does Brown inscribe what I recite. A hundred years hence who shall read his scribbles? What tidy wisdoms shall I impart to those waiting down the years? P'raps nought. P'raps civilised men will have no need of scribbles, being that all conundrums upon earth shall by then have been solved, discoveries all discovered, progress all progressed and phenomena all, long since, deciphered.

Involuntary writing is the rage. They say it is electrical, magnetical, just as with the rapping and the table-turning. No sooner is a phenomenon unleashed upon the world than another is found waiting in the wings.

'We should include some involuntary writing, should we not, Tuesday?'

'We have involuntary writing, Mister George,' he replies. 'I am the sole volunteer.'

I esteem an honest man who is sensible
in regard to glory ~ King Stanislas I

The morning sky is blue yet clouding in the west. A fitful breeze spooks the cab horses.

I sit with Ferrières. My forbearance is little short of remarkable. I watch his eye flick across the page. He considers the French blatherings of my royal dwarf. His lips move silently. He takes a breath. He begins.

'The heart is the most irritable organ. It convulses for an unbroken lifetime—'

I halt Ferrières with my upright hand. Are these the words, the very words?

However should I tell? Is he speaking in haste? I will not be his bloody fool.

155

He tells me these are the very words writ down before him, the self-same. My translation is faithful, he says.

I tell him I do not believe him. Ought I? He cares nothing for me. What if I am tricked?

'To what purpose should I speak it otherwise?' he asks. He sounds weary as a judge.

'Continue,' I say. 'Proceed more slowly!' I tell him. I set down half a crown.

I reason that it is certain to be a more irksome task to invent words than to translate what is already there, and I am heartened by this realisation.

Château de Lunéville, 1748

The heart is the most irritable organ. It convulses for an unbroken lifetime. Scientists have confirmed this along with the notion that fire is the principal component of the sun.

The Marquise, Émilie du Châtelet, informs me of this. I am dazzled by her beauty and brilliance.

I tell her so.

The weather is fine. Here among roses, myrtle and oleanders sit I. The king settles himself en plein air surrounded by his architects and a handful of Jesuits.

One points, another examines, another speaks while yet another interrupts. My king coughs. The rooks fall silent. One of the architects repeats a phrase, his attitude is impatient, his tone petulant.

I laugh! Quite unexpectedly and the timing is exquisite. Ha ha! My king laughs.

We are amused.

In this way I consider myself a jester apothecary, I calculate, formulate, dispense. I dance a jig. It is the sound of bells they wish to hear.

He puffs his tobacco pipe and is returned, in a plume of smoke, to Alsace and the kindness of the Countess of Andlau and her household. He remembers the castle and its deep moat, the rise of the land, thickly swathed in trees, the valley with its village spires and many a fair abbaye. A multitude of green fed by modest streams, a league or so to the south of Cernay. Stanislas speaks and his words part the pillows of smoke.

'I will pine for it forever,' he says.

The architects nod, yawn, endure.

The king is disordered by a surfeit of memory, it troubles his soul. That which took place and that which might have taken place, and that which ought to have taken place. A long life lived is a game of Tric-Trac.

King Stanislas, himself, is a sweet concoction created by his chef, Gilliers. The mouth, a raspberry, is ready to compliment, discourse, laugh. The face is a doughy pyramid of cream pastry, dusted with sugar powder. The eyes, two blueberries, are quick and kind. He is a man of great appetites! Though his satin shoes are small, his body is over-stuffed. He sways, like a sea captain, challenging himself to the next event. He seeks always to refine, enhance. He seeks gaiety, profundity, pleasure. He is partial to philosophers, mathematicians, poets, artists. He patronises them and founds their colleges.

His favourites are the philosophers. Their conversation is a game of sallies, reparts, en-gardes. This is their task: to examine, refute, reveal, entertain. To this end the philosophers are dwarves. To this end I am a philosopher. Philosophy is to extract the knowable from the unknowable as if it were a matter of arithmetic. At no point must the philosopher unequivocally discern but only dissemble. At this I am expert.

The Hawk is the name I have given him.

He possesses the quick eye and beaked profile of that raptor bird.

To others he is Arouet, the Seigneur of Ferney. To the world he is Voltaire.

To his enemies he is orang-outang. Ha ha!

Correspondingly, he has names for his enemies. One of these is the critic (*'pamphleteer!'* the Hawk corrects me) Fréron, whom the Hawk calls Frelon– the Hornet. Ha ha!

And myself, whom he calls Pou. Où est le petit pou? the Hawk enquires.

Un pou, or beaucoup de poux make you itch. Je vais ronger votre cul, Monsieur, is my cordial reply. Arouet-the-Hawk hates to be called Monsieur!

The Hawk arrives with the Duc de Luynes! They receive a cannon salute from the terrace. The noise startles poor Arouet, he grimaces, cringes. I hear him murmur, 'I prefer calm suppers and the charm of friendship to these fêtes.' I laugh mockingly so that others might know his ingratitude. I am disregarded by all.

I play my whistle to make my shoes dance. It is I, Bébé, the halfwit!

It is a fine tune. My feet skip rapidly to the sound. My feet are a miracle.

I leap around the Hawk, though I know Voltaire does not seek entertainment. I am juggler, conjuror, I remind him! Tumbler, acrobat!

The Hawk proceeds purposefully, guardedly, his upper body forwardly inclined, as if the ground were not level but steepening. His arms hang in their sleeves. The folded mouth, a straight seam, offers no clues to his disposition. The hooded eyes, the brows, are fixed in their attitude of detachment, enlivening only upon the appearance of a friend, when his smile breaks genially, or when a handsome lady of rank appears, when his gaze betrays a glitter of expectation.

I bow. His eye narrows. His mouth smiles thinly, without mirth.

158

'Ah, Bébé.' He speaks my name, neither bored nor amused. 'You are without a task?' he enquires. 'Shall I provide you with some small employment?'

A hawk never takes his eye off the target. The word 'small' comes with emphasis, an eyebrow rising.

'If it pleases the king I shall be glad to do it,' I reply.

I fetch out my whistle.

'No, no, no.' He waves away the flute. 'None of that. My head!' he says. 'My ears!' And he strokes his face and sighs, the weight of his achievements pressing heavily upon him.

I offer my hand but he reaches instead for my head, placing his palm flat upon my skull, and in this way we proceed towards the supper and evening entertainments.

Though he is bloodless and frail as a consumptive, the Hawk's mind is lively and fattened. It is his wit that is prized. To sniff out bores and accuse them where they stand is his task. The Hawk is not the only learned monkey at Lunéville: he must compete firstly with his adored Émilie du Châtelet, and then the reputations, if not the actual presence, of Montesquieu, Fréron, Helvétius, La Condamine, Maupertuis, Desmarets.

All have visited the table of King Stanislas and each bend to kiss his imbecilic dwarf upon the head. Ha ha!

For the servants it is the visits of King Louis of France, Queen Marie and the royal princesses that are remembered in detail. Many speak of Prince Charles Stuart, whom the Englander foreigners called Bonnie, and who stayed many long months. He sang to me, sweetly as a linnet, in a childish voice, and learned to name each of the star constellations.

The heads of forest boar are served with roasted meats, partridge pâté, grenades with blood, green truffles, quail birds, artichokes and salads.

The talk is of the gentleman Locke and his essay, which is no essay but a book and not merely one but four books, a weapon!

Voltaire-the-Hawk picks at the candied flowers served in drifts of sugar-sand upon mirrors: orange blossom, violet, marigold, rose. He has the tooth of a child.

It is the Hawk who is speaking. He speaks of hawks!

'A type of hawking and hunting, wherein the very pursuit makes a great part of the pleasure.' He quotes Locke. The Hawk is discomforted by the quotes of others. He winces and squeezes shut his eyes, but quotes on through his teeth. His pointing finger, unusually unoccupied, rests with the figs upon his plate. His eyes are two sewn purses.

'Searches after truth are a sort of hawking and hunting. Every step the mind takes in its progress towards knowledge makes some discovery.'

He speaks so that no-one else will. He approves of the gentleman essayist, yet would not choose to quote him so liberally at table. It is only that the Duc de Luynes quoted that hunchback vole, Descartes, thereby exciting the Hawk into a passion of indigestion and necessitating the swift disablement of de Luynes before the entrance of the fruits.

At the card table after supper, beneath the hot blaze of a torch, the Hawk regards with one eye open while the other, at rest, is closed. He allows himself a thin smile. He rubs his knuckles, twisting a ring, breathing through his teeth. Tonight he will play Tric-Trac. Last time he lost more than one hundred Louis. On that occasion he read aloud some stanzas from La Pucelle in a bad humour, while I performed an unrehearsed ballet around him. Ha ha!

Émilie du Châtelet considers herself the possessor of a fine mind.

In this and all else she is unerring. The ink is never washed entirely from her hands so that we might guess at the brilliance of her calculations.

She admires Descartes and his Géometrie. She discusses mathematical problems with Maupertuis, philosophy and court gossip with the Hawk, and the opéra with Moncrif. All agree that she has aptitude for letters, the metaphysical and geometry.

Though I am just a boy, Émilie du Châtelet does not address me as a child.

I watch her as an astronomer observes the night sky, with constancy and wonder.

Émilie does not allow me under her skirts but tolerates me upon her knee and congratulates me upon scribbles I feign to be mathematical calculations. She affects to study them with solemn expression.

Ha ha! I fall in love. I am a boy. She is my first. I clean my sword.

My rivals are Arouet-the-Hawk and Saint-Lambert. I warn them that blood will spill. Their howls of laughter follow me to the Grand Canal but I cannot, in defence of my feeble dignity, drown myself while knowing the terrible suffering it will visit upon the king. Like a caged nightingale I am trapped!

Catherine, Marquise de Boufflers, gentle mistress of my king, is a delicate beauty whose cheekbones spread beneath her skin like roots under snow. She writes verse, paints pastels, and falls in love. Her face shines as the moon. Once they end she reads her books again, from the beginning. This dame de volupté has hooked the heart of my king, yet the Hawk whispers in my ear that she has no livres to buy herself a new skirt.

'The idol of the temple!' he cries. 'In rags!' The Hawk admires de Boufflers.

Her beauty has stupefied him. Though his heart belongs to Émilie du Châtelet he is unable to prevent himself flattering de Boufflers, 'La première dame du palais!'

He considers it courteous. He confronts her unexpectedly with newly composed poetry:

'You please the libertines, You captivate the sages . . . '

Words cast by the Hawk are blades forged to injure but he has no defence against the Marquise's beauty, whereupon his sabres tumble lightly as feathers.

Together they walk, de Boufflers and du Châtelet, steady as swans, heads borne high upon their long necks, towards the water. I observe as their skirts are scooped by the wind, disrupting their elegance. The same wind carries their shrieks of laughter to me. I watch. I wait. I endure.

While the sun and stars swap places, Émilie du Châtelet does not move from her desk. Upon a chair of tapestried walnut she sits daily, nightly. The only sound is the scratch of her pen, the slide of silk as she moves her arm, the creak of wood as she leans.

Her breathing, like her thinking, is silent – it moves as clouds pass, without affray.

I am just a boy. I am tolerated only if I do not speak or sneeze. Ha ha! Or laugh.

I crawl upon the floor so that I may be invisible.

Émilie has translated the entire *Principia Mathematica* into French. She reads Locke, Newton and Pope in the original.

At her feet, upon my back, I eat a fly to gain her attention.

'She is a woman and therefore there exists no expectation!' Stanislas reminds us, without malice. To which the Hawk responds, sharply as the bee stings, 'We are men and there exists, therefore, no impartiality.' All must beware his swift processes.

The old king laughs. He understands a woman such as Émilie must be defended.

Her concerns are God, space, time, matter. Émilie is a creature who might, in a moment of leisure, translate Virgil or

Lucretius. She has read Descartes and Leibniz, she does not deny God as the Creator.

'Something exists since I exist,' we hear her say, 'and successive existence makes Time.'

Through her microscope she considers a bead of blood and observes entities within entities. She concludes that within matter there exists hierarchy. She wonders if this persistent hierarchy is the state of all matter on earth.

At three o'clock she takes her coffee; she is partial to cream and a small bread roll.

She allows me to lick the spoon. I gallop on all fours to make her laugh.

Émilie explains that, when working well, she imagines her chair to gather itself and fly as a winged horse.

'She was born for truth,' says the Hawk.

Voltaire-the-Hawk is in love. I am in love.

An old man and a dwarf. How fortunate is she.

I crawl beneath her desk so that I may observe an angle of her face. Émilie frowns over binomes and trigonomes. She does not always agree with Newton, she is queen of her own realm. She attends to angles, and cylinders, polygons, prisms and spheres.

I wish I were a sphere not a dwarf. She might see me.

Her smell is jasmine, oil of clove, and a woman's sweat. Scratch-scratch goes her pen until, beneath her desk, I fall asleep.

One swims perpetually in a sea of
uncertainty ~ Émilie du Châtelet

Here the gens de qualités, thinkers, brutes and dwarves alike, may feel themselves touched by revelation. Here art and nature conjoin in celebration of geometric regularity. Here upon closing my eyes, save for the thunder of water, I am returned to the plateau beneath the mountains of my home, so sweet is the air.

Among the groves and arbours, waterways and cascades, I take my thoughtful strolls and pray I do not encounter abbés or priests at their furtive business.

I allow my step to falter upon sighting the spread of crimson anemones and tulips that are red as my steady heart, each inscribed within by an engraver's tooling of gold. Here lies logic, perfect and divine. God's work.

From the sheep flocks tended by bonneted girls, the dairy farm, meadows and forests, to the faux pyramids, pagodas, false ruins and the cottages where high-ranking mesdames play at shepherdesses or dairy maids, all is a costume fantasy for la noblesse. How they adore the dirty fingernails! How they display their blisters with pride! Ha ha! Though, bien sûr, there is never more than one injury.

'The King of Prussia,' announces the Hawk at supper, partridge leg in hand, 'holds within his heart as many conflicts as the ones he fights with his sword. Ah, yes!' the Hawk agrees with himself. 'He is a man who speaks upon one impulse and acts upon another. And his father was viler still!' The Hawk bites, chews his bird, surveys his audience. He continues. 'Yes, a man of excessive thrift, quick-tempered and cruel. He had a school master's daughter horse-whipped for inexpertly playing the harpsichord.'

At this, one of the Mesdames cries, *'Oh!'*

'Furthermore!' he adds, hesitating for dramatic satisfaction. 'He executed his son's dearest friend for putting ideas into his head.'

There are gasps and murmurs from the Mesdames.

'Ha ha!' I laugh.

It is necessary. Who else may laugh? I am disregarded, but the room is gayer.

A violet cream is served with sugared peach beignets and orange-flower marmalade. Bell pear compote, powdered with sugar, is served alongside cherry pâté, a sweet Muscat from Lunel, and mousses of vanilla, saffron and ambergris.

The Hawk has the attention of all. His eyes dart, face to face. But not to mine. His voice is satisfied in tone. He talks of miracles. Of Seneca. Of Paul.

'It is important to consider the letters, the authenticity.'

Nobody seems able to agree or disagree. Arouet-the-Hawk presses his lips together and smiles; he closes his eyes, clasps his hands. He suspects he might have been resplendent as an abbé or a cardinal, though he detests such gentlemen (and in particular Desfontaines), being, as they are, self-regarding, self-elected and answering to no-one.

'Are not the philosophers themselves guilty of the same offences?' I once asked, expecting amusement to follow. Expecting to be fêted for my impudent wit, my dwarfish credulity!

Arouet whipped me about the face with his hat on that occasion, delighting the assembled company. Ha ha! Sauvage! they cried. Passionné! Vulgaire! Merveilleux!

Now the stage is set. He finds himself upon his feet. There is laughter, though he is yet to begin. Arouet-the-Hawk pauses until the amusement subsides.

'Ô sainte vertu! Ô sainte vertu!'

Ha ha! The Hawk has the gift of comedy.

'Au nom de la sainte vertu, Amen!'

He caricatures well. He should present himself upon the stage.

'Bannissez d'entre vous la raison et la philosophie!'

Poor Rousseau! How he is mocked! Ha ha!

For this performance Arouet, gazing piously Heavenward,

presents us his Docteur Pansophe, the sermonising professor, rolling of eye, stooping of shoulder, praying of hand.

'Ô mes enfants, restez dans les bois! Les bois sont la place de l'homme!'

A jeer of laughter, followed by hoots and cackles. The Hawk pauses until it fades, as if stagecraft were his art. I think to myself, The Hawk is a cat and Rousseau is a mouse. Ah, but I am a fox. You shall not see me. Yet here I am.

My fine legs are become magnificent in their hosiery as they patrol the gaming tables.

With mournful wariness Griffon observes me. Flaming torches fashion dragons that writhe upon the darkened walls.

At the tables the queens, kings and diamonds fall. Comète, Ombre, Piquet, Tric-Trac.

Madame de Graffigny shrieks, frightening my monkey, who bolts, dragging his shredded wig behind him.

The king does not ever cheat at cards. Perhaps to spare the blushes of a guest, if necessary, he may permit adjustments. Unlike the Baron de Montmorency, who is cheating before he has lowered his considerable arse upon the velvet. For gain or loss, the consequence is nil. The king is winning. He bids the string players to brighten their tune. He removes his pipe to laugh at his good fortune, as if fortune itself were wit.

Lansquenet and love: this is Lunéville. So says the Hawk with a flick of his hand and a slow smile.

Émilie prefers Tric-Trac or Comète to Lansquenet, which makes noble gentlemen curse foully in frustration. At the card table she has a swift hand and a flashing woodcock's eye that, beneath the torches, glitters blackly. She rarely loses. I watch her resisting a smile. She allows me to glimpse her cards. The Hawk narrows his eye. I am in love.

St Mary, Islington, 1879

The dwarf in his French idyll is the very essence of joy. He speaks and my senses sharpen. He dances and my spirits rise. He laughs and my heart sings. He is an exquisite toy, a capricious elf! What I would not give to welcome him here, or to visit him there. I catch my breath. What an honour. How I would grasp it!

His musings ... can it all be true? Does he sing false, or is the tune a faithful one? Who shall say? Ought I care? Must his tale be faithful? His people and his wax lights have lit a lamp in me. At night I tuck the edition into bed with the coin-purse and my penknife. Queer, that these old pages daubed in foreign and smelling of saddlery should stir the heart so.

And meanwhile the time has come.

The calendar notifies us tomorrow is the day. We shall ably assist the professor in his noteworthy experiment. We are rehearsed. Success awaits. Cold coins shall soon be warming in my pocket. Hip-ho.

We rise at dawn. I did not rest the night long, though I seem none the worse. A tingling in my blood tells me all will be well.

A south-westerly has arrived, rough as robbery. The wind tears at my coat as if it means to have my watch as I walk. Violent gusts assault horses and traders alike, chimney soot whirls. Has the Lord sent one of His plagues? Now it snatches my hat so that I must grasp my head and shout like a madman.

I hurry across Alfred Street, causing my almost-collision in the dark with a shit-eyed witless fadger and his cart. I curse him, being that my mind today is chock with torment.

At Quick Street Amen Steps jigs about on his long legs. '*Son of man, I am sending you to the Israelites*,' he mutters. His hair will not lie flat though he smears it down with oil and his restless hands find his Bible, forget it, remember it, and hurry to find it again. His scourge? Collywobbles.

'Has the Lord sent you?' I enquire. A jest, referring to the Bible: intended to unburden him. He does not grasp it. He has vexation in his blood that no tomfoolery will rub out.

I pray he will not disappoint. A deal is a deal. A handshake went upon it. Though doubt creeps at this hour, and miracles are for the Redeemer.

We share the bittersweet ale which I purchased earlier in the wind and dark. In this hour I am the daring acrobat of all my days. Teetering upon a wire. Praying not to fall.

We Two Gentlemen of Unease drain our cups as the sky turns pink in the east. We step arm in arm, hats clamped on. Bird follows, slithering on icy cobbles, wrapped against the chill in two broad shawls and a preposterously feathered hat, which I am obliged to remove. Each slip of her boot produces a shriek.

'Wait for me, then. Dear me! Oh! What a palaver!'

We board a two-horse omnibus in the dark. Experts in the field of all things unusual and remarkable are required. Aye! Present and correct. That is us.

Success shall belong to Professor Stanwick if he can prove, by experimental means, that psychic phenomena exist as certainly as Heavenly bodies hang in the night sky, as sure as gravity pins men and women to the earth. Stanwick, the crafty goat, has added the element of drama. He hopes for newspaper interest. By lunchtime we three will be heavy with shilling.

The increasing moon plumps up the
slippery oyster ~ Horace

The omnibus rattles and toils its way to Hampstead. The air is crisp. The greenery lavish.

Here the trees stand taller than church steeples. The leafy canopies hiss in the wind.

We meet at the appointed place, a wild corner, far from the paths and ponds. A mist stands. The shape of a man emerges from it as a cuckoo begins his call.

'All is well?' says Mister Cox, shaking my hand.

'All is well,' I confirm.

I think of Flora at the institute with the young Belgian doctor, whose task it is to unfasten whatever hex silenced her while she was performing her psychical duties there.

'How is Miss Flora Wickes?' I enquire.

'Recovered,' he murmurs. 'Another day. P'raps two.'

'Miraculous!' I reply.

His eye flickers. He turns away.

There, by the giant beeches, is the professor in an overcoat, smoking a small cigar. Another gentleman stands at his side. A photographer bends to his contraption. The professor approaches. I nod in greeting. I warranted a photograph'd be created, afterward. I am wearing a buttonhole.

Professor Stanwick, upon catching sight of Bird, pauses for a moment before placing a fingertip upon her cheek.

'Delightful and dear as a little thrush,' he murmurs.

Bird laughs. I nudge her.

'Indeed, sir,' I confirm. 'Sweet as raspberries, sir!'

I nudge her again and she curtsies abruptly, which makes her laugh out loud, revealing her ample rack of teeth. The professor turns away, deep in his thoughts.

Beneath a giant beech stand five men with spades; I look none directly in the eye. Nor do I look at the hole in the ground. The men are assembled in a semi-circle, obscuring it. Bird's 'kerchief is her blindfold; we tie it firm.

I remind myself we are well practised in stage illusion. Popular, we are. We shall not fail. Rose will take a knife to the eels in her bucket this afternoon and we shall have a stew fit for kings at suppertime.

Amen stands before me. He removes his hat and holds it to his chest. His left eye flutters.

'Belief is all,' I say.

I shake his hand. I would embrace him but we are observed. I step back. The professor positions himself before Amen. He raises his hand. The gesture seems holy, a blessing.

'Trust in me. I am here to guide you,' the professor says. His finger rests upon Amen's forehead. He begins to speak. The sound is drowsy and deep as the lowing of cattle. After which he begins to swerve his hands over Amen's face, as if he pulled invisible yarn from within. It appears even stranger than before: the setting, p'raps. I decide to flit sharpish, before I am mistakenly entranced.

When it comes to mesmerism none can resist Professor Stanwick's persuasive talents: young, old, men, women and fools, all set sail to oblivion. The professor said that himself.

Steps climbs into the coffin.

The professor murmurs once more. I hear Steps' reply.

'I am.'

Mr Cox replaces the lid. The coffin containing Steps is lowered into the ground.

The professor's arms are wings. He spreads them. A pause. His right hand gives the command.

The soil is shovelled quickly. Blindfolded, Bird turns her head at the sound of earth falling upon wood.

Out of the mist the crows arrive, one by one, clerical in black. Flap-flap. I watch them strut, flick a polished eye at the dug earth, tumbled with earthworms.

The men smooth the soil. They leave no mound. The cuts of turf are invisibly replaced. Now you may not ever know there is a living man who lies beneath.

I want to shout out. Stop! But I do not.

Bird is released upon the heath to find the spot where Amen Steps rests. No clue is offered as to his location. By psychic means shall she locate him. For his part, Steps will communicate his whereabouts by use of clairaudience. Bird, by the use of her psychic gift and her spirit guides, shall hear all and find him. A thousand times they have performed the like. Steps in a box. Bird reading his thoughts. Bird in a box. Steps guessing her cards. Neither makes a mistake. Not ever.

The photographer leans against a tree. The minutes have slowed.

Mister Cox checks his watch. The professor talks in a murmur to his colleague.

I walk in circles, as if I too mark the minutes. Tick-tock.

Thoroughly churned, my mind leaps about. Long have I observed mesmerists, enchanters, mentalists and necromancers. I recall Doctor Randall Kettle at the Royal Aquarium, performing between Benotti's Aerial High Wire and The Olympian Quintet. Only Kettle could produce bona fide uproar with his quick temper and rousing techniques, though he had not the scientific reputation of Professor Stanwick.

When my glance returns to where Amen lies I note, with a start, that I cannot tell where the turf has been disturbed. No clue exists.

Bird walks in a straight line towards the beeches. She halts. The trees hiss. Does she hesitate? She moves to the left. Returns to the right. Halts again.

How shall Bird find him if the psychic signal between them wavers? Weakens?

I try to recall the exact terms of Mister Cox's proposal.

Bird is walking in circles. Here then there. There then here.

'Find him!' I shout.

'Quiet!' calls Mister Cox.

Bird continues walking. Halting. Waiting. Walking once more.

I think, Has the mist interfered with the signal? Is the coffin buried too deep?

I am aware of smoke rising in slow hoops from the professor's cigar. Vacant is my head. I feel my blood swing.

I walk. I have no direction, no plan. I stride towards Bird.

'Find him!' I hiss. 'Have you no spirit guide?'

Mister Cox waves his arms. 'Quiet, please!'

Does she not hear him beneath the earth? A hundred times they have performed this.

'I do not hear him,' she says.

I run. The limbs are liquid. I arrive at Mister Cox. He is expressionless.

'We must dig!' I shout.

Then comes a cry. Bird crumples, her face twists.

And . . . mercifully, the sweetness of it.

'Here!' she cries. 'He is here!'

The professor's regard for science is so great that, momentarily, he is blind to the actual.

'Dig!' I shout.

Unusual is what we do. I gasp to catch my breath. Unusual is my middle name.

'Enough! Dig! Dig!' I yell. My hands are raised.

The men dig. An eternity begins. I am shouting. What, I cannot tell. Upon my knees I dig with my bare hands. The earth is freshly turned; this is the place.

I think, Amen! Hear me! Has the Lord sent His chariot? Hear me! Do not climb aboard! I forbid you to climb aboard!

It is Mister Cox who removes the lid. I have not the boldness left to do so.

I know from Cox's face that Steps is feeble.

'Give him air! Sit him up! Back off! Give him air!'

Someone says, 'Come along, Mister Steps. Take a breath.'

I see him. A mirror is produced. He is labouring.

'He breathes! Look!'

In my Sunday trousers I kneel in the earth. Sure as a pound I knew he would not let us down. He has performed it marvellously, bang-up.

'Hip-Hip-Hooray for Mister Steps!'

There is soft applause.

Lord, our merciful Father. Humbly, we give thanks to You for preserving our brother, Amen.

*

The professor poses at the graveside. An elegant tableau. I am not required, the photograph is created without me. I do not fret. It is only an image!

Afterwards the gentlemen shake hands. Mister Cox calls out an announcement: 'By the miracles of mesmerism and telepathic phenomena a theory is proved!'

A tidy headline, I wager.

'Three cheers for the professor. Hip-hip!'

A double stout and porter for our surviving hero, Amen Steps. At The Firkin we give him a cheer, a rendition of *Brightly Gleams*, and a plate of bread and cheese. Tye-diddy-o.

'Amen!' I call. 'A long life to you! I am proud to call you friend.' I raise my pot.

A grin opens on his face. He raises his mug, likewise. 'I am grateful for the opportunity, Mister George,' he says. 'For by grace are ye saved through faith!'

Upon the White Lion Road, returning home, we are sprightly. *Her Ladyship's Daisy* is our song. Robustly we sing it. Not long afterwards Amen sickens and deposits his luncheon on the roadside. Oh, the pity!

'Too much merrymaking,' says Ruby, back at home. She has named the culprit, bang-up.

Bella will not engage me in conversation, though I regard her most civilly and attentively. The stout, porter and bag of warm shillings has brightened my outlook.

I stand before her while she stabbingly darns. I sway my arm and chirrup a jaunty tune. I try a gentle jig.

'Bella, dearest!' I entreat her. 'Have you no words for a man who has put a ham upon the table?'

'No,' she replies, without an upward glance.

I remind her that the day after tomorrow we collect

Flora, good as new, from the institute. 'Won't that be a blessing?' I chirp.

She offers no response. I hum the opening of our favourite old ballad. After which I give up. Bird counts her coins and begins again.

A fire is lit. Amen is put to bed, his own full purse beside him.

A body without a heart ~ Ovid

I have a fresh shilling for Ferrières. The world contains sparks and bangs. Sovereign. I shall enquire of my clock-fiddler, most civilly, whether he might read to me in his preposterous accent more of the gamesome Gallic dwarf. More of this pot-sized Unusual would be a tonic for us both. A restorative!

I shall perform my broadest grin, usually reserved for young ladies and widows.

Whereupon, in a flash, I recall the steps for the polka. One and two and. Upon the kitchen flags I demonstrate, albeit none attend my display. Three and four and. As I skip, a sea-faring tableau forms in my mind, as if the journey of my life were taken aboard a three-masted schooner; its bow slicing through swell towards a spectacular sunset. There am I, the captain at the wheel. My course is charted. The omens are fair! One and two and.

Château de Lunéville, 1746–1748

The men of science have discovered the fashion of feeling in the body of living things and that living things must breathe air. They have proved it. Cats and birds are stifled in an air pump.

I catch my breath. I heard it spoken of this morning. I cannot banish the words from my mind.

I wonder if I might find myself, one day, gasping within an air pump. The Hawk observes my discomfort. 'Poor little Bébé,' he says. 'Ah, Pou. Le pauvre.' And goes enthusiastically on to describe how a living hound was affixed to a table by a scientist and opened with a knife to reveal a system of living cords within that can feel pain.

I am not the halfwit he thinks I am, as, plainly, I do not believe he is speaking the truth.

I have frightened the little powdered abbé with my flute. Ha! Observe him.

See his black wings flap! In his clerical attire he whirls like a dark bird.

'Maquereau! Maquereau!' I cry. As the sun rises, he bolts.

I have a marvellous shriek, it affrights all who skulk. The joie of the game is all!

I pursue the abbé and the joy of my laughter is the chime of a Sanctus bell.

We recline together after dawn prayers. I slurp warm bouillon from my king's bowl.

He smokes his pipe. The dogs stretch and yawn.

The rook bird calls from the cypress tree, his rasps echo across these wide rooms and remind us of the sleeping dead within the crypt, who wait upon our company.

Above us, preserved on canvas, ancestors regard us mirthlessly. Stanislas lights his pipe beneath portraits of Charles XII and Frédéric II. For Charles of Sweden I might sing a line. *Chacun juge le roi, fou, fou, fou!*

At his desk after Low Mass, Stanislas dips his pen and scratches his *Manuel de dévotion*, word by word. My king-the-duc has sympathy with Father de Menoux and his Jesuit horror of games, pleasure and sleep. My king has a soft heart. He feels sympathy for Jesuits. He feels pity for Rousseau. Poor Jean-Jacques, he says. Everybody laughs like magpies at Jean-Jacques and his wild woodlands, forest and rivers; at his wild man, naked as a slow worm. Ha ha! Jean-Jacques will not tolerate science nor that which is scholarly.

Says Menoux, 'Knowledge erases the stains of leisure and ignorance.'

'What knows Menoux of knowledge?' cries the Hawk. 'False brother!'

The priest has enemies. The Comte de Tressan will not speak the name de Menoux.

Upon the subject my king-the-duc is serene. 'The goat must graze where it is tethered,' he says, and disappears within a cloud of pipesmoke.

At his desk, my king covers sheets with his urgent scrawl. Words of advice and comfort to Queen Marie, who must lie with the King of France but prefers to wash the naked feet of poor children, whether or not it be Maundy Thursday.

Poor Marie, she has renounced decorum, leisure, entertainment. A simple 'kerchief lies upon her head, leaving the Pompadourette to flaunt the jewels. Oh! How I should like to kiss the poisson that is Pompadour! There are other names, too foul to mention, used upon the street. Pompadour-the-Reinette appears not to mind, though the Hawk insists she does, blushing when he scolds her for her lapses into bourgoise-speak.

'She expresses herself as a cailette!' he says, and cackles at the thought.

This month my king-the-duc will publish his latest, *Thoughts Upon the Dangers of Wit*.

The ladies pick at the fattened hen, while the Hawk is taken with the pigeon tart, artichokes, green truffles and garden salads. He drinks a wine of the Beaune region.

Sun glares off the table crystal. I shield my eyes, having once been blinded already this day by the Princesse de Talmont's beauty.

His Majesty Stanislas the Uncrowned sucks and slurps at the shellfish and crustaceans. He speaks. 'It is imperative for France that her people return to the yoke and plough, where her dignity and destiny lie,' he says. Around the table there is a rumble of assent as a beef madrilène soup with gold leaf fleck arrives.

I watch Arouet chew the pigeon. He opens a fig. Philosophy creates a hunger in the monsieur. Perhaps to understand the height and width of everything creates in him an emptiness. He speaks of sheep.

'Sheep,' he reminds us, 'commune placidly. Sheep represent, in truth, the perfect community.'

'Ha ha!' I laugh at his comedy and am violently shushed by the others.

'Sheep,' he continues, 'are the republic.'

'Ha ha!' I laugh helplessly. And am shushed once more.

The Hawk slurps at the crayfish tail in his hand; he loops his tongue beneath to catch the drips. Long have I admired his perceptual powers! In honour of this I rise in order to make my reverence.

'Sit, dwarf!'

'I stand only to honour your wit, Monsieur.'

'And I sit to withstand your honour. Sit! How else may you be tall?'

It is the wave of laughter that unseats me, blowing me off my feet. Amusing, yes! How may a dwarf appear tall unless he sits? Ha ha!

To follow, a bombardment of fruit missiles. Each hurled, with intermittent accuracy, in my direction. 'Barbarians!' I cry. I duck. Yet when I rise again a quince strikes me upon the forehead, followed by a volley of stony apricots! *'Aggh!'* I cry. 'Barbarians!' I feign injury and fright, which escalates the frenzy most agreeably. Ha ha!

I play along gamefully. Horreur! Meurtre! A boost to the amusement of all.

It is said Émilie du Châtelet learned to speak and read English in fifteen days.

It is said she learned Italian in eighteen days. Indeed, she gave advice to Algarotti.

If the earth is indeed a sphere it grows fuller because Émilie stands upon it.

The Hawk describes her thus: 'This woman, in imagination and in reason, surpasses the men who like to think they know a lot about the one and the other. Clarity, precision and elegance are the essence of her style,' he adds.

I have not the gift to arrange words as musical notes, as he does.

The Hawk composes for Émilie odes and quatrains in the style of Virgil, Horace, Ovid.

For my own courtship I will crawl upon my knees and try to catch her eye.

The freedom of numbers is her joy.

The numbers that tell the mysteries of the earth and all upon it. Every man, bird, river, valley and hillside are numbers in their dividing sub-parts. Every aria, poem and syllabub represent numbers tumbled in alternative fashion.

179

The world becomes a formula. A wind blows and the numbers alter.

I ask her, 'Did numbers assemble me as a dwarf?'

She replied, 'The numbers forged you, Bébé, and God gave His Holy blessing.'

The sun, according to Émilie, consists of particles of fire, for its rays produce the effect of fire. The earth's shadow makes an arc, so the earth must be a sphere.

God in His Heaven presides. Émilie calculates. Voltaire sighs.

'Hers is the most beautiful soul in the world.'

I watch her walking by the bosquets where the wind lifts the corner of her gold silk cape and I try to recall the name of a gilded bird, whose wings might lift it Heavenwards, when I realise no such bird exists upon the earth.

Fréron is here. How the Hawk detests him, taking his meals in his room, refusing to emerge unless a servant reassures him the coast is clear! Ha ha!

The esteemed critic, meanwhile, escorts his multitude of chins around the park with my king-the-duc, seemingly unable to glance either left or right, staring fixedly ahead, rigid as a cardinal, startled of expression, as if he espies something frightful that is invisible to the rest of us.

Monsieur Fréron thinks less of the Hawk than the Hawk thinks of Fréron, conceding that if Voltaire had only stuck to verses he may have retained his reputation. Fréron for his part cheats at the card table.

For myself I observe that his wig is poor and that he smells of something over-ripened.

'That will be his reputation!' cries the Hawk when I tell him, beneath a hoot of laughter. 'It poisons the air!'

Truly there is something decomposed in Fréron, as debauched as rotted pears. Moreover, he does not smile. Not even when I emerge unexpectedly, in a spray of foam, cream and meringue, from the pastillage pièce montée at a crowded supper table, ha ha! The spectacle of which reduced all, but he, to helpless convulsions. Ha ha!

I am told by Madame de Bercheny that my voice sweetens the air she breathes.

I tell her she is milk upon which roses float.

I press my lips upon her fingers and tell her that her face sweetens the blood in my . . .

Her breathing hesitates. I insert the tip of my tongue between her fingers, as a cat takes the first taste of milk and then I say . . . heart. Her eyes close and her lips part to display her little ivories. I tell her I will die of love for her.

She declares she is grown bored of our game.

'Enough talk!' she squawks in my ear, pinching my nose, laughing at my startlement.

'Play!' she commands me, spanking my cheek with her fan. 'Sing!'

She falls upon the chaise and I, having lost a shoe during my jig, dash unevenly across the room to fetch my flute.

I play a sad fugue. I observe her eyes closing and wonder if she may slide into a sleep.

I desist playing and begin a song in a breathy soprano alto.

On goutte tous les jours,
Mille délices,
Qu'assaisonne l'amour . . .
À ce Dieu si propice . . .

The ill-mannered de Desmarets interrupts us, the Vicomte speaks boldly, as if I do not exist. He spoils the song, ruins the game.

181

He considers his speech to contain phrases of such beauty and merit that no marquis, prince or duc may dream to compare himself to this esteemed gentleman of the noblesse d'extraction. No matter that his mother was the daughter of a Bordelaise tailleur, the Vicomte now orders his chemises from Paris.

I scream!

I throw my flute at him. I stab him in the thigh with my shoe. He converses in flowery verbioses, as long as an ass's prick. I tell him so. I run from the room.

I comfort myself in the cabinet de Chinoiserie with bowls of sugared almonds and Jacquot, who is costumed as a hussar and has soiled himself, in his usual habit.

I recall there was, last night, a vicious child, pretty of face, exquisitely mouthed ... the tiniest rosebud! This child, amply rouged with tilted eyes and brows of fur, examined me as if I were an animal, poking my ribs and opening my mouth with her fingers.

She impersonated my voice in a mockingly high register, squeaking, tittering, to the amusement of all. 'A demon!' she screamed, upon seeing me happily astride my cushions. 'A monster!'

In response to this outburst I was obliged to break wind loudly, in order to rescue my dignity, trumping her little act, and receiving a satisfying storm of amusement from the assembled noblesse.

They are calling for me. I do not respond.

At night I think of home. In search of sleep I recall the sunsets on the heath.

A scent of briars, woodruff. Horses at the ponds, geese in the sky. Gypsies hang their kettles at dusk. A shepherd's horn beyond the hill, where cattle are pastured.

I re-plait the strands of my father's whip and look up at the Roche, from whose heights you may view the smoky summits of the Vosges, and there I fall asleep in the midday heat to the scratch of crickets and the distant croaking, from a nearby ditch, of a solitary frog.

St Mary, Islington, 1879

There may hang upon a wall, somewhere in France, a likeness of my midget. My dainty morsel of a man. I see him, princely in his threads, haughty of eye, uppity, cocksure . . . dwarfish, that's him!

Curious, I'd wager my midget would know me on the street just as well as his own mother. Uncanny. I fancy he'd look up at me and say, There you are, Mister George! And take my hand. I do not know why I reason it, yet I do.

How gentle is the uncrowned monarch with his dwarf. How wise and kind to his guests and advisors. I cannot disregard the fancy that I too should have made an excellent king, well-nigh the twin of King Stan. But for the torment of running this many shows a day, I too should have written philosophy, poetry and pamphlets, entertained royalty, designed gardens and fashioned philosophical frippery.

A benign royal I should have been, in the manner of this royal Pole. I'd have conversed on politics and war, quoted Seneca, Horace, et cetera. I too might have spoken Latin, Italian, French, made princesses laugh. Men of the clergy and science alike would kiss my ring in gratitude. Ladies of the nobility would set sail from the Bay of Biscay to pay me a visit. I should charm them with my manners and my peculiar little dwarf. All would know my name. How I would cherish it. How merry to be celebrated, how merry to be heard!

The dwarf is heard. His words have journeyed far. I hear him through the barriers of language, time and place. When I am bones, might any fellow know of me? Though I am buried shall I cavort once more? Shall I be flesh again? Then watch me caper and spout like a living man!

As a boy I considered time as a wheel upon which the minutes went around and began again. I remember the one-legged showman in Clerk'nwell with his cage of scrabbling squirrels, ringing bells and spy-hole box of story pictures. A blast on his bugle brought us running and he spoke his stories as a clergyman might preach, head back, arms wide, eyes closed. As if words were truth. Miraculous! And I was caught, as a rabbit in a net. And wished to draw a crowd of my own, and tell them tales for chink.

A few more hours and we shall collect Flora, jolly as a cockle once more, from the institute. Bella shall see how well I have contrived it all. Harmony shall return and contentment will abide. Sovereign. I fill my pipe.

I observe Jim, the pyke'art, carrying our buckets across the cobbles between a jostle of advertisement boards. Will he never grow taller? Already in that low stride do I perceive the buckled old man he will become. His years are rolling backwards. Only his bones know it. Time is a slippery scurf. How deft is the cunning minute's sleight of hand! At my age you know the game: too late to dodge, too soon for laudanum. Patiently shall I wait till the clock finishes me, by tick or tock. Time alone decides. Time has within its net each of us already captured.

Château de Lunéville, 1747–1759

Émilie raises her chin and smiles before she quotes Locke.

I watch her. I chew bread. I would prefer to fashion an uproar to gain her attention, but she is discoursing. Her voice is a small bell. Her throat moves as she speaks.

'Knowledge comes from the senses and is filtered through reason's reflections,' she says.

A quarter of veal arrives at the table to follow the rabbit, with rissoles, cabbage, salads.

I lie my head upon the table, while keeping her in sight. Another quote follows. I watch her throat. My eyelids grow heavy.

'We will never know enough by the light of mere reason to assert that God cannot grant the gift of feeling and thought to the being known as matter.'

'Ah! Again! Locke!' calls a voice. The Comte de Croix. 'Yes, Locke, indeed!' he cries.

The Hawk makes a clattering upon his dish, sighs, wipes his mouth. He is an admirer of Locke but becomes restless when his own work is set aside for an entire course.

Moreover, the mention of Locke reminds poor Arouet that his own article in support of Locke unleashed a storm in Paris at the time. It gives him indigestion still.

An atheist, they called him, a bad poet, the son of a peasant. Ha ha! I laugh aloud while affecting to sleep upon my plate. The Hawk assessed the indisposition of his accusers thus: his recent stage plays had enjoyed success, voilà! It was jealousy. Fin.

She sings Zirphé from *Zélindor*. There are guests in the outdoor green theatre, a thousand wax lights, torches, orange trees and ribboned nymphs leading lambs.

There are dancers, musicians, silver bowls of peaches and figs and a firework display.

I consume three plates of peaches and am violently sick into an arbour of jasmine, while Émilie sings once more – an aria from *Issé*– with Madame de Lutzelbourg.

After vomiting, I inform her that her performance expertly captured the nobility of Zirphé, as exquisitely as if she were the mortal beauty herself. This appraisal I overheard the Hawk deliver aloud to the Prince de Craon. I bolted, thereafter, to Émilie to convey the compliment as my own. She kisses my head and takes my hand.

I am raised upon wings!

At supper, among scatterings of jonquils and roses, surrounded by vines, turfs and arbours, I pick at a pigeon. There is a scent of burning wax, cedar and musk.

The Hawk sucks at three young partridges, his lace amply stained. His mouth purses as he gossips, ' . . . car il espère l'e poser . . . je dirais même qu'il compte dessus!'

I should prefer something jocular. I shall sit elsewhere.

I climb upon the table, it is the swiftest route. Only Bébé may step among the goblets, porcelain and vermeil. I have the dancer's gait, the dainty foot.

From here I catch the sound of the Baron de Montmorency. *'Meh. Meun!'*

This is the sound of the baron. Ha ha! I shall impersonate him as I step. Close your eyes!

'Meh. Meun!' A true likeness. The Mesdames laugh! It is the sound of bells. Listen!

I may stroll upon the table, sit where I please, or draw my sword upon any gentleman, whether or not it shall offend. My king's orchestra conductor, Monsieur de La Pierre, is a small crow with a single tooth and a short stick. I prick him, nightly, with my weapon. Ha ha! My swordsmanship is excellent. It amuses all. The blood stains his chemise.

Ah. I have caught the eye of the comeliest musician, whose

sweet face appears to slumber against his viol as he plays. He thinks I am a cockerel bird! I display the he-bird strut. I flap my little wings. Ha! I shriek the cock-bird sound. My impersonation is astonishing. I repeat until the Mesdames are squawking like she-pheasants!

At dusk the waterways and fountains glow from the lights of ten thousand flickering lamps. The sun slides into the Grand Canal and the ivory swans are washed pink.

At my throat hangs an outburst of Brussels lace. Beneath my coat shines a weave of Siamese silk and broderie d'or. I am exquisite. A treasure.

A hundred columns of water climb Heavenwards, while yet more water tumbles to earth in foaming plumes. The air is glittered.

Ladies curtsey in their dresses to our crownless king, crushing the satin that falls over their hoops. Within gondoliers are ladies in the English fashions and their cavaliers setting straight their swords. Musicians match sight with celestial string sound, while boatmen push against long poles. Guests step into barouches, while still others stroll towards the cascades, the pavilions, or the little palace of Chanteheux.

A tall ship sails sedately up the canal, while sea horses rear out of the water, ridden beneath by water divers.

'The most adorned sitting room in Europe,' comments the Hawk. He smiles and rests his arm upon my head.

A great crack, and the arch that is decorated with the royal coat of arms takes flame.

The crowd gasps. I hear myself scream. Ha ha!

Fireballs, nimble as bats, flee Heavenwards. A sound like cannons. A blaze of fire, tall as Olympus. The screams of mesdames! Feathers of fire burst into a million stars above us. Hot loops of red and orange twist in the sky and fall into the

187

canals, where they rest, burning upon the water. Alive is the night with the crack and roar of beasts until, from the Heavens, a gentle rain of gold bids them calm their ardour and, in a magical smoke, disappear.

I too am a single flame made for the sky.

Just after midnight the fortune-teller strokes her fingers beneath my chin. It is amusing.

'Fie sorceress!' I warn. 'I shall draw my sword! Ha ha!'

I shall hear first what she has to say. Stanislas laughs, everyone laughs.

Her eyelid trembles, she smells of the dug earth.

A voice calls. 'Attends! All gather around. She speaks!'

'A little Frenchman,' she says, 'will change the fates of France. His name will live. All will know him.' And, as if she saw the future standing in bold satins before her, she adds, 'The little Frenchman will have a pet name referring to his short stature. The letter of his first name is N, yet his second name, which contains two meanings, begins with a B. The world shall know him.'

She smiles. I stare at the dark hole of her mouth beneath the black bowl of star-filled sky. She bends to kiss the rings of la noblesse, to touch the jewels, the satins and lace. While guests chatter, laugh and drift away, I stand alone. Bewitched.

It is me. N. Nicolas.

I am he. B. Bébé. Whose meaning is two. A baby. And an illustrious dwarf. Myself!

Speak my name. Speak it! It is I.

I inform my king-the-duc I am to lead France. I require an army.

I have need of advisors. We must discuss these matters urgently. What! Does he dispute the fortune-teller's prophecy? All there assembled heard it spoken.

My king regards me solemnly.

His face lowers to mine. His Majesty examines me through the reds of his blue eyes.

Beads of sweat rise through the blanc. His breath? A sardine. His neat mouth? A raspberry. Ha ha! It arrives. I close my eyes. It kisses my forehead.

'You shall lead no-one, Bébé. No armies. A goat and a monkey, you have.'

He kisses me again.

'The King of France is upon the throne,' he says. 'At his right sits my daughter. I do not wish to see you horse-whipped, Bébé.'

And then he laughs, revealing a mouth ill-furnished with teeth, shot out at intervals by gaps. And I too laugh gaily. Ha ha! Yes indeed! A once-upon-a-time king may be proven wrong. No? Why (if he were unfailingly correct) is not the crown resting upon his own head? Ha ha! Yes, I will reward my champions when it is time for me to lead France.

It shall follow.

Saint-Lambert keeps a torment in his face. His unquiet eyes and agitated brow all serve to arouse pity in the ladies and suspicion in the gentlemen. His eyes are wide, their gaze restless. He smiles often, yet remains detached.

Inexplicably, Émilie has fallen in love with him.

His conversation? Commonplace. His poetry? Poor. He is an officer of the Gardes de Lorraine and talks of military service in Bohemia and elsewhere. Ha ha! How is this possible? His health is feeble and he coughs like a hound!

Émilie can think of little else. They leave notes for one another within a harp.

The paper she writes upon is lace-edged, tied with a pale blue ribbon. Au nom de Dieu!

His valet and her maid know their secret. As do I. She

wounds me. I say nothing. It is an infatuation. I will wait, with sharpened blade.

François-Maximilien de Tenczyn-Ossolinski stoops under the weight of his titles, allowances, lands and castles awarded to him by his cousin King Stanislas, my king.

During his flight to Konigsberg, Monsieur le Duc d'Ossolinski utilised his long fingers in the pilfering of crown jewels, diamonds, relics and the financial registers. Yesterday he dangled those same fingers into my wine goblet, withdrawing them suddenly to flick a stinging quantity of it into my eyes, whereupon he laughed like a peacock.

Now it is he, Ossolinski, who calls me.

'Dwarf! Dwarf!'

I do not obey.

Ossolinski believes my relatives are monkeys, this much he would like to prove. From the Chinese Trèfle he has chased me. Paix! My dress is in disarray, my wig a-fly. He commands me to climb the silks, as Jacquot does. The ladies' laughter follows me as far as marbled Jupiter on his plinth. Here too sneers Charles of Sweden in his gilded frame. I flick my glove at him.

My steps are rapid. God sees me, pities me. A miniature hostage to a stateless king.

Ossolinski calls. The Comte has joined him. They wish to instruct me, I shall not be instructed. I am a dwarf of quality, of the sword. My king-the-duc's child is Queen of France! Ossolinski beats his hunting dogs. He shall not beat me.

Here is a vale of linden trees, straight as a rapier, almost three miles long. At its end a mist hangs. There is a bowl of sky, where starlings make their geometry, as Émilie, on paper, sketches hers. The birds do not acknowledge the accuracy of their angles, effecting them carelessly, unheeded and free of vanity. Their place in Heaven's sky is unassailed. See me. I run. I weep. Not for myself but for these execrable mediocrities, these misguided wretches who consider themselves ingenious, those whom once I admired and for whom I became a hare-brained witless fool.

*

An educated dwarf, Polish by birth and esteemed in the courts of Europe, is to visit France. After presenting himself at Versailles he is to travel to Lunéville, where he hopes to deliver his most gracious compliments to King Stanislas.

That I, Bébé, Dwarf of France, must be subjected to such inglorious humiliation is intolerable. The creature they speak of will arrive this week accompanied by his attendants and the Countess Humiecka. I am measured for a brocaded coat and breeches in a dazzling shade of seafoam, a silk and cap, cane, ribbons.

How I wish Montesquieu were here. It is his kindly face I wish to see. It is a face made feminine in its quest to co-operate. Tides move beneath him. His gaze, like his mind, sees both the immediate and the distant: the left eye fixing upon you, while the other alters perspective to contemplate beyond. He is wise enough for three men. He has an upright bearing, for one so old, moving nimbly yet discreetly. He carries himself as one who has heard his name called for an important honour.

In the afternoon I hide in the Chinese Trèfle pavilion, whose design is a copy of the Japanese teahouse of Frederick the Great. This is apt, as the talk, lately, is all of Frederick the Great and his invasion. I consider that this monstrous dwarf shall be here for a short time and will, almost certainly, have contemptible French.

When I emerge for supper not a soul appears to have noticed my absence. I affect detachment. The strings play, the wax lights flicker, the Mesdames chatter.

I execute a slow ballet, whose movements are dictated by the agony of my wounded soul.

I hear it said that Monsieur le Duc d'Ossolinski has died suddenly of a cough in La Malgrange.

I take this as a good omen.

*

Saints in Heaven! The visiting dwarf, Józef, is monstrously vain. See!

How he cavorts and struts.

On his behalf I am ashamed. He does not appear injured by my expressions of horror. Such vanity! Such pride!

This imposter shall now take counsel from a bona fide dwarf. I will be patient with the poor wretch. I shall not display my contempt but only pity. Poor Józef Boruwłaski, how unnaturally tall you are, impertinent and unamusing, barely a dwarf at all. How the fortunes have shone on this rogue and assisted him in his subterfuge. Aderat fortuna etiam. God in His Kingdom of Heaven will forgive you. Poor Józef! Truly he has brought this upon himself.

I am instructed to entertain our foreign visitor after Mass. I begin with an old folk song from my childhood. He appears to admire it. I conclude it before the seventh verse, in order to execute the manoeuvres of my new dance, which I have rehearsed, in preparation.

The brief ballet is the story of an orphan boy who, after gaining the love of a beneficent king, becomes lost in the forest and is saved by the wandering spirit of a wolf that is revealed to be the spirit of the beneficent king, who died, upon losing the boy, of a broken heart.

An exquisite tragedy!

The Polish dwarf appears deeply moved.

I am instructed to escort our visitor to the gardens.

Liberated in the leafy bosquets, among the groves and allées, softened by the scent of jasmine and lime, I take his arm and lead him to the distant view of the Vosges and the horizon beyond. I take my small knife to cut for him a ripened plum, mopping his chin with my own silk 'kerchief and waving away inconvenient insects.

In response the foreign dwarf speaks of nought but himself.

'I am to receive mention in the encyclopédie, the Comte de Tressan informs me,' he bleats.

This, a contemptuously uncivil boast, is audacious in its inferred mockery of myself. The encyclopédie, a work compiled by Diderot and d'Alembert, cites anyone of note.

I laugh gaily. 'A marvellous advancement,' I say, 'and befitting.'

I swat a wasp away from his head.

The dwarf darts swiftly to his next boast, clasping his hands in delight.

'Yes! I fear I am to be flattered once more by the Countess Humiecka, as she informs me she is to present me a second time at Versailles to the Queen, for which I am most humbly honoured, for I did not expect to be favoured so!'

I decline to mention the impeccable manners of our Queen, which prevent Her Royal Highness from pleasing herself in her duties.

A queasiness is upon me. He opens his rosebud mouth. I fear he will announce another unspeakable glory, shortly to be bestowed upon him.

I slap him hard upon the nose.

'Aagh!' he shrieks, stumbles, clasping at his face.

'A hornet,' I explain. 'As our honoured guest, I should not have you stung.'

Some affliction claws my gut. I am ailing.

Later with the Mesdames he behaves odiously! Kissing each of their fingers, though it is, of course, the jewels upon their fingers he slobbers upon.

He speaks of Vienna, where he was taught dancing by the great Angelini, ballet-master to the court. Of how he sat upon the lap of Her Imperial Majesty, Maria Theresa, Queen of Bohemia and Hungary, remarking to her how extraordinary it was to behold so little a man upon the knee of so great a woman.

So sickened am I, necessity bids me close my eyes.

He brags of his success in Bavaria, where he was graciously welcomed by His Electoral Highness, Maximilian III, and, naturally, he brags of Versailles, where he was first presented to Queen Marie and the princesses and where, he claims, he was named 'the little prodigy'.

At this, I collapse.

I am put to bed.

He has captured my king. Together they recline to discuss poetry and politics, agriculture and architecture. An outrage.

I might discuss these things, often have I cared to. Yet the king has never wished it!

He prefers me halfwitted, for amusement, for diversion. My duty is to offend, terrorise. This is my task. Impeccably have I played my part. The king instructed me in the art of devilry yet he praises Józef for his manners, charm, intellect. And now this false toy, this crippled fish, leans upon his elbow to smoke a pipe and wave his arm and pretends he is a great wit, a philosopher, a theorist!

How must I respond?

The king has created a pet name for him, as he once created one for me.

Joujou. Toy.

A toy is more amusing than a baby, no?

I cannot eat nor sleep! I would flay him. Stick him. Disappear him.

As a cordial host, and under instruction from my king, I have made gifts to the dwarf of my feather pillows, my gold enamelled pocket watch and a likeness of myself in oils by Trubenbach.

I am most regretful about the watch, which I donated in haste.

I ask that he return it, it is my favourite item! For this he scandalises me, fetching it out and consulting it countless times a day, causing me to weep great gasps of tears until I am lightheaded.

'How can I express to you my grateful sentiments for these numerous favours?'

The dwarf speaks not to me but to my king. He speaks of Charles XII, for it was he who first appointed Stanislas Leszczynski to the crown of Poland. Józef flatters my king. He speaks of his exceeding wisdom, tolerance and fortitude as a king in exile, a scholar of law, a reformer who speaks four languages. He compliments my king upon his purchases of wheat for the poor, for in his dukedom nobody shall starve. He commends Stanislas upon his founding of the college of medicine in Nancy, in the grand square Stanislas himself built. He reminds him that his patronage has built schools, buildings, libraries, training for clerics and architects, not to mention a college for artists, and a seminary run by Jesuit priests. Moreover, he compliments my once-king upon his noble aspect, his serenity, dignity, deportment. It is true. He is not a duc, not a king, he is a *saint*.

And I am his singular dwarf. He belongs to *me!*

The vines and arbours are aflame with wax lights and Chinese lanterns. Nymphs carry cages of birds while reciting poems upon the subject of sweet slavery and freedom.

In the bosquets the sound of oboes and flutes fill the air while, within a tent of damask, a ballet is performed to the harp and lute.

At the Salon Carré, beneath a ceiling fresco of Apollo in his chariot, a fried crème of citron and rose is served with macarons de fleurs d'orange and biscuits d'amandes.

The Comte de Tressan is speaking. I do not attend him at first, as I am observing Józef, as he consumes a neige de bergamote. Yet gradually, through the disorder of violin, harp, laughter and chatter, Tressan's words reach me.

'There can be few better examples and no better proof in support of the theories of Descartes, when he describes the lack of a soul in animals, than Bébé himself. This you must consider! If a monkey or a poodle has no soul it is, in effect, a machine, well ... In consideration of his base behaviours ... so then is Bébé!'

A gentle ripple of laughter.

I think, Can he be referring to me? De Tressan continues.

'Bébé represents the degradation of the human existence, whereas the Pole dwarf, Józef, instils pleasure with his appearance and intellect, he arouses interest in his feelings and evokes a desire to soothe all pain and indignity such as his fate may entail. He represents well his species.'

A rumble of assent follows. And afterwards, further down the table, a sudden, misplaced hoot of laughter.

I stand upon a rock whereupon waterfalls cascade and sheep graze. No sound is made save for the grinding of wheels, for all is mechanism. Here nature is painted, carved and operated by pinion. Beside me appears, haltingly, the figure of the miller's wife: reproachful in expression, sagging in bosom. We stand equal in stature and share a moment of eye contact before I provoke her with my tongue and eye until she, in her mechanical habit, returns woodenly, upon her hinges, into the mill. Whereupon emerges the miller, downcast of expression, leading a donkey laden with overflowing baskets of grain. I throw a stone at him and another.

*

I remind myself de Tressan's mother was fathered by a black-smith. Indeed, perhaps she was. The relationships betwixt courtiers and comédiennes are become so numerous as to be considered commonplace. Truly, if a comédienne of merit has triumphed on stage in recent times she may rest assured that her star is in the ascendant and take her pick of titled courtiers with whom she may liaise.

I listen to the click of my heel on the parquet. My step is slow.

My punishment was delivered to my mother upon the day of my birth. Now I am at liberty to speak truths. They shall listen.

They see the cruel work of fate before them and they shall beg my forgiveness.

I discover them, Stanislas and Józef, reclined together upon the daybed.

I shout his name.

'Stab me! I fall at your feet!' I open my chemise. Upon my knees I implore my king. 'Cut out my heart,' I say. 'Do it swiftly.'

My king sighs. The Polish dwarf laughs, before quickly silencing himself.

The king turns to me. His blue eyes are rubbed pink. He speaks to me in a kindly voice.

'Bébé! Come to me! Yes, come!'

I run to him and fall into his arms. He continues to speak softly.

'Ah, little Bébé. You see what a difference lies between Joujou and you?'

He strokes my hair as I listen. I keep one eye fixed, as a blade-tip, upon the foreign imposter.

'Joujou is amiable, cheerful, entertaining and well informed, is he not?'

197

There exists, abruptly, an unpleasant texture to the air. I sit upright. I look at my king.

'Yes. Whereas you, Bébé, are but a little machine.'

A melancholy countenance arranges itself in his face at the final words. He sighs.

He rises to leave.

'You disappoint me, Bébé.'

I make no reply.

Stanislas moves to the door. The footman steps back.

A small fire burns in the fireplace. I shall throw myself upon the flames. All is done.

I turn to Józef. I am a royal dwarf. I shall deport myself with dignity.

I reach out to him. He takes my hands. And here, upon the tick-tock of the clock, my consideration alters. With both hands I snatch him about the waist and drag him to the fireplace, whereupon, with a desperate effort, I push him into the fire.

Or would if I were able.

He clings on to the wall hook that secures the fire irons and in this fixed position, groaning with exertion, we remain, while he begins to shriek. His lamenting brings the king hurrying into the room, and the precious Joujou is saved.

*

I am accused.

I will be whipped today at the chime of five.

I would appeal to my king-the-duc, yet he will not have me in his sight.

This very same week His Majesty's essay, *Incredulity Combatted By Sheer Common Sense*, will be published by the royal printer. I had hoped to mark the occasion by his side.

I smell first the fire, peat and fir.

The milk from our cow is in the kessel warming. From this

my mother will make curds. In season she will have collected herbs, flowers and blueberries. Upon our bread she drips a cheese from the goat. In September there will be other berries: plums, red currants, white currants. In June my father may catch a trout from one of the waterways at the base of the ballons and when the days grow shorter they will dig up tubers for soup. I close my eyes and consider the voice of my mother. I was her favourite.

In the palm of her hand I lay. God, by His grace, gave her a masterpiece made miniature by His love. And it was I.

I am whipped. The sun moves behind a cloud during my beating.

All nature turns away. I endure my punishment. Afterwards my wounds are washed and wrapped. I cry as loudly as if the whip were falling still.

My king-the-duc does not visit me. He is ashamed. He is disappointed.

I am told my screams could be heard from the northern apartments. Screams so terrible, they say, that flocks of herons lifted off the water and the wild pigs fled deeper into the forest.

I am pleased.

St Mary, Islington, 1879

My heart is a stone. Poor Bébé. I rest my head in my hands.

How these miseries torment my impish boy. How the poor creature suffers as the superior dwarf charms the king and sways his affections! Only this morning I hurried to

Ferrières for the comfort of hearing my prankish miniature speak of his royal frivolities.

What a tonic! I thought. He shall calm my nerves, I wager'd. He shall soothe my soul.

I could not have imagined the arrival of these unexpected mishaps.

My sweet boy, would that I had been there. None would hurt you, as I would disallow it in my kingdom. There'd be no more weeping. I should crown you as my heir, and you would love me as a son. There. A tender picture. A century has pulled us apart.

Timely is the misfortune that assails my dwarf, as a tragedy of our own unfolds.

For it follows, as if by sorcery, that we too are struck down. Here I shall reveal it . . .

After the success of the precarious experiment, Amen confessed, upon our return home, that he felt unwell. Ruby named the culprit: 'Too much merrymaking.'

Apt, as we were indeed a pinch blustered. And so we put Amen Steps to bed.

And here is how it went:

Once tidily abed Amen asks for a sip of water, after which he lays his head down, cheerful as a duck. You would not consider this same man found himself buried in the ground, in the name of science, that very day.

'Did I do well?' he asks.

'Splendid well!' we tell him. 'No doubt your name will feature in the article.'

He asks for his fiddle, though he does not wish to play. At around midnight he laughs, albeit nobody has told a joke. Thereafter he is quiet.

The next morning he is dead.

What horrible fate has led us here? Over the girls'

weeping I raise my voice to God. I ask, In what aspect might we have displeased our Heavenly Father? Upon my knees I humbly ask Almighty God why He chose to seize Amen from us? What is the sin that has been committed? I ask. How do we deserve this judgement? Is the sin my own?

I consider my misdeeds. I wonder whether the professor's scientifics may have given Heavenly offence. Yet all is guided by His hand alone! The Almighty it is who designs the mysteries. I cannot fathom it. What are we to do?

Upon our knees we raise our prayers. Only Amen's face, serene in its final slumber, gives me comfort. And his voice recollected, *Did I do well, Mister George?*

During the night I hear the sound of his fiddle so distinctly that I sit breathlessly upright and call out his name.

Oh Holy Spirit. Beloved of my soul. Enlighten me. Guide me. Strengthen me and console me. Together we murmur his favourites. The girls join hands to weep. A space exists, I fancy, where Ames ought to be.

The next morning Mister Cox arrives, holding his hat.

He tells us that, according to Professor Stanwick, the death is quite unrelated to the experiment. An unfortunate coincidence, nothing more, he explains. What a pity, he adds.

He rubs his pink eye.

Bella spits on his coat; whereupon, in startlement, I make a swift and forthright apology. 'She is distraught!' I explain. I drag at her arm. 'We are in turmoil,' I say.

Mister Cox nods once. His glance remains fixed upon Bella. 'Tomorrow,' he says, and glances at me.

Later we gather around the bed.

Our Father, Who art in Heaven.

I recall his breath, how it fogged the mirror glass at his mouth, now it seems like a miracle.

Our Saviour weeps! Oh, Mister George, I did not ring the bell this time.

Clear as day, I hear him. As if he sat beside me, pipe lit.

For thine is the Kingdom, The power and the glory, For ever and ever. Amen Horatio Stepman. Gone but not forgotten. He sacrificed himself for progress. In his place we have the heavy shilling many times over. Cold coins. No matter how swiftly they warm in the hand they shall not replace him. My dear pal, Amen.

A south-westerly. Clouds chase. Sky white as bone. Geraniums are flowering in our yard. A rattle and clang from the street.

By the window I wait.

I have it in my hand, *Borders, Spirit and Light.* It is the photograph I dwell upon. In their dark attire they are rigid, the professor and his colleague, polished as ravens, stern of gaze, hands at their backs. Deep in the ground is Amen. He sits upright, one eye is closed, almost a wink! His hands are gesturing, two blurred moths. His mouth is open, as if he were about to sing.

For Apollo had made her to be a true
prophetess ~ Tryphiodorus

A low sky, blackening in the west. Treetops and spires are vanished in the fog. In the east a wash of pewtery light falls upon St Mary's, silvering the churchyard, sharpening the names upon the tombstones. At Quick Street the clock tocks, weary as Methuselah.

Bella and I have closed an upstairs door for a moment's peace.

We lean against opposite walls. We have grieved this way together before. Four infants. Now Amen.

She does not look at me.

'A better man than you we have lost,' she says.

This is despair talking. I glance at her. She seems to tremble in her grief. Her eyes, washed with tears, hold all the light.

'D'you see what has been taken from us? I hope you are satisfied?'

I move to explain, to uphold the particulars. Yet not a word forms in my head. I am transfixed, agog, like Jim in the morning when confronted by his own boots.

'Have you nothing to say?' She is looking at me now, her eyes widening in disbelief.

I spread my arms in the manner of a reputable showman, which is plumb what I am.

I look up for inspiration. Where are my phrases? My spoutings? I am mute as Flora.

Bella's face is composed but her dead eye warns me, a shiver moves on her lip.

'Did I not tell you?' she gasps. 'Did I not beg you a dozen times?' Her volume rises. 'Are you not sorry for what you have done?'

'Bella, I did what ... I have tried to ... Had I been aware ... I have always ... As well you know ...'

For a moment I imagine she is about to smile but an alarming grimace appears in its place.

I am unprepared for the moment she lunges, swiping and clawing. I am obliged to wrestle her firmly. I pin her arms, grip hard and hold on, so she may not struggle.

'Stop!' I breathe into her hair. 'I loved Amen as a brother. Would you have us starve?'

She does not answer. I breathe her in and remember what it was to comfort her.

She stiffens. 'Let me go.' I dare not look at her directly. I am about to say something befitting and astounding, it is on the tip of my tongue. I release her.

'I have an appointment with the professor,' she announces, smoothing her skirt.

'What?'

'Yes. Today. I am to pay him a visit. See for myself. I'll fetch Flora home from the institute. I shall deal him what's-what-and-proper, in a flash.'

'I forbid you to do that,' I tell her. 'I am instructed by Cox to fetch Flora at twelve.'

'If he is misbehaving,' she says, 'he will be sorry for it.' She laughs at the thought.

'I strictly forbid you to go.'

'Woe betide him if I find the cure is shabby.'

'Do you not hear me?' I cry.

'Ought I listen? To you? A skipping fool! Flo is my sister. She is ill. I will fetch her.'

'She is cured!' I insist. 'And Cox instructed me to fetch her. *Me.*'

'You. Aye, the bobbing pyke who gave her up. I am her family. I will go.'

'Watch your tongue, Bella. I've denied you nothing.'

'I daresay that's right. Albeit you lend us out for ha'pennies.'

'Guineas.'

'You haven't an idea what goes on!' she cries.

'Scientifics! Scientifics! Scientifics!' I roar. 'Can a man be plainer?'

'Well, he hasn't met the science of me yet,' she says. 'P'raps he'll wish he never had.'

'I forbid you to go! These are gentlemanly transactions. Is that clear?'

But I am shouting at the back of her head. She has scurried.

Tap tap tap, go her boots. She is deaf to common sense, blind to facts. I watch her skirts swing as she bolts. I call to her fleeing figure.

'I shall not have you back if you shame me! Not this time! Do you hear!'

A body without a heart ~ Ovid

She has stung me with her accusation. Do I not weep nightly for Amen? Do I not daily accuse myself? Am I not a man who year-on-year cares for them all? Have I not done my utmost? Time and again? My heart could break for the pity of it.

I shall not intervene. Let her go to the institute. Let her tell the professor what's what. I should like to see that. How the professor will quake! By'n'by she will come begging to me for help. I shall abide. She'll return. Forbearance is my middle name.

Rookbird observes me with interest: he rasps, ticks and sidles to examine me in my dejected repose. I listen to his tuts, croaks, gargles. 'Well now,' I say. 'Enough.'

I wipe my eyes and pocket my pipe. 'This way shall nought get done!' I tell him, struggling to my feet. He bounces away, crawing raucously. It is the precise sound of my torment. Artful corvid. Noble consort. In this way do man and creature become fastened.

*

They accompany me, Tuesday and Pie Clark. What a forlorn trio! Beggarly, bound in grief. We drain jugs and pots, porter, stout and brandy. We toast our pal, Amen. We honour him and his timely contribution to scientific phenomena. To Amen! God rest his soul. And the others reply in recognition of the same. Amen. Amen. Amen.

Finding ourselves on White Lion Street, soothed by ale and stout, Tuesday and I note that the Ship tavern is so brightly lit you might imagine it is an actual vessel set sail towards you on a dark night. In a room therein, bull-dogs are set-to barking for the entertainment yet to come. Louder here than the dogs and wheels and harness rattle, is a woman's shrill laugh, on and on it goes, unguarded, lit by gin.

Around the next corner on darkened streets my thoughts begin to boil. Bella shall make a fool of me. Yes. A disaster awaits. The esteemed professor shall wonder that a man of my reputation cannot keep a woman's nose out of gentlemanly business. He shall consider me feeble (albeit Field Marshalls would quake in the windstorm of her temper).

Shall my reputation fall this way? Shall Bella drag me into the mud? For what? A spot of mesmerism, a pinch of levitation, a few guineas in the pot. What a bloody mischief. There is meat and gravy upon the professor's table each day and cinnamon puddings to follow.

I have not even mentioned the fruit pastries.

Bella is an impractical woman who keeps not a shred of common sense. She is wild as October storms. How I have loved so untamed a creature for so long I do not know.

~

Farewell to the fictions of the
poets ~ Ovid

No sooner do I arrive home and remove my hat before a fresh skirmish occurs.

An item in flight. Misses my head by a narrow margin. I swivel. A boot was it?

I am unsteady.

'Who threw it? Have you gone soft! Has she gone soft?'

'Oh, go lie down!' Bella yells.

Chaffy jay.

'Watch your mouth!' I shout it twice.

I shall not rise to it. She is restive on account of losing our previous quarrel.

'How is the professor?' I ask, chirpy of tone, turning on my heel.

It is this she deplores most. I have won this race tidily. She follows me.

'They would not let me see her. Yet I am her own sister. You must interfere!'

I turn. 'Interfere? Who am I to interfere with science? I bid you not meddle, yet you did.'

Hands upon her hips. Now her finger points.

'I shall do as I like! Ask anyone! Chippin' me!'

'I see you have entirely forgot you are employed by one of London's foremost,' I quip.

'Don't flatter yourself, Percival George. There are those who coin heavier than you.'

I halt at this. 'Name him.'

'And Flora?' she barks. 'Would you rather the shilling than she?'

'What! Have I not cared for her? For you? How many times over?'

Once Bella had a heart. Now it is all spout.

'Do you not have it all?' I say. 'Must I deliver more?'

'Don't fly to pieces!' she cries. 'Bit of chaff! Where's your spark? Flat man!'

She has the wit to inflame me. I shall not rise to it.

Bella scoops up the sewing and threads from the table. She turns to speak again yet I do not recognise her voice; some demon has choked it.

'Daft little man! All puff inside your head. You and your rotted bones! Who'd have you?'

'Now, now,' I reply. 'Settle down. This is gibberish.'

I walk away.

'Is it?' she says. And swings me a decent punch to the head.

I stumble sideways. A moment while I steady. And now my equilibrium is undone. She has raised a heat in me. 'What have we here?' I shout. 'A red-faced hag, well-shillinged, past her prime, ungrateful. A fright!'

'Will I show you then?' she says. 'Shall you see for your-self what I'll do?'

'Stuff your wailing,' I tell her. 'Now!'

'Come on, then.'

A woman who has lost her sense of propriety requires sensitive but firm handling. No shilly-shallying. I take hold of Bella by the arm and turn her so that I have a proper grip.

'There!'

A sharp smack on the backside, and another.

'Don't you dare touch me! Look at you, brimful of brandy while Flora suffers!'

She wheels around and hits me hard across the face. The evening's refreshments have oiled me, I take a moment to adjust.

'That's enough, now!' Tuesday calls out.

'Yes, that's enough!' I command.

'Have you lost your wits? Do you not see?' I protest. 'Flora is softly landed in the good professor's employ!'

She comes at me, fists up, and wallops me good again. My blood whips.

'Oh, I see!' I tell her. 'That's your game!' At which I hit her back. She lunges. And now we are fighting like dolly-mops, slapping and gasping.

'That'll be enough, now!' Tuesday grabs at us.

Ruby arrives, shrieking, jiggling on her toes. 'Come on, Bell! Pop him sideways!'

'Stop it! Ha ha! Stop!' Bird's voice, frantic, shrill.

'Enough! Enough!' Tuesday continues to shout. And now the dog is barking.

'Com' on, Bell!'

'Stop it! Stop!'

She hits me again, across the temple, hard with her fist.

'Dodge, Mister George! Remember to dodge!'

It is Jim calling out. I turn to him and she clobbers me again, another blow to the side of the head. And now my temper frays.

I do not recall taking hold of Bella, but I know that I swung hard for her. I remember her scream. The screams of others. The dog barking. Crow flapping. I recall turning to Tuesday and asking him to assist me.

'Brown, take my arm!'

And this is when Bella rushes at me. She hits me hard in my side. Ruby screams.

'There! Snipe! Slang! Vile little man!' Bella shouts.

I recoil. I push her away. Again she swings her fist into my side. I feel the thump, the burn.

'Don't you touch me again!' she shrieks.

The pain, sharp as a hornet's sting, twists fiercer. My hand finds nothing there, yet my legs weaken.

209

'Mister George!' Ruby runs to me, Bird follows. And here I note their faces alter.

There is blood arriving upon my clothes. She came at me with the sewing scissors.

I am stabbed. I hear myself say it aloud.

'I am stabbed.' Feeble, it sounds.

Ruby falls to her knees. 'Percy! Look. He is stabbed, see!'

'Hold your jaw,' I say. 'This is not a theatrical. Daft wench. Where is she?'

We turn to see that Bella has fled. 'Fetch her back!' I hear myself shout. 'Fetch her!'

She hoped to harm me, nothing more. I should've clung to her. Why didn't I?

I am bandaged, tightly bound. The bleeding is staunched. It burns at the site, yet the wound is not so deep. I ought to have hung on. Threatened her with a constable. A hiding she deserved. And now? Scarpered. No word since. I daresay Ruby and Bird have a clue yet their lips are sealed. Their voices follow me. 'Oh, Mister George! Wherever is she gone?'

As if they don't have the foggiest. Times such as these women bond tight; I hear them murmuring then hushing whenever I approach.

Where is she bolted? I suspect I already know.

I send Tuesday to fetch Flora from the institute.

'If Bella is there with her,' I tell him, 'bring them both home.'

What have I done to deserve the devil's own luck? I cannot tell. The wound is two punctures; one has the sharper nip, it throbs and burns. It might as well be Bella's own fangs.

Ruby finds the arse-wedge doctor up Caledonian Road

way. He arrives with his bag. Clink-clink. He applies a salve and bandages, he takes payment. He says it could take days. As if I have days to convalesce! I have a powder for the pain, though it has taken little effect.

I send Jim to Ferrières, in Clerk'nwell, to request he visit me here due to my being ill-disposed. No doubt it will cost a peg more.

I ask Bird for hymn sheets, so that I might sing to keep up the spirits.

She obliges. 'Hop-dilly, Sir Percival. Hum it in your gizzard,' she advises.

The afternoon is saved by a meat broth and *We Plough The Fields And Scatter*.

Followed by *Ride On, Ride On, In Majesty*, after which I sleep sound as a hound.

I am awoken by a sharp sensation, as if I am stabbed anew. A north wind is here, black rain, the streets are slicked. Bella has been gone a day and a half. And something else is different. I sense it immediately.

Flora. She is returned.

She sits, quiet as a dormouse, sewing by the fire as if she'd never left.

I want to call out to her. Yet I am cautious. I do not wish to disrupt her composure nor frighten her with my injury. None are as frail as Flo when it comes to calamity.

The wound throbs, bites. I catch my breath.

'Flora!' I gasp, as cheerfully as I can.

She turns. Her eye-glance is steady. She smiles. A miracle. A blessing.

'Flora,' I repeat. I move towards her. It is a gift to see the blueness of her eyes. I place a kiss upon her head, and she whispers my name. *Mister George.*

'Where is Bella?' I ask. She does not reply: returns to her stitching. I shall not press it.

Tuesday hunches in a chair, a face like a river rat. He grieves for Amen. A week now. Nothing is the same. I take a powder. Restless I am, used-up. Must I merely loiter here and fret? I cannot wait here any longer for that pyke, Ferrières. Presently I fetch my coat and hat.

On the street I am wild of hair, collar a-flap. Owing to the wound I am obliged to use my walking cane. All about shines with a dark grease, horses slide and fall. One is down on the Goswell Road, it will not stand and a crowd is gathered. Without my cane I should be tumbled beside it in the mud, the whole world looking on.

Groans, whistles and hoots from the river. The temperature turns skittish hot, cold. I remove my coat only to replace it moments later, as if a victim of the fever.

I find a wall to lean against. A river bird drags over the water, wailing like an infant. I must catch my breath. How I gasp! My strength is gone.

The travails of my royal midget shall distract from my own. I shall lay down the coin to hear how fortune will bless or blight my miniature. In my head a picture forms ... I am rigged in wig and satins, running over parquet and marble and laughing at kings. Time runs backwards and I see myself anew. Not a man but a child. Not English but French. Not here but there. And I am stranger than a sphinx.

I find Ferrières at his bench, his face turned to gilt in the gaslight.

Upon seeing me he hurries to take my arm and assist me to a chair.

'Did you not see my boy, Jim?'

'We are busy, Monsieur!' he replies. As if mending time is all that matters, when time itself is the culprit, playing merry havoc with us all. On the other hand p'raps he has counted his shillings and concluded that by now he could buy a farm. Or two. He fetches me a jug of stout before he begins and I am obliged.

Château de Lunéville, 1749–1764

Émilie once explained that a scientist, who was also a priest, discovered that a plant may breathe just like a man. This same man discovered mysterious pressures in the blood of living things. He bled sheep and horses to death in England to demonstrate the mysterious fact, for which he was awarded a medal. God forgive me but now that Saint-Lambert has fallen ill I pray that he will bleed to death. I send a whispered curse.

Émilie visits his room in her billowing cloak, like a demon, like an angel. She carries a herb soup and a wing of partridge to him. Everyone speaks of it.

A storm turns the sky black. The wind laments in the trees. In the morning a mist stands. A single rook calls. My prayers have not risen.

Together they picnic in the forest, they row upon the Grand Canal. I follow, I observe. I watch them disappear into the mist upon horseback.

She gives Saint-Lambert a portrait concealed in a watch. I pity the Hawk. Years before she gave an identical one to him. He displays it with pride almost daily.

The Hawk becomes kindly towards me. We share an injury. We hold one another's gaze. Now he does not whip me about the face with his hat.

'Help me,' he says.

I do. I lead him to a little boudoir at the end of a cold corridor, where he discovers them together upon a sofa, entwined, discussing neither poetry nor philosophy.

The Hawk becomes enraged. I leave him there, his voice rising against the walls.

I creep away. I feel his words spread hotly in my throat, as if they were my own.

Mademoiselle de Thil is summoned from Paris.

In September the child is born to Émilie, a daughter, Stanislas-Adélaïde.

They lay her upon a volume of geometry.

She is baptised in the chapel before she is put out to nurse.

Six days later Émilie dies of a fever.

Arouet's cries carry across the bosquets, allées and canals. So terrible are his shrieks rooks lift from trees and grazing herds raise their heads.

I am just a boy, a story ought not end this way. I run to Stanislas.

In the chapel we lay ourselves upon the stone. Together we weep, we pray.

The Hawk, in his grief, leaves Lunéville three days later. He does not ever return.

Long ago. I remember it still. My devilry is vanished of late, some affliction grips me. My dancing legs, my wit, charm, impudence, all are fled. I am buckled, withered. I have grown weary.

I am put to bed.

Matilde brings soup, bread, Listlen biscuits. My bones are firewood, my lungs, sacking. Within my ribs my heart writhes. Shall I be an old man at twenty-two? I weep.

I dream my bones walk from the room. I listen to them clatter across the floor.

*

My king brings me his completed *Masterpieces of the Beneficent Philosopher.*

I hold it in my hands, it is a stout item, the pages stiff as wings.

He has forgiven me. I forgive him. He is a king. He is sorrowful.

The Polish jadebird has left for Paris.

Now we are two once more, he and I. He offers to read his essay to me.

I fall asleep.

St Mary, Islington, 1879

My French dwarf ails. Though he dallies a century behind, his future appears gloomy. Meanwhile, brown as brick is the sky over London and a grumble of thunder can be heard on the river. Shouts and bells on the street, horses are urged on. A chill damp has gripped.

I take a powder for pain. The wound, I note, swells. It throbs. Dew sparkled the wool collar of my coat this morning, albeit it hung by the fireside the night.

Do I shiver at the prospect of ill luck? Is my story to become tragic hereabouts?

Impossible. I am a nib, a cove. A bang-up king. Gentlemen nobs and professors of high rank seek me out. My name was coined to linger, my reputation to endure. A better day awaits around the corner. I tip three powders into a jug of cognac and drink.

I call out to the others, 'I shall be off out on my business, then.' Each and all are subdued. 'The sun will deliver his compliments shortly!' I add, for cheer.

Ruby affects not to listen. A state of sorrow has settled on her. She misses Bella. She grieves for Amen. Her stare troubles me with its lack of enquiry. She holds a broom but does not rise from the chair to use it but only picks at her shawl and whispers old rhymes.

Rookbird perches on the back of her chair, fusses his feathers, rasps to himself.

I am quite maddened by the sound of Jim snivelling, Ruby sighing, Bird blethering.

I spot Pie Clark, my remaining dwarf, sat on the edge of the stove smoking a long pipe, like a hobgoblin. The cognac has lit a fire within me.

'Shall we have a rousing song?' I call out. 'To blow away the rags of grief? To bolt some steel to our hearts? How about *Drunken Ned*? Well?' A pause.

'Who shall play fiddle?' slurs Pie, pipe stem between his teeth.

And his name fills our thoughts instantly: Amen Steps.

'I can bang the drum!' Jim startles us all by leaping up from the floor where he is cleaning cages. Nobody heeds him.

Bird uncurls from a chair. 'It's not the time, Mister George,' she says, 'albeit p'raps tomorrow. We shall wear ribbons and be gay, only not today. Bearing in view of what's-what of late.'

'Very well,' I reply.

'Bird,' I say, considering her. 'Sweet girl. Shall you try the cabinet? A gifted performer like you?'

'No. She shan't.' Ruby is on her feet, hair a-fly, sending the crow skipping.

216

'Ah!' I comment. 'She breathes! She speaks! She lives!'

'She is owed four days' wages!' Ruby calls back.

Sharp as knives, my girls.

'Five,' mumbles Pie. 'We are owed five.'

Jim stumbles at me, his brush dripping, his eye in a spasm of twitching. 'Are you to The Hat? Shall I accompany you, Mister George?'

'No, for the merciful love of Christ. Look at the floor! Get the cages done.'

I turn.

'Ruby? Here's enough for buns.' I hand her the coins with a wink. She curtsies in a grotesque mockery and flashes her teeth.

'Charmed,' I say.

'I'll go to The Hat with you,' mutters Pie.

'None shall go!' I say. 'God above! Look at the clock.'

Is my heart a stone? It is not. But a crowd shall not gather for nought, nor a show perform itself neither. And who shall chase the demons of grief away but me? My duty is done. Coins shall tumble.

'Where is Rose Burton?' I ask. None reply. She has not come for laundering, nor yesterday.

'Smallpurse!' I call him. He knows his name. He hops, flaps. His glassy eye finds me.

'Where is she, rookbird?' He blinks, considers.

I do recall that Rose, upon observing my injuries on Thursday, closed her eyes in an attitude of theatrical contempt and said, 'You have brought it all upon yourself, George Percy.'

'It is Percy George!' I cried. 'Why do you belittle me?'

To which she answered, with flaring of both nostrils, 'The Lord hears not your shrieks, George, but only your prayers.'

217

God in Heaven. Many prayers have I intoned at night concerning Rose Burton and am splendidly punished for them now. Suffice to say my passion for her has dwindled and quietly died.

With the assistance of my cane I walk. My pace is timid, excruciating. Why so slow to heal? Penance perhaps. The cost is dear. Heavenly Father, have mercy on a repentant man, Amen. Does the Lord see me shambling the muddy streets to the tap of a stick? Where skips that artful dodge whom once they called the bang-up king? Here I am.

I halt. Distinctly, I hear music playing. The fog has crept and crouched. Barge horns sound, boatmen are blinded. The river is chilled and its currents drag at the mudsides. Yet music plays on, I hear it, fiddle, drum and whistle, pursuing me.

Tap tap. I shall gasp and stumble towards the sound of my dwarf's enchanting voice. My good man, Ferrières, shall deliver the imp upon his tongue. Only my miniature brings solace. He alone is the remedy.

Château de Lunéville, 1764

A play by Palissot: *Les Philosophes*.

It is performed especially for King Stanislas and his guests at the opening, in Nancy, of the Palace Royale. I am wrapped in skins and laid upon a daybed beside the king.

The play is amusing. Diderot is mocked! Helvétius is mocked! The Hawk is spared!

Crispin, the natural man, crawls upon all fours and eats leaves. Everyone knows it is Rousseau. Ha ha! They say that, when he saw it at the Comédie Française, the Hawk laughed longest and loudest. Afterwards, they say, he affected to be mortally offended on behalf of the other philosophers! I miss him. I would embrace him. Grief has entwined us.

With a blade I am bled. I weep, for it pierces me hotly. Doctor Rönnow proclaims my veins unsatisfactory, insists they must be strengthened by further bleeding.

The room tumbles, as if some fool uprighted himself while gondoliering upon the Grand Canal. Ha ha! Yet there is no amusement here but only a whirling of walls and chairs.

While the blood drips I squirm and whimper. Doctor Rönnow speaks of the inclement weather. The sky is yellow in the north, he says, foaming over the eastern hills. He says tomorrow the weather ought to improve in the west. Thereafter, he tells me I have an accumulation of black bile. He will administer ash bark to purge and reduce the bile.

This never fails.

My king prays. I pray. Our prayers rise sweetly. I watch them drift across the room, out over the trees and up to the soft-clouded Heavens. Together His Majesty and I drink coffee, bitter as cardamon, beside the window where we may view the gardens and distant hills. I kiss his hands. He lights his pipe. Sunlight illuminates the swag of smoke and His Majesty, blurred in his bright clothes, within. There can be no more than love in this narrow life, for it is all.

A frosted sky. A cold brass sun. Madame de Graffigny has returned from Paris in her carriage that is hung in Spanish lace. I am carried to the window by Matilde to watch. The horses below blow the breath of dragons. Boxes are unloaded, foot-men hurry left and right. Madame has purchased Dutch linen, Persian silks, laces, fans. A valet carries a box filled with roses and pairs of billing doves. I observe a balding parrot, hunched miserably in his cage, and a vision of myself appears in my mind: wigless, frail, legs a-dangle, a puff of hair upon my scalp, my curving spine, my small hot eyes.

I dream of my mother. I dream of home: orchards, meadows, ploughlands. Forest, hills, lakes. The slate-roofed villages. The fires burning. A poacher's full moon. A rabbit opened by my father with his hunting knife, skinned, and laid upon the fire. At her sewing under smoke-stained rafters is my mother. Michaelmas. Charred potatoes from the fire embers. The blacksmith and a priest and my father, with his pipe, playing cards. I hear again the springtime warblers, plovers and kites, the winter grebes and pochards.

I recall Montesquieu's death. He did not conduct himself as clever men do, with rapid gestures and ready argument, but only as a gentleman of deep curiosity and steady disposition. He could be roused but I never saw him disordered. I recall his gentle blind gaze and timid smile. I speak a prayer.

While thinkers die royals are born. Another great-grandchild for my king-the-duc. Maria Josepha of Saxony gives birth to Princess Élisabeth at Versailles.

I am bled once more. I am bandaged. I float into sleep.

The maid brings chocolate. She places it on the little rognon table. She is wearing a new bonnet. I do not know her name.

'Please,' she says. 'For strength.'

St Mary, Islington, 1879

> It is not easy to fly without
> wings ~ Plautus

Hold the funeral horses! God in His divine mercy has shown pity on us all.

Bella is home. The sun rises. Good fortune is returned!

I observe her from the corner of my eye, murmuring in a low voice to the girls, peeling an apple with her small knife. The bruise upon her hand darkens each time I glance. Her hair is swept up in a tidy style, a new gleam is about her.

Sweet Flora, returned home almost three days, is cured of the manias. She is returned to her whispers and numbers, her twirls and skips, her slow smiles and baffled stares. Like a girl who never frowns, Flo cannot recall the merest discontentment.

I wager'd it all along. I spoke it yet none listened.

'I wager'd it!' I call out. 'I wager'd Flo would return shiny as a new penny!' The others pay me no heed. They bustle with private business.

'Bella!' I cry. 'D'you hear me?'

I watch her pretend not to listen as she sprinkles seed for the doves, slams a cupboard, chatters and fetches her shawl.

Is she contrite? She angles her head and will not meet my eye. P'raps she will beg my forgiveness, meek as a mouse. How genial. P'raps she could not withstand our separation. P'raps she needs me more than she imagined. I am buoyed. She has crawled home upon her hands and knees. I am content. Charity I have by the barrel in my heart. I shall forgive her! Albeit . . . not just yet. She shall make her apology first, whereupon I shall take her in my arms and pardon her for the wickedness and violence. Tender, it shall be! Though she will resist. Then she will yield! Percy, she will say, I love you more than any man who lived. I shall not demean you again. There. What a mild scene. She loves me. I shall forgive her.

I listen for her voice. I can no longer catch the sound of it. Where is she?

A thing with teeth and appetite, the wound chews at my side, it gnaws until I cry out.

Jim, the lurk, is fearful. He rocks and twitches and mutters to himself. Ruby bides with me, lays on a poultice, calms my groaning. 'Where is Bella?' I enquire.

'Upstairs. She needs a spell alone. Do not fret. All in good time, Mister George.'

The door bangs.

'Blessings and cheer, Bird here.' She has brought me a drop of warm milk from the Welsh girl on Cross Street. 'You are a pigeon,' I tell her. And Bird coos, obligingly. She calls out.

'How do I seem in these?' She is wearing Amen's coat and bowler.

'Take 'em off,' Ruby instructs. 'Put them back, before I make you.'

'Yes, your please-sir, ladyship. In a tilly-tally spit, dear.'

'Now!'

'Calm yourself! Don't get a fizz on!'

Jim holds out his hands. 'I'll have 'em.'

Bird jumps. 'Cost you five for them live-in-the-brine, sir!'

Ruby closes her eyes. 'No-one takes his things! Is that clear!'

'Clear-very-dear. Very hoo-ha-hat.' Bird dashes the gloves out of sight.

'Hush!' I call. 'Does nobody heed the sore and injured laid among you?'

'Aye. Shut your lid, all!' cries Ruby.

Smallpurse mutters at the window; he watches the street. 'Does he look for the reaper?' I ask. Nobody replies.

I have drunk a pot of brandy. P'raps it was gin. Manias. Are they not a mild affliction? Flora is not stabbed abed and laid out like a carcass, as I am. A mania is a fimsy, no? Chased away in an eyeblink. I wager I had a mania not three weeks ago. Ale and a song shall take care of it. And yet I am grateful to the professor for the medical assistance. What scientifical times are these. What bewildering feats of astoundment are upon us. How fresh is our time. What year is it? Eighteen hundred and thereabouts. I pray my wounds will heal. Bella shall throw her arms about my neck and thank me for her blessings. Top brass. I should dance a polka if I had the strength.

I bid Tuesday fetch the pen and journal. I take a powder for the pain, washed down with a dark cognac. I can no longer walk without my cane.

'Fashion some new words to write,' I tell Tuesday. 'I cannot speak aloud today.'

He dips the pen. The sound of his scratches upon the page soothes me.

I cast myself into the first gently lapping wave of sleep when, in a door slam, Ferrières arrives.

In my hour of need the Frenchman is persuaded by the clink of coins. Tick-tock. He has fetched himself sharpish today.

'Furrier,' I rasp. At the foot of my sickbed he stands, shifty as a butcher at the ballet. It gladdens me to see him looking so ill at ease. Ha. I tell him so.

'Furrier,' I instruct him. 'Read on. I suffer. And my dwarf ails too.'

And he begins.

Château de Lunéville, 1764

Doctor Rönnow listens to the pulse beats. An excess of blood, he says. A pronounced fever. A bad fermentation within the blood.

As he speaks two horns grow from his head and his eyes turn onyx black. Ha ha! With interest I observe him. Skin from his left hand falls away, revealing bird bones and feathers and long tapered claws.

I have the fever.

A purge of bark, resins and amber empties me of all but my weary soul. I suffer from a profusion of yellow bile. An enema of vinegar is introduced. I am dosed with quinine.

I suffer from dysentery. Poor humours. A syrup of violets and white whale meat is given. Afterwards, a powder of chalk, coral and syrup of ivy.

I am bled again.

In freezing water I am bathed. I cry out. My skin burns. My bones turn to stone. My teeth rattle a terrible violence, as if they mean to devour me, bite off my own head and burst from my skull, bouncing like pearls.

For the cough I receive a medicine made from the droppings

224

of white hens and a tincture of fox lungs and birch to which has been added the blood of a he-goat.

I would prefer a sweet-smelling cure, a syrup made from nutmeg, honey and lime.

The king arrives with an abbé. At the foot of my bed they pray. I sleep.

I dream of the Hawk: 'Bébé,' he says. 'Where is your flute? Your joie? Your dancing feet?' I reach out for him. He smiles.

How long have I lain? My fingers are become ancient willows. My head is a plinth.

Peasants come to be blessed. *Ora pronobis Deum.* Are they peasants?

No, it is Doctor Rönnow and my king-the-duc, an abbé, a bishop, a cardinal.

My willow hand signs the Cross upon them. *Christum Dominum nostrum.*

My hands are become Crucifixes. Do I weep? A wind is here, the room is blown.

They talk in murmurs. I raise my finger. They are silenced.

Quia surrexit Dominus vere.

What floats on high? My bones! How they hang upon the air. Alleluia! Ha ha!

Doctor Rönnow! Au nom de Dieu!

I observe the doctor's eyes are become smooth marble! Blank as Apollo's! His wig melts, drips as candle wax, onto the floor.

My heart is an eel grown too big for its cave; it squirms. My teeth are diamonds.

My eyes? Sapphires. My mouth? A single garnet.

At my head stands a blind dove.

Music drifts from my ribs wherein plays a violinist, no taller than a dragonfly. A dwarf within a dwarf. Bienheureusement.

A single flame stands upon my bed.

St Mary, Islington, 1879

My eyes are closed. Ferrières imagines I sleep. He has stopped speaking the words aloud.

'Continue,' I hear myself whisper.

My eyelids are sealed but he cannot refuse me, being that I am horribly stabbed.

I hear him sigh. I command my eyes to open, my voice to speak.

'Continue, please.'

'There is no more to tell,' Ferrières says. 'We have reached the conclusion. The dwarf must have died.'

'Died?'

'There remains just a few lines, no more,' he says.

'Read them.'

He reads.

Nicolas Ferry died upon the evening of 8th June 1764.

At the order of His Polish Majesty, King Stanislas, the bones of Nicolas Ferry were entrusted to the Comte de Saint-Florentin, secretary of foreign affairs, for safe passage to the Comte de Buffon at the King's Cabinet in Paris, while the remains were buried at Lunéville.

The body was dissected in the presence of Doctor Rönnow, and the flesh removed from the bones. His Polish Majesty, attentive to the progress of science, and encouraged by the Comte de Tressan, ordered that the skeleton of Nicolas Ferry be preserved and mounted. A study of the skeleton was written by the Comte de Buffon.

Signed, Peter Joseph de La Pimpie, Chevalier de Solignac, Secretary to His Majesty King Stanislas I of Poland. 1st July 1764

'Voilà. The fairy tale is over.' Ferrières closes the book.

I do not respond. My dwarf is gone. Scarpered, along with Steps. Along with Bella, yet, unlike she, he will not return. My mind falls, a kite without wind.

Bébé. Beloved dwarf. Sweet boy. Where are you? 'Where is he?' I demand to know.

I hear feet moving around my bed. I picture Bébé, my jaunty imp, a young man, yet he may recline within a teacup. And a roaring begins. A terrible din. I gasp to breathe and I realise the sound is me. I hear my own voice rising, howling.

'Where is my boy? Where is my boy? Where is my boy!'

No answer comes. Only shuffling feet, murmuring voices, boots on the stairs. A door slams.

I gasp. Do I weep? Ferrières is nearby, he clears his throat. I have embarrassed him.

I collect myself.

'Furrier?' I say. I speak to keep him by me. 'Furrier?'

'I am here.'

'We shall not find a replacement,' I rasp. 'A remarkability, par excellence. Was he not?'

I wait for him to admire my foreign phrasing.

'There is only one, Monsieur.'

'Have you spoke the words of my dwarf exactly as they were writ, Furrier?'

'I have performed the task, Monsieur.'

'We have wound back your broken clocks a hundred years. Have we not?'

'Perhaps,' he replies.

'Aye. We have!' I confirm.

227

He lays the edition upon the bed.

'Perhaps?' I repeat.

'Perhaps I tell you the story you wish to hear, Monsieur George.'

I wipe my eyes. What is he saying? Blether-blether-chirrup. Does he not see a stricken man, an unblemished hard-toiling man, laid abed before him through the malice of happenstance?

'Speak up,' I say.

'My translation is perfect. A little invention is part of the translator's art.'

'Invention?'

'Here and there, perhaps, I have perfected, Monsieur.'

I must steady the tide in my blood. 'Furrier. Have you or have you not translated the dwarf thoroughly, as agreed, for which I paid you handsomely? Yes or no?'

'Of course, Monsieur.'

'We are obliged.'

'On occasion . . .' He hesitates, '. . . perhaps I shine the translator's lamp upon a darkened page.'

'Do I understand you? Is your translation true or false?'

'I have played the game, Monsieur.'

'What game?'

Is he soothed by my tribulation? How French! His moral superiority is haughtily played.

'Does it not occur to you, Monsieur George, that your dwarf, too, invents? How would you tell the story of your life, Monsieur? Without invention? Would that not be a little dull?'

His words hang in the air. I consider them. My journal. Am I truthful? To a fault? Always?

'Good day, Monsieur.' He reaches for his hat.

'Good day to you, Furrier.'

I listen to his footsteps.

'You are a gentleman!' I call out. 'My French pyke'art. I shall miss you, my friend!'

I realise it is true.

Ferrières' footsteps return. He leans at my bedside. He places his hand upon my shoulder.

'It is your story, Monsieur. I have honoured it,' he says kindly. 'I wish you well. Good day.'

I examine his face. I remember that first glimpse, lit by gas, bronze and gold. And the sound of his clocks: tick tick tick. The frantic minutes, days and hours. Counting us down.

'Good day, Furrier,' I say.

A tear creeps into my beard, and another. But for the pain I should be ashamed.

'I shall miss you,' I say again.

Barely do I have the opportunity to mourn my dwarf, no sooner has my clock-fiddler departed than Jim creeps in. Like a lurk, he waits. Twitch-twitch goes his eye.

He holds out a paper.

'What is it?' I gasp.

Like a halfwit at the Easter Fair, Jim jinks, contorts, wrings his hands.

'Just say it!' I bark.

'From the professor, Mister George,' he says. 'A delivery from the professor.' And he covers his twitching eye with his hand as he passes the envelope to me.

'Brought here by Mister Cox,' he clucks.

Cox. Like a bad penny.

'Do not tell him I lay abed, knifed!' I say. 'Let him think I am gone gambling at a gentleman's salon. Tell him receipts are up. Off you go.'

'Cox,' bleats Jim. 'He said it is settlement for Bella. Upon her own instruction, delivered.'

He nods, coughs. And out he lopes, a broken hat stand.

Cox crept to my door. What's this? Doubtless he examined the contents with his pink eye. This is misfortune. For Bella? I take a breath and open the envelope. Six guineas I find.

'She is gone, Percy.'

Ruby's face, a sketch of dismay. You may not even admire her freckles, so pale is her skin, eyes glassy, a hand upon her cheek, hair tumbled around her neck.

'No, no. What? I saw her myself. Bella is returned to beg my forgiveness. Send her in.'

'She is gone!' Ruby repeats.

And as she turns to go she shrieks it again, *'She is gone!'* Frightening me monstrously and rousing the pain to its heights once more.

I cry for mercy, the suffering is cruel. They urge me to try the hospital. Do they suppose I will allow some pin-eyed butcher set about me with his bag of knives and a rag of ether? From my bed I swing my cane like a sabre, so that they cannot take me by force.

'Stop that now! Look who it is to see you, Mister George. Look! Happy as a hen's egg.'

I stop. I hear myself wheeze. I open a single eye.

Flora.

'There, now,' says Ruby. 'We shall all be steadied in a tick, won't we?'

The girls flutter out. Their murmurings continue beyond the door.

'Flora.' It is a consolation to say her name. 'Give me

your hand,' I breathe. I cannot prevent an old man's sob. A fool I am.

A shy smile she gives.

'Blessings shall come, Mister George,' she says. 'Shan't they?'

'Flora. I meant no harm. You must believe me. Forgive me. I shall ask for nothing until you say I am forgiven.'

The sky bursts and several inches of torrential rain fall upon London.

Bella. I think of her. She ought to be home in this weather. She ought to be home with me, where she belongs. I shall return the six guineas to the professor, for I don't doubt the institute is where she is gone to ground.

We are assailed by wind and rain. I think to look for my Holy Bible. A man might have a quote, times such as these, yet I cannot locate it. Amen would've spoke three by now.

Whole streets are disappearing and re-fashioning themselves as rivers. Thunder overhead, a sudden bang. The girls' screams come next, followed by more thunder, a stumbling crash this time and a blaze of lightning.

Between the flashes, rumbles and bangs I find my hat and cane. My steps are lead-footed. Only rookbird notices me leave.

The raging weather and discomfort from the wound bids me creep, as slow as an insect, inspecting as I go for holes that would tumble me to the ground. The fog is swollen with rain. It blinds, chokes. There is panic. Carriages, pedestrians, carts, all are in disarray. I cannot tell if I am lost. I step as if I am creeping along a perilous cliff path. I see only the reassuring silver-top flash of my cane through the fog, as it guides me.

*

A servant opens the door. I hesitate. Water flows from the brim of my hat. Bogged and marshed I stand, a creature from the river. I'd hoped for the professor.

I spy the staircase within, the mahogany bannister lit by the lamps and the glow of a fire. My breath is gone. All I can manage is her name. I speak it.

'Bella. Bella.' I tap my cane. Then I shout. *'Bella!'*

I am aware of figures, voices, out of sight, within. Beyond the servant I see someone hurriedly approaching in his shirtsleeves. Cox.

'John!' I croak. 'Cox! My friend! It is me, Percy.'

I am sufficiently rain-soaked that I fear he might mistake me for a beggar. But no, he speaks before he reaches me. The downpour bids me lean to catch his words.

'Go,' he says. 'You must leave. The professor has guests.'

'Yes,' I reply. 'Of course. But, Cox,' I say, 'I am here to accompany Bella home.'

'She is working,' he replies. 'Off you slope. Go on. She is resident here.'

'Resident? Working? For whom?'

Cox leans out of the door, half-closes it behind him. He shouts over the clatter of the rain. 'She volunteered herself. In exchange for your cabinet girl. Bella is working for the professor. Now then. Time to vanish, Percy. Off you go!'

'You allowed this?'

'I am being patient! Hear me! She came of her own free will. You took payment today.'

'Yes,' I gasp. 'But I was not consulted. I had no prior warning. Here!'

I offer him the six guineas, wrapped against the damp. 'Here!' I repeat. 'Take it!'

Cox edges out of the rain, patting his splashed sleeve,

wiping his hair. 'Now then! That's enough! The professor is busy. You are paid. Keep the money. Off you go. Shoo. Go on!'

'I do not give permission! Bella is not available! She is unsuitable for this kind of appointment!' But I am shouting at the door, now firmly closed.

'Bella Wickes is not currently for hire!'

Not Heaven will render ineffectual
what is past . . .

That creaking sound is a cry in my throat. My head burns to ice, cracks apart. I shiver.

Ruby and Bird move about the room, blethering, 'Bloody foolish idea. Soaked to the skin. Dear me. Look at the state. Why would you? What on earth?'

Tuesday waits, frowning, head bowed.

A sensation prevails, as if pins are scouring my veins. In my hand lies a weight yet when I look it grasps nought but air. Curious. Heavy blood hauls me under to sleep.

The doctor brings a stronger ointment and more powders. Ruby shows him in.

'A little chicken tea,' the doctor says.

I vomit. The doctor approves. 'The fever will purge,' he says. 'It is progress.'

'Bring me inside!' I say. 'I am frozen.' My voice is a child's plea.

'But you are inside,' they say. 'You are abed, Percy. It's the fever, is all.'

〜

233

> ... nor undo what the fleeting hour has
> once carried away with it ~ Horace

I wake, cry out. I drift. The head throbs, my bones prick.

The wound is tight as leather, it chews upon me, observes me with its animal eye. A foul smell emits, the stink of my own troubles. What is the time? The day? I see my leg is darkening to the colour of late cherries.

I think of her. Merciful God. She will kick and argue. She is too contrary for the professor. They shall have to discipline her. This will reveal itself to be a shoddy turn of events.

Tuesday brings beef tea. He sits with pen and journal. He thinks p'raps the fever is cooled. My strength is gone.

I cannot drink. The girls stand at my bedside with Jim. I listen to the mutterings of Ruby and Bird.

'Have I died?' I whisper. 'Is that why you each look on with orphaned expression?'

It is my wellbeing they fret upon. Would I care for a song? A powder? Ought I sleep?

The wound festers. My senses fray. My mind is wax. I am horribly swelled. I have an inkling of what shall follow ... Presently the fever shall roar a final time.

'Out,' I say. 'All of you. Out, Jim. Look to the girls.'

Once I charged a troupe of Remarkables. Fine they were, cut from paper. Their home was my boot. The bang-up king I was, even then. My paper players: see them leap, flit, dance and tumble. What talents. Peerless! Such dazzling careers! When they were damaged, torn, bent, I cut them anew. Began afresh. Nought else is as easily mended.

He has paid for her in guineas. She who is priceless. She who would not be bought.

234

I call her name. Where is she? My thoughts spill. I cry out. Why does she torment me?

I call her. Why does she not come? Bella!

'I am here, Percy.' She steps from the shadow on the floor.

I hear her breath catch as she reaches me. Her eyes are wept red.

'Sweet girl, do you weep for me?'

I am cheered at the thought. How I long for her compassion.

A flute, I hear, gentle as moonlight. A flock of dark birds swoop from the ceiling.

'The wound,' I say. 'It pains me. Shall we pray together?' I reach for Bella.

I close my eyes. 'Lord God, our merciful Father in Heaven,' I begin.

She makes no sound. I open one eye in time to see her walk through the wall.

'Give us Your comfort, we beg—'

I stop. A fiddle plays. A whistle. I hear it. The room fills with the sound of birds, or is it the roar of water? The voice of a child. Clouds run over the sun, a darkening.

And there, at the foot of the bed, no higher than the bedstead, stands my French dwarf.

Bébé.

I try to speak his name but my voice is vanished, bubbles and gargles is all I have.

The French dwarf observes me with interest and suspicion. What quick blue eyes!

My miniature! My prankish dwarf! Will he speak? Will he dance? He approaches.

He is dainty, powdered as a harlequin. There is a sharp smell of nutmeg.

'Are you the king?' he asks, in his Punch and Judy voice.

I nod.

He laughs.

'I am the king,' I confirm, as nobly as I may.

'Well,' he squeaks. 'I am your humble servant, my king-the-duc. Ha ha!'

He bows deeply. I blink. I smile. When I look again he is vanished.

Cries and rattles upon the street yet the house is silenced. Are they all disappeared? Where?

Fled to Dick Fisher? Surely not.

'You wished to see me?' She stands by the wall, hands folded.

'Bella?'

'Percy George.'

A vision? Must be. Was she here before? Not exactly. A vision then? I wait.

She moves closer, touches the blanket. Upon her face I note an expression of concern.

'Calm yourself,' I whisper. 'I will be well again. You are not to blame.'

If she is a vision it is a sweet one. Bella, my own. Shall I take her in my arms? Surely now we shall be reconciled. Is this the moment?

She does not meet my eye. Her sorrow pierces me.

'Here are arms,' I say. 'Lay yourself in this embrace. You shall be loved. I swear it. You shall be happy.'

Shall I lure her? I know how. *'Give a man,'* I quaver, *'a girl he can love,'* raspily I sing it, *'As I, O my love, love thee,'* till I have no more breath.

The weight of her in my arms. How I have longed for it. She is with me, my Bell.

Yet here the sweetness changes. She lifts her head from my chest to look directly at me.

Her eyes are hot wax. Her teeth are canine. I freeze. She speaks. *No son of mine will prance the boards theatrical with bangtails and Marys*, she rumbles. A deep voice. His. My father. *I shall put a stop to it!* she growls. *I will punish you once only! I will do a proper job, so that you will always remember.* She stands, her back to me, brushes down her skirts. I think, Oh merciful God protect me. The walls are alight, I note. All about is soft with flames. The floor is ash. She turns. She speaks . . . *You shall not touch him again!* It is the breathy voice of my mother. *If you do, I will kill you*, she gasps. I look at her directly. And her eyes turn to pearls.

The fever withdraws. I disperse three powders in a jug of gin and drink it down.

The girls are weeping. Is calamity visiting us here once more?

I call for Tuesday. He sits by me. He speaks the words. I listen.

'A girl was dragged from the river. She was found in the mud tides by the pier at Allhallow's, beyond Southwark Bridge. The girls are panicked. You might prepare yourself.'

'Prepare?'

'In the event . . .'

'What event?'

'God forbid the unfortunate girl may be Bella,' he says.

And I see that he fears the worst. Yet how? Why would? Ought I to know? I see it now.

Doubtless she would not tolerate the discipline. P'raps they were obliged to use the restraint chair. A freezing bath? Were punishments inflicted? Purgatives?

I am the inventor of this catastrophe. She is right. I am a simple, savage little man. I have managed nothing with proficiency. I have created mishaps, horrors, and lost those whom I loved. I don't like to think of her. Did she run through streets? Did she stumble? Shout?

Was she afraid? Where was I, Bella? Your bang-up king?

A pain in my legs travels, forks and splits my chest, as lightning splits a tree. My bones boil, soften. A roar gathers within my head. I burn.

'Rookbird?' I cry. He ticks and gargles.

He is stood upon his pin legs. He jumps closer. 'Mister George,' he mutters. His inky eye observes. 'I shall abide with you,' he says.

I reach to touch him. His eye is a mirror. I see myself reflected, tilting, weepy as a beggar.

'Look who's here!' he cries.

'Percy George. Fancy finding you.'

I turn.

There she stands, in her best hat and shawl.

'Stand back!' I say. 'Is it you?' I gasp.

'Well, well. Ain't you the shilling?' she says. 'On the deathbed, are we?'

'Is it you?' I say. 'I must know. I've had visitations. Visions! Here. In this room. Twice.'

Bella gives me her hand. 'Here I am. Touch me.'

'We feared you drowned.'

'Drowned? Dear me, no. I'm too quick for that.'

She kneels by the bed. I take her hand; our fingers knot.

'That'd be some poor soul with no-one and nothing,' she says.

'Bella, is this you? Oh please let it be. God, let it be you.'

'It's me, Percy. See?' She moves closer and her breath is warm. 'Hush your fretting. Budge up.' She pulls off her shawl and climbs into the bed beside me, boots and all.

238

'There now,' she says. '*Give a man a girl*,' breathily she sings. 'See? It's me. No other. 'Well?' She nods for me to sing the next line.

I open my mouth. A gargle.

She kisses my knuckle. 'I am here,' she says.

How I have dreamt of this, I think.

'Forgive me, Bell,' I rasp.

She wraps around me. Tenderly, we lie.

'We have wound back the clock,' I say.

'We have.'

'No other woman but you have I loved.'

'None other would suffer you,' she says. Her eyebrow jinks.

I kiss her fingers. I consider what I might give her, my few items.

'My journal,' I whisper.

'Don't fret,' she says. 'I'll keep it.'

'Bella. Here under the mattress, with my knife, is a purse of money. Have it. Use it.'

She sits up and looks at me. She squeezes my hands.

'Where'd you like to be, Percy?' she asks. 'Will you rest at St Mary's?'

'No. Don't put me in the grave, Bell. I shall be alone. Don't part us again.'

'Well then?'

'Find a spot for me here,' I say. 'Near to you. I should like to be close by. Unforgotten.'

She smiles. 'Percy George,' she says. 'Flat man. How I loved you.'

'Might you not love me still?'

Upon my shoulder she lays her head. 'Time'll tell.'

I wrap her in my arms and we rest. We listen to the peaceful sound of our breathing.

'Find them, Percy,' she whispers into my neck. 'Our little ones. Hold them. Till I come.'

I turn to her. I wipe her quick tears with my hand.

'I shall do.'

'You'll know them. Small as doves.'

'I'll know them.'

'They've waited for loving arms.'

'By the grace of God,' I breathe.

'Robert is in his Baptism gown,' she reminds me.

'I'll tell him his mother loves him.'

'He might cry for his daddy.'

'I'll hold him.'

'Promise?'

'I'll find them.'

Her tears are warm on my fingers. 'Tell them I'll come,' she says.

'You have my word, I'll find our babes.'

She closes her eyes. I watch her face.

'You are my queen, Mrs George,' I say. Look at me, my Bell.' She does. 'And here am I. Your bang-up king.'

There is nothing assured to
mortals ~ Ovid

'Bella?' She must hear me shuffling outside the door.

'Tuesday Brown?' She hisses my name. I whisper back.

'Bella?' I open the door and lean in.

Percy George lies heavily in her arms. I watch as gently she frees herself, at which I step away.

On the landing she finds me. 'I want to speak with you, Tuesday Brown,' she says.

She smooths her hair, wipes the tears from her face. 'Where is your pen?'

'Here,' I say, pulling it from my pocket.

'Percy would have the journal completed,' she says. 'Will you oblige him?'

'Of course,' I whisper. 'How is he?'

She replies. 'It's Mrs George now, if you please. He is peaceful. With Jesus. He has our firstborn son upon his knee.'

Here am I, Tuesday Brown, at my usual spot with pen and ink jar. At your service.

This afternoon, 14th October 1879, at four and twenty past, Mister Percy George died.

We gather around his bed, myself and Mrs George, Ruby, Jim, Bird, Pie, Flora.

The rookbird observes from the window cove. He gargles and fidgets.

We bow our heads. 'Heavenly Father, take into Your merciful arms this son and loyal servant. Forgive him his transgressions. Fill him with Your Heavenly Light. Bless him with Your Holy Spirit. Grant him peace and serenity in Your Holy Kingdom. Forgive him his sins, Lord. Amen.'

As his employee and secretary, it is my duty to conclude this journal, belonging to Mister George and dictated by the same, much of it written in my own hand, and entrusted to me by Mrs George upon his death.

Herewith I do so.

A few days after the demise of Percival George, Bella (the newly re-coined Mrs George) and myself set off for the establishment of Mister A.L. Goffe, on the Water-loo Bridge.

Our intention? To sell back the midget skeleton in order to raise enough to pay ourselves, as we remained unpaid by Mister George that month or the previous, due to the dearth of shows following Flora's incapacitation, Amen's death and Bella's disappearance.

Despite performing a card routine with a rabbit in a hat and a basket of doves, Bird and I discovered we were several crowd members (and performers) short. By and large response was poor, shillings were few, and crowds dwindled.

I had understood the dwarf skeleton to be valuable and Mrs George agreed. Below are my notes taken immediately after our meeting with proprietor, A.L. Goffe, Esquire.

To our astonishment Mister Albert Goffe of Waterloo tells us, happy as a starling, that he cannot guarantee the bones of the royal midget are authentic. He cannot purchase them back, yet he agrees to cancel the payment instalments. *I am fair to a fault!* he says.

I produce the documents he gave to Mister George. To our stunned surprise Mister Goffe tells me there is no relia-ble method of authenticating the authenticating documents, nor authenticating the authenticated bones either.

For all we know, he says, *the royal midget's bones lie in French soil or under glass at an academy, or p'raps they were thrown to dogs! Oh dear!*

'You pyke!' snaps Mrs George. For a minute I think she may cause a scene.

'I see,' she continues. 'Well, snark this! We have a con-stable, too dear to mention, and won't you be surprised when he trots in for a visit?'

I am obliged to interrupt hereabouts for fear she may

foster increasingly unpalatable threats. I remind Mister Goffe that there exists the printed edition, published upon royal edict, containing the French words of the dwarf who lived at Lunéville, known as Bébé.

He concedes that this might be authentic. *Yet I offer no guarantee!* he laughs. *The manuscript is printed in the French language!*

'What of it? You scurf!' blasts Mrs George. 'We had it jigged in the English off a superior Frenchman.'

I hold my hat between them. A temporary halt. And I beg of him an explanation.

He came upon the printed edition, he says. *Yet the book is writ in the foreign*, he says. *Ah!* he replies to himself. *But a set of bones shall ring the bell*, he explains. *Bones add magic*, he adds. *A bit of wallop! A set of bones shall make a story talk. Simply add a measure of the bone fide* (he winks) *and a pinch of the uncertain.* He winks again. Mrs George rolls her eyes. *This is the fancy of the crowd*, he says. *Percy was a fool but he understood that. Not that his shows were anyone's fancy! Abominable!* he shrieks. *There were those who'd pay to avoid them!* And he laughs merrily.

'I shall have you reprimanded!' stamps Mrs George. 'Unusual George was four square,' she continues, 'whereas you are a common lurk. Look to it! And watch your back.'

I conclude that it is time to take our leave of Mister Goffe. I bid him an abrupt farewell and escort Mrs George from the premises.

'*Pyke'art!*' she calls over her shoulder and offers an obscene gesture as we go.

I carry the unauthenticated articles, while Mrs George leads on apace.

'Shall we have a word, Tuesday, you and I?' she calls, striding ahead across cobbles.

I dash after her.

'I have a scheme,' she cries. 'Hurry up.'

The mind heaves. I think to myself, Percy would be proud.

We return to Quick Street.

'Now then,' she says as we step inside the house, unpinning her hair, loosening her boots and poking the fire.

'Bella!' Bird and Flora rush to her. The girls are happy to have her home. They are pleased at her comings and goings. There is tranquillity about the house: rabbits yawn, doves roost, the clock ticks.

I fetch the journal and pen.

The girls have prepared Mister George. We file in to admire him.

He is smart in his best, tidied and polished, restful of mien (somewhat blackberried about the neck from the fever), hair neatly waxed, pipe in hand, notwithstanding his missing cane.

'He shan't need it now,' says Mrs George, who has taken command of it herself. Tap tap.

'Jim,' she says. 'Take the girls to the baker's boy on Canal Street. Fetch us each a pastry. Pie will accompany you. Here is coins.'

Bird gets to her feet. 'Joy and cheer! What have we done to deserve it, Bell?'

'Never you mind.'

'Told you.' Ruby nods to Bird, picks up her shawl and narrows an eye. 'What are you rigging then, Bella?'

'Piracy!' squawks Bird. 'Jiggery-pokery!'

'Shall I stay with you, Bella?' Flora tugs at her sleeve.

'Anyone still standing here in one fadging minute gets no pastry at all,' shouts Mrs George.

I dip the pen and begin to write.

244

A roll of the eyes from Ruby. 'Yes, m'lady.' A curtsey. A rush of boots. Mrs George kisses Flora's head and releases her. The door bangs.

'They needn't hear it, need they?' Mrs George explains, smiling.

I nod and yet I understand nothing. I stare at her and blink.

'Sit down, Tuesday.'

Journal and pen in hand, I settle upon Percy's chair with the unauthenticated articles.

'Well now,' Mrs George pronounces. 'Have you a scheme of your own, Tuesday Brown?'

The rookbird steps, blinks. I open my mouth.

'No?' she interrupts. 'Lucky bugger you, then. Here is one I've prepared for you and I. Listen carefully.'

Bella makes herself comfortable in the other chair.

'A dying man may have his final wish, mightn't he?' She doesn't wait for a reply. 'And Percy George wishes to remain here with us. Don't look so fuddled. This is the last request of our own Mister George and our solemn duty it is to fulfil it. Listen sharp then, for it's a scheme that should make us all fortunate. And make Percival a happy man. Would you have it so?'

'Well, yes, I—'

'Here it is, then. For no ears other than our own. Do I have your word?'

I nod. 'Of course,' I say.

And she begins.

'Tomorrow, at dawn, Tuesday, you shall take the carcass of Mister George to Norman Jackson's son, Tom, at the yard on Wilderness Row. Very well do they remember Percy George. Obliging they'll be. You shall give him this note, signed by me. It describes herein how we shall have our Mister George prepared. Tom Jackson shall do the necessaries: he knows his work. Afterwards, you shall take Mister George to the other address, writ here, to Mister J.F. Dawson, where Mister George shall be further prepared before he is articulated. Now, here is the third fellow's address in Clerk'nwell who will do the sketch, John Finch. He is the least dear in London for the advertisement. I have prepared the wording – you shall jig the spelling – as follows . . .

His Majesty King Stanislas the Unusual of Poland & His Beloved Royal Dwarf, Bébé – A Historical Masterpiece.

'He shall have absolution and blessings by the reverend this afternoon.'

'Of course.'

'Not a word to anyone. Not a word shall be said about it. Is that understood?'

'Not a word,' I repeat.

'Percy spoke it to me himself,' she continues. 'Don't put me in a grave, he said. Let me stay by you. I shall not be alone, he said. Rather I'd be unforgotten! Well then? Oughtn't we to honour his final wishes? Why might we not?'

Bella taps the cane twice. The rookbird blinks. She continues.

'Percy wanted it. He shall have it. Why so blank, Tuesday Brown?'

'I, well. I think . . . Naturally you might . . . Well, I am quite certain—'

'Do you recall Stepney Fair?' she interrupts.

'I do,' I reply.

'Mister George found you. Fed you. Did he take you in?'

'He did.'

'And is it not a glory to deliver him this way? Is he not a bang-up king after all? A king he was. A king he shall be always. On the stage with his French babe. There's nought as unforgot as bones. Well, is there?'

I look at her for some moments before I say, 'No.'

'So. Dip your pen, Tuesday. Sharpish. Write something nice. Something cheerful.'

Here am I, Tuesday Brown with pen and ink jar.

The skeletal remains of Mister George shall be articulated in the proper fashion and presented as those of the celebrated exiled King of Poland. He of the unpronounceable name. Father-in-law to the King of France. Friend to the kings and queens of Europe. Royal. Distinguished. Eminent.

There are none who know otherwise. And none shall argue. Mrs George has spoke it.

He shall be exhibited and toured together with the bones of the French baby.

On the day Percy died, Bella Wickes became Mrs George. And this became her miraculous plan.

'Exhibition halls are best,' she exclaims, 'the crowds are large. The Egyptian Hall,' she says. 'America!' she cries. 'Why ever not?'

Picture me listening to her feverish words while taking it in.

She sounds just like him. And here I consider how much he might approve.

'They must exhibit together at all times,' she informs me. 'Do not separate them. Together they are the act. Alone they are average. Together they shall lead the main bill, as royalty takes precedence. Name me another royal skeleton exhibition currently touring.'

I appraise her, my mind a blank.

'There. See? None exist! Until now. The coins shall clatter! Do you see it? Do you hear it?'

She speaks and I write it down. It appears that everything is just as it always was.

'Here is payment. Enough for Jackson, Dawes, Finch. Enough to set up. Begin a tour. Think of it, Tuesday Brown. How they will talk!'

In a quiet spot with pen and ink jar, I write. I decide that I shall put down the truth, as Mister George was a great admirer of it. Let the hereafter be the judge.

I have found a secure box for the safekeeping of this journal and the antique French edition. I have played my part.

Before I sign off, I should like to be forthright.

Mister George enjoyed only limited success as a showman. His career and that of his performers never *rang the bell*, as Mister Goffe would have it. Many was the time we did not eat a meal. For all that we were not the very worst show in town. We attracted modest crowds and Mister George tolerated no fist fights nor dippers.

I for one support Bella's ingenious plan. I stand up square to inform her.

'Mrs George,' I say, 'your plan is premium. You may count on me.'

And she smiles. 'Well,' she replies. 'We shall need more ink then, Brown.'

On this and other items, she was right.

And here with my pen and blank page I consider that everything is just as it always was.

My name is Bella Wickes. You may call me Mrs George, for I am the guv'nor now.

God bless Percival George. He was not as unusual as his visions nor as remarkable as his dreams. Which of us truly are? He was a fanciful man and yet. A scheme begets another scheme. And here we stand at the end, delivered. Albeit we remember that we are all forgotten in the end.

May they find Blessings. Dear Amen. My Percy. And his precious dwarf.

May miracles both Unusual and Remarkable honour them in the Afterlife.

May they Ring the Bells of Heaven, Swing wide the Joyful Gates and Ride upon the Backs of Angels. Remarkable and Unusual it Shall Be.

This is the story of my Unusual George. True as church, I shall miss him.

The clock chimes, the crowd awaits. Tap tap. This silver-top cane leads me on.

Bang! Bang! goes my man, Tuesday Brown, on the drum.

Walk up! Walk up! This way for The Strange! The Hideous! The Obscene!

The Peculiar, The Remarkable. The world for a penny! Unusuals, novelties, prodigies!

My name is Mrs Exceptional George.

Hats off, Gentlemen! Prepare to be astonished, amazed, horrified and astounded!

For mine are Remarkables ... *all*.

I declare
That later on,
Even in an age unlike our own,
Someone will remember who we are

Sappho, Stung With Love: Poems
and Fragments

EGYPTIAN HALL
PICCADILLY LONDON

GENUINE ROYAL SKELETONS!

HIS MAJESTY KING STANISLAS THE UNUSUAL OF
POLAND & HIS BELOVED ROYAL DWARF, BÉBÉ

A HISTORICAL MASTERPIECE!

Author's Note

The Lunéville chapters contained in *The Wisdom of Bones* are based on actual events and involve some notable historical figures, all of whom are reimagined here and presented as part of the personal remembrances of Bébé, in the form of a fictional journal. All events mentioned did take place at Lunéville within Bébé's lifetime, 1741–1764, but are informally recounted in the style of memoirs, and therefore do not necessarily follow in the precise order of historical sequence.

I have used the French spelling of King Stanislas Leszczynski, and the Polish spelling of Józef Boruwłaski.

Acknowledgements

Thank you to Dr Alex Windscheffel, Senior Lecturer in Modern History at Royal Holloway, University of London, to Rachel Benoit of New College, Oxford, for her French translation and corrections, and also to Lou Broadbent for French translation. My grateful thanks to Lady Antonia Fraser (a fortuitous encounter) for suggesting that a French-speaking researcher might be helpful, and to Natasha Fraser-Cavassoni for helping me locate that researcher. Thank you to Caroline Kageneck, researcher and translator in Paris, for the numerous documents and searches.

My heartfelt thanks to the indomitable Clare Alexander, who has championed this book through storms and high seas. I am grateful for her counsel, insightful draft-reading and encouragement.

Thank you to James Gurbutt and to Olivia Hutchings and all at Corsair. Thank you to sharp-eyed copy-editor Tamsin Shelton.

My love and thanks to my family, and especially to Mark for his humour and support.

And variously, for IT support, babysitting, notes, advice, assistance and draft-reading: Esther Freud, Dan Souza, Phil Davis, Robyn Becker, Marylou Soto.

Thank you to Olivia Bell at www.oliviabelldesigns.com for her hand-drawn maps and Victorian skeletons.

The author gratefully acknowledges the following publications, in particular, among the many books and journals consulted for this novel:

Stanislas Leszczynski by Anne Muratori-Philip
The Story of an Architect King: Stanislas Leszczynski in Lorraine 1737–1766 by Renata Tyszczuk
Lunéville: Fastes du Versailles lorrain by Jacques Charles-Gaffiot
Les Jardins du Roi Stanislas en Lorraine by Stéphanie Chapotot
La Dame d'Esprit: A Biography of the Marquise Du Châtelet by Judith P. Zinsser
Memoirs of the Life of Monsieur de Voltaire: Written by Himself. Translated by Andrew Brown. Foreword by Ruth Scurr
Eighteenth-Century France by Frederick C. Green
Victorian Magic by Geoffrey Lamb
Phantasms of the Living by Edmund Gurney, Frederic W.H. Myers and Frank Podmore
Le Cannameliste Français (1751) by Joseph Gilliers